Jean Colombier
novelist. He was
novel. He won th
second novel, *Le*

JEAN COLOMBIER

# The Photograph

Translated by Tony Hartley

An Abacus Book

*Les Matins Céladon* first published in France by Calmann-Lévy 1988
This translation first published in Great Britain by
Hamish Hamilton Ltd 1990
Published in Abacus by Sphere Books Ltd 1991

Copyright © Calmann-Lévy 1988
Translation copyright © Tony Hartley 1990

Acknowledgement is made for permission to quote, on pp. 165–6, part of the original text by Christopher Hogwood accompanying the recording of *Nisi Dominus* by The Academy of Ancient Music, directed by Hogwood. © 1976 by Éditions de L'Oiseau DSLO, Decca Record Company Ltd.

The right of Jean Colombier to be identified as author of this work has been asserted by him in accordance with the Copyright, Designs and Patents Act 1988.

*All characters in this publication are fictitious and any resemblance to real persons, living or dead, is purely coincidental.*

All rights reserved.
No part of this publication may be reproduced, stored in a retrieval system, or transmitted, in any form or by any means without the prior permission in writing of the publisher, nor be otherwise circulated in any form of binding or cover other than that in which it is published and without a similar condition including this condition being imposed on the subsequent purchaser.

ISBN 0 349 10266 X

Printed and bound in Great Britain by
Cox & Wyman Ltd, Reading

Sphere Books Ltd
A Division of
Macdonald & Co (Publishers) Ltd
165 Great Dover Street
London SE1 4YA
A member of Maxwell Macmillan Publishing Corporation

# The Photograph

— I —

The ample-thighed women slithered silently by ... Ample-thighed women.

Paul was getting impatient. He couldn't dismiss from his mind this doggerel that came from God knows where and wouldn't leave him be. Of course he had better things to do than recite such rubbish. But, for all that, the women he dismissed by the door kept reappearing by the window, trying to arouse in him memories still too confused not to be disturbing. He pulled himself together and returned to his post.

Not before time. From the depths of the reddened water the fog – assiduous, stubborn – was rising very slowly. It blanketed the cobblestones and the footbridge with a strange hum. It magnified the shadow of the trees along the Quai. It invested the night with dreams long-forgotten in its surrender to the cries of the city and its desertion by man. The fog made the dim light of the street lamps flicker. Only the bottom steps of the footbridge could be made out, glisteningly obligingly; he was tempted to cross it. He was tempted to leave and never come back.

This time he had got his fog – he had it! His success made him jumpy. Glancing in the mirror, he was taken by the image of himself bent over his trays; he allowed his face to show the simple joy of someone who has almost made it. Anyhow, the fog was fully deserved. The time he'd devoted to it! Just a second – was it ample-thighed or dimple-thighed? It had to be ample-thighed, or it would sound even uglier. Whether it was ample-thighed or dimple-thighed, the problem remained the same – he didn't care for fleshy women. Roll on Sunday. Armand would have to eat his words. He'd always maintained that Paul was out of his depth here, that a victory over night and fog demanded experience and skill far beyond him as yet. Still, before crowing, he had to see how things looked under a naked light.

The photo was now fully developed. He rinsed it and dropped it into the tray of fixer. He sat down to wait until the processing was finished. He forced himself to recall the disillusionment so often heralded by the return of unfiltered light, that unforgiving denouncer of flaws masked by the red bulb. He also told himself some sad jokes to subdue the excitement caused by his eventual mastery of the fog. He checked off the difficulties of execution that Armand had drummed into him – photo too dark or too light, balance of light and shade upset by a poorly judged exposure, black not black enough and white not white enough. He scratched a buttock, but his mind was elsewhere. Which was a mistake. Life is made of such small satisfactions; one should learn to grant them their due importance, use them to detach oneself from futile concerns. A finger-nail, a buttock

that's the way of the world, its pains and its joys. Won round, he lifted his leg again to scratch where it itched. But it itched no longer. This prompted a certain resentment within him. The lack of synchronization between desire and pleasure, these clumsy efforts to grasp *the* moment, worried him more each day and heightened the melancholy he felt at watching himself pass himself by. He vowed to take stock at the earliest opportunity, with total dispassion and equal resolve.

He peered over the dish. That was enough. All that remained was to rinse the print in the sink. Time was starting to drag. What was it? Two o'clock! He'd been in there five hours – he'd be in great shape at work. He sat motionless, resigned, his elbows on his knees, facing down towards where the shadow of the bidet and the glow of the red bulb contested the tiling. With one hand he conjured up on the wall the shadow of a bird whose short-lived flight was interrupted by a corner; the doomed creature crashed in a flurry of feathers and blood. Shit, what an auspicious beginning for a photo, the death of a bird. It's worse than the slithering of ample thighs. He awarded his antics a highish mark and went into his bedroom.

He could have turned on the light. Instead he fetched a can of beer, settled comfortably on his bed and savoured his drink. In fact he was postponing the moment of truth, he no longer felt impatient.

It was Armand who had instilled in Paul Pervenche his love for photography. He who had taught him the pleasures of composition and especially of enlarging. He who would hold forth on the metaphysical aspect of the matter, that absolute instant when a sheet of paper submerged in a bath of chemicals authenticates or betrays the soul of the photographer. Armand was fascinated by the performance, before his very eyes, of a disturbing alchemy. Looking from his bed through the half-open bathroom door, Paul considered the glowing crucible where he had just been officiating, a womb cut off from the world, a guardian of the mysteries of creation. He had stripped naked, as always when a session was proving delicate: it made him feel more fragile, more receptive, more artistic; he was better able to attend and participate in the birth of his works. He had the feeling that, had he been a writer, he could only have worked naked. He plumped up his pillow, stood the beer on his stomach to make himself suffer, in moderation – today he only wished himself well; is it possible to wish ill on the father of a masterpiece? He took a long swig with the sole aim of titillating his imagination. Yes, nakedness fuelled the emotions, of both expectancy and regret. Mustn't forget to talk it over with Armand, a lively debate in the offing.

The leaden light falling into the room did nothing to ennoble the epidermis of the recumbent thinker: bushy hairs on legs, pasty white chest, indolent penis, empty beer can – he despaired at the assessment. With praiseworthy objectivity he recognized that he was unprepossessing to the point where he should get on with putting the finishing touches to his thing of beauty, as François would say. A last gulp to check the can really wasn't hiding any more liquid, a glance at the ceiling, towards the stage of his daily shadow show. Every night the lamp on the far side of the street gave him, courtesy of the ever-open shutters, a show of branches bowing to the whims of the wind. On occasion the headlights of some passing vehicle multiplied the effects, making them describe across the wall two unvarying trajectories. He imposed a pre-condition on getting up to switch on the light: a car had to pass. This hard bargaining was brought to an abrupt end. A car had just left the Quai de Jemmapes and turned into the Avenue Richerand. The branches, crucified for a split second above his head in the halo of the headlights, climbed the wall before disappearing in the middle of the ceiling just as the car roared underneath his window. At peace with his conscience, Pervenche got up and went back into the bathroom. He indulged himself in the flattery of the sensual light that bathed the room, assured himself in the mirror that he wasn't as bad-looking as all that, confirmed to himself that it wasn't dimple-thighed women but definitely ample-thighed women – though that did nothing for the lameness of the line of verse – counted up to three and turned on the light. The red bulb, caught unawares, lifted its spell.

He craned over the photo, held it at arm's length under the ceiling light, making no concessions, impressed by its self-assurance. It was good, it was as he'd hoped, and Armand, without doubt, would be knocked out. No question about it: a nice piece of work. The fog, beneath the two lights on the footbridge, was weaving a sort of motionless golden rain, in so far as a black and white photo could leave a choice between silver and gold. It cast over the pavement, the cobblestones, the trees, the footbridge, the street lamps, over the darkness itself, a luminescent unreality.

Nice one, Paul. Another print, a small one, and then to bed. He didn't argue with himself; he started on it after putting the first print to dry. While the second print was coming to life, Paul's thoughts turned to his success, to the photo drying behind him, stuck to the wall tiles in the renewed darkness. He was overcome by an unpleasant feeling, but without knowing why. He hurried to get the second one done, switched on the light as soon as he could and returned to his creation. He couldn't understand – technically it struck him as perfect, aesthetically too, yet something bothered him. Was it a flaw that eluded him? He looked more closely. No, no white spots, no intrusive object, no, nothing. He peeled it off the wall, laid it under the bright light and concentrated. He still liked the photo just as much, and still the uneasiness persisted, like a diffuse threat, like a distant clap of thunder in a cloudless sky. Did his disquiet come from the light patch in the foreground? No, it didn't detract at all from the photo as a whole. All this spoilt his pleasure. For once he couldn't find any fault with his efforts, yet he couldn't revel in the elation of work well done. Something obscure, unfathomably obscure, punctured his joy, and his pride at muzzling Armand. Forget it – Armand would explain everything, he must have had his jaded moments too. Come on, bedtime everyone.

Paul Pervenche slipped between his sheets with a wry smile. Three o'clock, God Almighty, he'd get less than three hours' sleep. The photo was quite something all right, ample-thighed, yes, no doubt about it, but what a bloody tragedy for the crashed bird, what a pity to celebrate a birth with a death. He'd forgotten to turn out the light in the bathroom. Grousing, he got up again. The red bulb next to the sink was pulsing, splashing the floor with the blood of the bird. Pervenche was suddenly afraid of this light whose evil spell had given no forewarning. Though it normally stayed open, he couldn't stop himself closing the door on the two photographs he'd caught sight of, backed against the end wall like grim sentinels.

## — 2 —

He was late. No time for deciding what colour morning it was. He threw on his jacket, slipping the smaller print into his inside pocket. He could take a closer look later, at the office, in a neutral context better suited to a detailed analysis. Maybe he'd show it to François.

With renewed enthusiasm he charged down the four flights of stairs, pausing stealthily at the second floor; he tiptoed up to the door on the left of the landing, which was ajar as always, banged it shut and ran off laughing to himself. The old lady would kick up a fuss again. The flat – second floor, left-hand door, you can't miss it, said the concierge – was occupied by a retired couple that no one showed any interest in but who took an interest in everyone. Old Ma Gautier, who was usually staked out at her window, would leave the front door open so as not to miss a trick, keeping tabs on life inside the building while watching the comings and goings of passers-by whose anonymity crumbled a little more each day under the battering of her mute interrogations. Pervenche had taken an instant dislike to the Gautiers. He made their life a misery whenever possible. And they complained about the lout from the fourth floor who slammed their door, tipped rubbish on their mat – I didn't see him but it couldn't be anyone else – posted porn magazines through their letter-box and made dubious gestures at them. They didn't like one another, ignored one another and in doing so thought about one another a great deal. Pervenche came rushing out on to the pavement, not needing to look up to know that, on the second floor, a furious face was scowling from behind a drawn-back curtain. He made an outrageously filthy sign; a passing young executive, thinking it intended for him, felt life was all of a sudden getting complicated.

Pervenche lengthened his stride. This episode, though nothing out of the ordinary, had put him in a good mood. He dashed up the footbridge steps, forced himself, despite the time, to make the mandatory stop above the Saint-Martin canal, took a deep breath of the bracing sea air, closed his eyes to listen to the gulls, but heard only the revving of land-borne motor vehicles. He hurried on. At the corner of the Rue de Marseille he came to a halt, seized by a terrible realization: he'd forgotten to feed Anne-Sophie, she would sulk for a whole week. Too bad, she'd have to look after herself, she was big enough.

He just made it to the office by nine, out of breath, pleased at being on time, at having brought his photo and having tormented old Ma Gautier. He ignored the lift and clambered up the four flights. His whole life was lived on the fourth floor, professional and private. He'd have to insist that Claire should move, there was no reason to live on the fourth floor, work on the fourth floor and screw on the eighth. An ultimatum. He would send it to her right away — why not? With growing self-satisfaction he ensconced himself in his chair, from where he greeted his colleagues, who, despite the early hour, were already becoming engulfed in piles of papers. He too put his head down, but only in order to concentrate better on the photo placed lovingly in a desk drawer. The fog, the light, the blank patch ... What's more, it was original. Beautiful and original. He addressed an obsequious 'hello' to Frigo, who had just sat down, before opening a file and telling himself there was a long day ahead. He didn't try to kid himself; his work was going to suffer from the elation with which his masterpiece overwhelmed him. The day proved even longer than he feared, interspersed with breaths of fresh air snatched from quick glances down to the drawer and quick glances up to the windows that kept the sky from coming in.

\*

Saturday seemed never-ending too. In the afternoon, feeling like an old man, Paul dragged himself to the Square Jules-Ferry. The September sun bestowed upon it an unaccustomed hint of festiveness. He sat down on a bench, next to the bandstand, half-asleep. He thumbed through the novel he'd brought along. Around him, the shouting of boisterous children, the growling of the traffic and the birds barracking the quiet. A ball rolled against his legs. He placed an authoritarian foot on it, waiting for someone to come and ask for it back, immersed himself in his reading once more, his ears pricked. Surprised at going unchallenged for so long, he lifted his gaze. She was there, hands behind her back, looking down, shifting from one foot to the other. A little further off some kids, her friends no doubt, were waiting with mocking smiles for her to pluck up courage.

'Hello.'
'H-hello.'
'Is this ball yours?'
'I-it's theirs.'
'Do you want it back?'
'Yes I do. P-please.'

She must have been five or six. He could remember meeting her on her way to school, escorted by her brother, sagging under the weight of an enormous satchel. Curly dark hair, huge blue eyes, long jet eyelashes – she would be breaking hearts before long. She looked at him unabashed. Her upper lip protruded slightly, reminding him, for some unknown reason, of a robin.

'What's your name?'
'Ella.'
'What?'
'Ella.'
'Ella?'
'Can I have my b-ball back, please?'
'Do you go to school?'
'I go to primary school . . . what about my ball?'

Pervenche handed her the ball. He felt the cold hand beneath his fingers. He would have liked to pursue the questioning, but she was getting impatient and her shy politeness would eventually turn into a tantrum. He didn't want to see a frown on that face for anything in the world. Ella: what an odd name for a small girl. He could see her, chasing the ball that the leaders of the gang had, as a precaution, taken far away from his bench. He would try to photograph her some day, if he saw her again. His book was boring him stiff. He unearthed three ants that he squashed between pages sixty-eight and sixty-nine to be sure not to forget. He left the square and Ella.

Anne-Sophie was sulking, no doubt about it. She had repaired to her refuge behind the hot-water pipe, near the ceiling; her web was deserted. Pervenche deposited the three flattened ants, summoned the tenant to show herself, but nothing doing. He had taken to the big, black spider one June evening. He had spotted her lurking in her corner, removed his shoes and perched on a chair. Then, after the customary injunctions, mercilessly brandishing a shoe, just as he was about to put an end to a life of ambushes and weaving, Claire had knocked at the door. He had explained and she had spared the evening spider's life. Since then Anne-Sophie and he had got to know one another. She never left her patch, never raised her voice, as discreet as could be. But she did have times when she was somewhat touchy. Pervenche put up with it. They got on with their lives, she not interfering in his business, nor he in hers. He examined his photo one last time, the large print, the one he was going to show Armand tomorrow. Great, great, a nice photo, no question. The after-taste of ashes in his mouth had completely disappeared. He fell asleep amidst prizes and plaudits.

A village church tower was sinking slowly behind the endless, rolling fields. A row of poplars promised a distant road, a tractor in a banked lane was seeking its raison d'être. The swallows, high in the sky, having enquired of the winds, would shortly be packing their bags. Summer sounds still hung on the air like capricious feathers. But he could feel that they did so on principle, that they had given up, that the autumn would soon impose its sham cheeriness and that its impalpable presence would mar the splendour of the countryside.

Pervenche resented this abdication by the summer, not that it was a season he held in great affection. But autumns disturbed him with their gentleness and calm so imcompatible with the promise of death they held. Their smiling threat scared him, suggesting they had the same poisonous charm that, two days earlier, his photo had exuded in the harsh brightness of the bathroom. Autumn was the time for romping through the woods with his grandfather, dew in the sunlight, mushrooms, transparent dawns that shimmered through the chestnut trees. That was long ago. It was over.

The excitement at seeing Armand again was faltering. And yet, for seven years, virtually every weekend he had taken the train to Meaux as today and every trip had been fun. The hour's journey wasn't long enough for him to go over what he had to say, to confide, to ask. Armand used to be waiting at the station and half an hour later they would be at his place. No one would be waiting today. In May, Armand had suffered a cerebral haemorrhage from which he had made a poor recovery. Half-paralysed, he got around only on crutches nowadays; he couldn't drive any more, he couldn't cycle any more, he wasn't Armand any more. Even so, Pervenche wasn't too worried by this physical decline. At seventy it's only natural, he explained to his friend, that you're not the man you were. You're not too far round the bend, you can talk and think straight, that's what counts. Armand didn't hold with this philosophy, he fumed, he swore, he laughed and he forgot his crutches.

Pervenche stayed for hours, for whole nights, settled in his host's armchair by the hearth where a fire encouraged the exchange of confidences. Armand, sitting on a pouffe, narrated. He took Paul to Indochina, Arabia, Afghanistan, China, everywhere. Everywhere except Africa. He wouldn't be drawn on his life there, Paul didn't know why. He had never been able to rid himself of a Parisian accent well matched to his irreverent wit and to a vocabulary where slang vied with home-grown expressions. The fire and his oratory parched his throat, wine came to the rescue and Pervenche, urged to fall in with the rhythm of his elder, soon felt overcome by a torpor swarming with jungles, raids, gun battles, hoaxes, girls conquered and abandoned. When he woke up in the early morning, he didn't have time to sort what he'd dreamed from what he'd heard. Armand, already on a war footing, was pumping up the bicycle tyres, coffee was steaming in the bowls, what's this you old woman, still hung over this morning? They mounted their steeds and took off along small roads where sleepy birds flew out from under their wheels.

They devoted Sundays to quieter activities: generally a visit to old André Véron, unless they'd paid it the day before. He was Armand's only real friend in the village. He took them to his basement, which he grandly called his wine cellar in memory of a small vineyard from which he had squeezed a few litres of wine. And then they would talk and talk about photography. Armand had taught Pervenche everything. He had detected in him a certain talent and had undertaken to instruct him. When Paul had proved himself, Armand gave him his old Leica, a camera that had witnessed his global adventures and that he treasured above all else. Pervenche had cried with joy and Armand with emotion, they had felt embarrassed at crying like that and had covered their embarrassment by knocking back a bottle of red.

The weekends would pass quickly. Armand drove Paul to the station on Sunday evenings. Once in the car they stopped speaking. When Paul got out, Armand would clutch his sleeve. Sparing of compliments, more in fun than in tenderness, Armand would then run his hand through his protégé's hair and say 'till Saturday?' As if Paul could have contemplated anything but coming back to see him.

In Meaux, Pervenche waited for the bus that would take him to Antigny. From there it was another two miles, which he walked, happy to renew acquaintance with the countryside and to see Armand again. He had stopped coming on Saturdays, since May: his visits, for all the pleasure they gave him, tired the old man. The home help who looked after Armand's needs had remarked on his exhaustion on Mondays. Pervenche had found some excuse to do with work and Armand hadn't pressed him. A page had been turned. The bicycle trips, the outings over hill and dale were gone for ever. Pervenche made every effort to persuade Armand that what they had left was more than enough to make them happy. It was hard going. Armand could not cope with the idea of going downhill physically. He claimed that old people should be killed off at the age of sixty-five. Throughout his life he had extolled the superiority of body over mind, and he wasn't going to change his spots at the age of seventy. Nonetheless, by dint of provocation, secrets confessed and secrets extorted, Paul managed to distract Armand from his dejection and the older man's face quickly became animated as the conversation went on.

It was ten o'clock when Pervenche arrived at the small house at the end of the tree-lined street. The garden at the front, the vegetable patch at the back always immaculate because Armand had never looked after it – he had entrusted this task to a neighbour – the wooden balcony where they took their aperitif when the weather was fine, all these little nothings that surround a house, that distinguish it from others, and that Armand had transfigured and immortalized in hundreds of photographs. The subject is of no great importance, he kept saying, what matters is the way you photograph it, the light, the soul. And that's why a dim-witted spider caught in wet paint on a fence, the garden seen through snowflakes, an egg, or a chair, had filled with wonder the visitors to the galleries where he exhibited. Armand was engrossed in reading Valéry's *Cimetière marin*:

'Ah, you've arrived! I won't get up, I'm pissed off, even my brain's going, I can't remember the *Cimetière* any more, hell, you turn into a bloody idiot when you get old . . .' It was something he prided himself on: he could recite the *Cimetière marin* from beginning to end without any hesitation and maintained that he'd bedded three tarts on the strength of it. Now Casanova had hung up his machine-gun. He moaned, swore that was that, it was a lousy way to die, can't you see what's left of me, I don't think I can stand it, I'm going to blow my brains out. He was relieved to be able to get if off his chest, to recount his woes to a sympathetic ear.

The ear was less sympathetic than he supposed. Pervenche had already taken the photo out of its envelope:

'Look.'

Cut off in his litany, Armand put on a brave face. He loved photography too much not to give it priority over his own infirmities. Paul felt himself shrink. He was sure to have neglected something, his stomach was tightening and still there was no verdict. Finally, Armand stood up. He grabbed one crutch and shuffled to the french window where he resumed his examination.

'It's not bad. It's good . . .'

Paul wanted to cry. Not only was his photo now an official success, but, more important, Armand had actually showered him with praise.

'Well done, well done, but there's something bothering me. What's this whitish patch in the foreground?'

'The light from a street lamp.'

'I see. Something's bothering me, damn it, and I can't figure what.'

Paul congratulated himself on not crying too soon. Yes, Armand too felt this inexplicable uneasiness. He preferred to say nothing.

'It's superb, I didn't think you'd manage to pull off a thing like that. Fog's the hardest thing there is to make something of. So what's wrong with it? I've got it! Something's missing. I don't know what or where, or why, but I can feel it, something's missing. It doesn't matter, the photo's superb.'

Yes, it did matter. Paul couldn't make do with an 'it doesn't matter' He had dreamed of perfection. Armand had granted it for a few seconds, he didn't want to resign himself to second best.

'Is Claire well?'

'Claire's well.'

Paul regretted the sharpness of his answer. It was due to his artistic disappointment and also to the fact that Armand and Claire just didn't click. He had brought her here once. Armand had found her ordinary, Claire had found him selfish. She had bad memories of the day because, with some justification, she had felt left out. She had realized that between Armand and Paul there was no room for anyone else. Since then she had organized her own weekends. The week belonged to her, the weekend belonged to Armand. For Paul the arrangement was too cut and dried, but he had avoided a discussion that would have led nowhere.

Armand was already broaching a more serious topic:

'André's expecting us for a drink. Give me a hand, I'd never make it on my own, I'm fucking fed up with this life . . .'

Gaining entry to the cellar was for Armand like a descent into hell, but between the four of them – André, Paul and the two crutches – they managed to get him safely down. Dust reigned supreme, bestowing value on the bottles carefully laid down along the wall, yet sparing the four stools and the chipped glasses hung up on nails. The empty barrel was a reminder of bygone glories.

The two elders soon set about another bottle, while listing the girls in the village worth bedding. There were seven, eight counting the baker's daughter, but you'd really have to be desperate. André was beaming. He was in his element, his glass safely stowed in his hand, his nose already livid, with hitched-up skirts on the horizon. Armand had been quiet for a while. Which surprised Paul. When there was talk of skirt, usually Armand just wouldn't keep quiet. Then suddenly, butting in on André who was dwelling on the curves of the young Mercier girl, he exclaimed:

'That's it, I've got it . . .'

Startled looks from his partners in crime. With difficulty Armand turned away from André and spoke to Pervenche:

'Your photo, that's it!'

'How d'you mean, that's it!'

'I know what's wrong. It's perfect, it just lacks a story. A great photo always tells a story, that's what's missing from yours. And it's all the more noticeable because that pool of light there in the foreground, looks like the circle made on a stage by the spotlight trained on the star. It's missing a hero. Without one it'll never have a soul.'

'What should I do, then?'

'Start again. Doctoring it is out of the question, you'll have to start from scratch with something or someone in this void, a shape, a girl lying there, something like that . . .'

Everyone remained silent. André couldn't follow a thing, Armand was pondering, Paul felt out of his depth. They all emptied their glasses. André was busy refilling them when Armand's voice broke the silence, almost reluctantly, muted:

'A corpse . . .'

'What?'

'A corpse, that's the foreground your photo needs. The foreground that would be most in keeping with the atmosphere. It would give your story its credibility, justify the uneasiness it filled me with.'

Pervenche would have liked to make light of it, to crack a sick joke. He couldn't. He recalled the disquiet he'd felt in his laboratory, the bad omens he'd foretold in jest, the suddenly threatening red of the bulb. He was anxious to look at his photo again, to try to imagine what Armand had seen more clearly than he had. Armand had already resumed his banter with André. Their voices were becoming excited, wagers abounded – I'll have her before the year's out; you must be joking! Pervenche had raised his glass to eye level. A beam of sunlight from the basement window embedded itself in the wine, which exploded into countless drops of blood. He held the glass to one eye, closed the other; the world was reeling – grotesque and crimson – to the rhythm of the liquid; he couldn't see any more, he was sinking irresistibly beyond the point of no return into a pinkish gelatine that was suffocating him. Next to him, he could hear the voices of the old men talking of love and youth, all the better to forget death. He felt her blond hair brush against his cheek, he could remember it well, just before the bend he had enjoyed this caress from breeze and hair in concert. He lowered the glass and downed it in one.

'Bloody hell, you can put it away,' came the compliment from André, who knew how to judge a man by his true qualities.

'Let's go.'

Armand had stood up. He ascended from hell more easily than he had entered it; alcohol is the friend of the infirm. On the way back home, his vigour regained, he enquired whether Paul might be in need – money, or anything else?

'No, no problem.'

Paul felt Armand's arm under his own. He snatched a surreptitious look at this small man, so fearsome and so frail, beret and spectacles, slippers that had the advantage of being easy to slide into. Like the baker's daughter, he invariably added, but he preferred slippers, they didn't gossip. The afternoon passed quickly. Armand had stopped complaining and Paul resented that he'd let himself go. The wine was proving more effective than all his arguments.

Paul took his leave.

'Don't you forget, think about your corpse!' called Armand, bursting out laughing.

'I won't forget, I won't.'

In the bus and on the train where the booming laugh stayed with him for some time, Pervenche turned the photo this way and that. The old guy was cracking up; a corpse – what next! Paul really couldn't see what story could come out of it. Give something a soul by means of a dead body, that would be the limit. His photo was perfect as it was. Reassured, he put the masterpiece away and immersed himself in contemplation of the light which, like him, was going.

— 3 —

He didn't need to open his eyes to decide: it was a celadon morning, which didn't mean a cloudless sky. At the moment of awakening, his first impressions as a recent sleeper, the noises in the street or in the building, the feel of the air and also its mood, the after-effects of the previous evening or night, simply everything contributed to his decision. A celadon morning was a good sign, a sign of vitality, plans, daring and certainly of fine weather. Wait and see.

Anne-Sophie was well. She had polished off her three ants and returned to her lair. She would probably show her nose at the window this evening, by way of thanks. Ah yes, the window. He opened it to air the room and lure in some unsuspecting midge that would end its days in the treacherous web.

He gulped down his coffee and sanctimoniously descended the stairs. He had plenty of time. Shit, the old lady had closed her door. On the way out, he glanced at the window, second floor left. On the lookout as ever, the old trout. He had the impression she was sporting a satisfied smile, which added to his frustration. In fact, for a celadon morning it was off to a bad start. He took stock, as prescribed, on top of the footbridge. The air was keen. In the woods, out there, the ponds must be steaming gently, the stars bowing out quietly.

Here, they'd upped and gone ages ago. But anyway, the canal was looking good, the pigeons were already attending to their business, the city was stretching in a clamorous yawn. He was early, so he allowed himself a coffee at his local bar. François was finishing his, which, like a genuine Breton, he'd followed up with a chaser, a short to give heart to his stomach, and anyhow it wakes you up, and it doesn't do any harm.

François, like Paul, had a job as a loss adjuster with Magistrale Insurance. He had shown the ropes to the trainee who, one day seven years ago, had sat down opposite him, withdrawn and overawed. Little by little a friendship was forged that was no longer confined to working hours.

They took their seats in unison. Each opened a file with a togetherness that was moving and turned over a couple of pages to impress Frigo, who seemed out of sorts.

Whereupon the two adjusters got down to real business:

'What did you do with your holidays?'

'Went sailing, what else!'

François Le Nabec, native of Lorient, deported much against his will to Paris, lived and breathed only for Brittany. His eyes were small and blue like those of true sailors, ones who have never really been to sea but who dream of it all their lives; thin lips clenched an unlikely sea dog's pipe. When he arrived in the morning, always in a rush, dishevelled, he would sit down quickly, open a file while keeping watch on Frigo out of the corner of his eye, and rattle off his news, because almost every morning he had something to relate:

'Hey, Paul, I scored last night.'

His eyes misted over with the pleasure and disgust of the repentant hell-raiser. He didn't go out on a binge, he went out on a sortie, preferably with a crew of fellow countrymen, and when he had the good fortune to meet a real sailor, he press-ganged him into the confessional and the next day recounted wondrous tales of derring-do at sea, though he was no longer sure by whom. In fact, he couldn't have sworn that it wasn't himself.

Lulled by François' confidences, Paul thought of Claire, and peeped at his photo. The obscurity which the neon lights could not quite dispel accentuated the sensation of unreality to which Paul was becoming increasingly sensitive. Not only that, it teemed with memories. It didn't have a story, but it had stories to tell – its conception, its birth, the reactions it had provoked, the comment aroused, the disagreements still surrounding it, and the doubts and certainties. Pervenche slid the drawer shut. Claire would like the photo. After all, she had acted as his model so often that she might be better at penetrating the secrets of another model, even if it were inanimate. And if she did agree with Armand, Paul could get her to lie down in this blank spot. She would provide the foreground. She would undress. A naked body is always more convincing, especially with a female. And she wouldn't be allowed to shiver even if it was cold, not allowed to make the slightest movement. There's nothing more obedient than a corpse.

In the afternoon there was no escaping work. Pervenche referred two touch-and-go claims to Frigo, to stretch his legs and for the pleasure of hearing him preface his reply by saying he was 'cool' about contesting it or about paying:

'What shall I do here, drop it or fight it?'

Frigo leafed through, scratching his head:

'Well, I'm cool about dropping it. And I'm even cooler about fighting it.'

It was to this lack of warmth that he owed his nickname. He had been wearing it like a millstone for years. Pervenche observed him. Right now Frigo couldn't give a damn about anything, it was tea-time, sacred, the only time he bent the rules in his exemplary executive's book.

Frigo's plastic cup, from which dangled a length of thread and a label, was steaming slightly. The smell of the concoction reached his nostrils and carried him back to that holiday in Britain which had shaken the bedrock of his existence. He appreciated his tea on two counts. He appreciated it for its Englishness, please and thank you. And he appreciated it even more because it came a few minutes before the ceremony by the mystical Breton, and coincided with the last peaceful period in his day as section manager in the loss adjustment department at Magistrale.

At five o'clock the hooter announced work was over. Pencils disappeared, files were shelved, foreheads uncreased, but no one got up. Work was over in Frigo's group – whatever his ideas on the matter – but it wasn't yet time to leave. The day did not finish officially until five-thirty.

At five, a suddenly feverish Le Nabec would consult his watch, place on his desk several blank sheets of paper, a pencil, a rubber, and take out a photo showing him leaning brazenly against the rail of a trawler.

'Booom . . .'

They were weighing anchor. The noise made Pervenche jump. After carefully clearing his nostrils, Le Nabec had given the signal. He had closed his eyes, cupped both hands in front of his mouth and thrice given the nostalgic blast of a fog-horn. It was deep – the ship must be big, leaving for many months. The women on the quayside waved their handkerchiefs, the seagulls escorted the crew bunched at the vessel's stern. The sun, masked no doubt by the clouds, failed to give the scene the colour one would have expected. After the final warning shot, Le Nabec remained motionless for a brief instant.

And then his pencil flew across the paper: that, do you see, is the small port of Saint-Goustan near Auray, you know I was born in Auray, I lived in Lorient afterwards, but I was born in Auray, and I spent all my childhood in Saint-Goustan. The pencil brought to life a jetty, rowing boats, yachts, the port's tiny square with its cobblestones, its old houses, its two bars, ah, old man Lecadec's bar, I'll take you some day, you'll see what Brittany's like . . .

Sometimes, when the westerlies were blowing, he would abruptly suspend whatever he was doing and freeze, his nose twitching:

'A-hah, mother's doing cod this evening. Which reminds me . . .'

Paul knew most of his friend's stories by heart. They had reverberated around this glass jail with its never-changing rituals. The air-conditioning hummed away. A few leafy plants carried on, from mother to daughter, a peaceable existence. The stacks of files served as a barometer for the occupiers: four adjusters and two secretaries face to face with Frigo, solitary and unquestioning. The next room was a carbon copy of Paul's and down the end a larger cage imprisoned the typing pool, eighteen of them under the stern gaze of Choufesse, their overseer.

Le Nabec could draw. Pervenche felt he knew southern Brittany as well as if he had been there. There was nothing he didn't know about the house where his friend had lived the childhood of a seafarer's son, about the life of the Bretons, about the return of the fishermen, the dreary evening gatherings in winter, the sea in its prime in summer. With François he dreamed, he no longer thought of his own village, nothing existed outside the noise of the surf and the sailors hoisting sail. The Breton half-hour passed quickly. At five-thirty, lights out, everyone packed up their things and went off to confront a destiny free from surprises.

Paul sauntered as far as the Rue Montmartre. It was mild. People thought they were on holiday. Briefcases swung from arms with rolled-up sleeves, stockings had not yet replaced the tan on trim calves, schoolchildren were extolling the virtues of their new friend to their mothers. The city was light-heartedly readying itself to brave the yellow of the leaves, the grey of the sky and the black of boredom. His head aching slightly, Pervenche quickened his pace: he detested this general good humour, especially when he sensed it was grounded on nothing firm. He must be mad, how could he not be happy when everyone was laughing? He had arrived. He climbed the stairs, recapping on what he had to say first – the move to the fourth floor, the photo of course.

Claire prepared the meal. Her movements revealed fleetingly the curve of a breast, the slimness of her waist. She had a new haircut, it suited her, set off the black eyes. Paul liked her this way, wearing just a T-shirt she'd pinched from him. It stopped half-way down her thighs. Her still-bronzed legs promised to astonish and Pervenche never ceased to be amazed that they always delivered. He savoured these minutes reverently, solemnly: they quavered, fragile and moving, huddled between the banalities of the meal and the passion of the embraces, they sang as a traveller sings while packing his bag. He lay on the cushion-covered bed, turned on his side, his head propped on one hand, running the other over the gentle slopes, hesitating at the hip, lingering at the waist. And he began to talk. Claire looked at the photo, long and hard. Pervenche could no longer feel her skin tingling beneath his hand; Claire was away, in the fog, near the pale void. She turned to Paul:

'I don't like your photo ... It's very beautiful, but I don't like it, and I don't like what Armand said to you.'

She remained pensive.

'I don't know, I feel something, no I don't feel anything, I don't know, I don't like your photo. It's sick, it's too sad. I don't know.'

Paul stayed silent. He had hoped they would both laugh at the figments of Armand's imagination. They weren't laughing, the evil spells of the photo couldn't be broken. Claire was right perhaps: the feeling of uneasiness came from the sadness of this stretch of the canal which was accentuated by the fog and the street lamps. The photo wasn't hostile or threatening, it was just sad, that's what Armand had failed to see.

Beneath his hand, Claire's skin started to tingle again.

'I want you.'

These were the first words she had uttered for a long while. With Claire, 'I want you' signalled an emotion that was not only physical. The photo had disturbed her. She came very quickly, placed her lips on Paul's. She didn't move, didn't breathe, didn't speak. Paul thought he was holding a dead woman in his arms. He shook her, she smiled at him, stretched out beside him, put an arm round his chest, laid her forehead against his shoulder, adopted the posture of an affectionate wife in fact, and abandoned Paul. In any case he didn't want to continue the lovemaking, the feeling was gone. He was going to walk out on Claire's perfume, her music, her skin. He could hear the city whispering below, the night was inviting him to pleasures with a complex taste. He would never resist. He rose soundlessly. Claire saw him dress hurriedly and disappear like a shadow. She hadn't tried to hold him back, she hadn't tried for a long time now.

Standing in front of the building, Pervenche breathed in the last fragrance of September. He plunged into the Rue d'Aboukir, not caring where he was going. He walked slowly, head down, oblivious to the goings-on in the street. His hand still thrilled at Claire's warmth, he caressed her breasts until he reached the end of the street, almost turned back, realized that he hadn't come, that his desire for her remained intense. In the Rue Saint-Denis he looked hard at two prostitutes. Neither resembled Claire. He moved on. The footbridge reminded him that the morning had been celadon. Correction, dark celadon. About to turn into the Avenue Richerand, he changed his mind, continued along the Quai de Jemmapes, passed the Rue de la Grange-aux-Belles and, just after, turned right into the Rue Monte-à-regret. It was here, in this narrow street, under the arch of this doorway that he had taken the photo.

No fog this evening. The cobbles weren't glinting, the neighbourhood was sleeping a sleep without nightmares; the pale void, paler than ever today, expected no one. Armand was sinking into senility, Claire had a delectable body, it was a pain in the arse to go drinking with François on Wednesday, the weather was really mild, and what if he pissed against the Gautiers' door on the way up?

It wasn't that late, hardly midnight. He spared the mat outside the second-floor flat, heard laughing voices on the third floor. So the ladies aren't asleep yet. He caught sight of Anne-Sophie scampering into her hole, undressed, kicked his clothes to one side, you dickhead, fished a sock out of the sink with its leaking tap, put some music on, took a few half-hearted dance steps, turned the light out, opened a can of beer by guesswork, sat crosswise in his armchair, his legs over the arm, and thought about nothing interesting, contrary to the expectations raised by his preparations. Aren't the tarts downstairs working tomorrow, then? That was what was eating him.

The Martin family proved the concierge right when she maintained there were still decent people about. Father, temples greying and shoes shining, mother always with a kind word to say, three clean, polite children. Pervenche was madly in love with the youngest. She wasn't particularly pretty, but she had a mouth and smile that were fatal. She seemed in the grip of perpetual motion. Occasionally he would follow her in the street, when he managed to leave at the same time. She strode along, her skirt beating time, her hair streaming in the wind. He could recognize her imperious ring of the bell, sharply followed by pitiless chivvying when her mother didn't open the door quickly enough. Her lilting voice soon cut short the maternal remonstrations. She seemed to have an answer for everything. Pervenche was dying for a set-to with her, a little spat to get into the mood, long, sweet kisses to make up, oh what a mouth, oh what teeth. But she wasn't in the bag yet. Here too, Pervenche was tracked by his reputation as an eccentric. Life is a bitch, isn't that right Arthur?

Rimbaud concurred in silence. He stood, hands in pockets, leaning against a wall near an arched entrance. The rear end of a car right next to him had made him change centuries. Pervenche worshipped this poster, had given it pride of place on the wall. The lamp in the street cast enough light for Pervenche to be able to make out, even at night, the features of the dreaming child. On this poster he had a totally disconcerting presence. His was an irresistible call to unleash body and imagination. He had forsaken the dust of books and museums to take his place beside that arch, in search of new adventures. His doorway resembled the one in the Rue Monte-à-regret; there was no fog or blank spot, but Pervenche had the feeling they shared the same street corner, the same universe. When he came home late at night, he wouldn't have been surprised to bump into Rimbaud, one leg folded up against a wall, his hands in his pockets.

Pervenche liked his bedsit with its fastidious disorder. The sofa, the desk miles from the window – on the rare occasions Pervenche had tried to string a few words together on paper, he had realized that the window was too distracting – the armchair, the television, the stereo: essential objects for someone not keen on looking passing time straight in the eye. His furniture would have delighted any mother with children, overjoyed at her offspring's lack of originality.

Apart from the poster of Rimbaud, Pervenche was very attached to another one, stolen during a Polish film festival: a small girl was crying for no apparent reason. A solitary but frightening tear ran down her cheek, she bore all the sadness in the world. No doubt Rimbaud was to blame. Paul had made a kind of cylindrical lampshade from red paper that projected on to each poster a circle of light as if from a spotlight, like a pale void. For the last few days Paul had shied from turning this lamp on. He made do with the bedside lamp, which washed its hands of the whole business.

He had also decorated the walls and ceiling with photographs, ribbons on which he'd written sacred things, and a bizarre assortment of objects. Everything was upside down, you had to climb on a chair or go on all fours to read a ribbon or study a photo.

He finished his beer, said goodnight to Arthur, then discovered a likeness between Petrushka – the crying girl – and Ella. It's true, he'd never noticed before, he'd have to photograph Ella crying. He got into bed, told himself off for not making love to Claire, and turned to the wall, with which he swiftly gave up exchanging ideas.

— 4 —

Paul Pervenche was content to lose himself once more in the humdrum routine of the passing weeks, now resumed after the summer. Autumn was upon him; so too, like the leaves on the pavements, were the files piling up on his desk.

Blandine poked out her tongue, as always when she was thinking. Calot, as always when he was thinking, twirled a pencil that he caught in mid-air, punctuating the revolutions of the projectile with 'bloody job'. Anyone overhearing was reminded of the worries of a loss adjuster still on probation, always on his toes because of the intricacies of the job and the ribbing of his established colleagues. The two secretaries swapped secrets over their typewriters. All around Pervenche, lives languished in bland routine. For years Paul had worked and lived among invisible people. He spoke to them, felt a liking for them that was probably mutual and promptly forgot them at five-thirty. Except for François, who could unlock the ocean and his dreams. He alone was alive among the dead, alone with Pervenche and his photograph.

Paul occasionally enjoyed these brief interludes of disillusioned philosophizing that spared only those he liked. The few there were. The telephone cut in just as he was deciding on the appropriate penalties for his colleagues' insipidness.

It was Armand. Pervenche didn't recognize his voice.
'Is that you, Paul? I'm buggered.'
Silence. Armand was waiting for Paul to rescue him – to

sympathize or to galvanize. Yet Paul could feel something welling slowly within him, preventing him from speaking, preventing him from hoping.

'I'm buggered. Can't walk, can't read any more.'

Then Pervenche came to; Armand was far from dead. He knew how he dramatized the slightest reduction of his physical capabilities. He opted for ridicule.

'Yes, but you can still bullshit . . .'

'That's right, you sod, laugh at me, take the piss.'

'How did you get to the phone?'

'I crawled, like a worm. It took me at least twenty minutes, and on top of that . . .'

The wheels were in motion, Armand was improving.

'Fancy coming on Saturday?'

'For the whole weekend?'

'I don't know, depends how I am.'

'Okay, see you Saturday.'

'See you Saturday, son.'

Pervenche was troubled less by Armand's complaints than by his closing words. It wasn't his style to call for help, even less to utter a word of affection. The main thing is to make him accept his relative decline, Paul reflected, not let him whinge, tell him about that new case, Bruno, the kid who's paralysed, that'll keep him quiet. In body, he's sound enough.

That evening Pervenche went out with François and a friend of his, Loïc, who was passing through town. After a quiet meal near Montparnasse to get up a head of steam, as the sailors put it, they tied up in a crowded harbour. The body heat fired their thirst. They came to a small creek at the corner of the bar and started to rehearse their repertoire. The yellow pastis brought a strangely red flush to their radiant faces. Pervenche was in a dream. His photograph, Claire, Armand, Ella – all held intriguing promises, fuelled by the alcohol, in store.

There was a scuffle behind him. Two rowdies were grappling in the centre of a circle of onlookers. Friends egged them on, the barman tried to pull them apart. Loïc, an habitué of brawls and seedy bars, broke the circle and grabbed the pair by the arms, come on boys, that's enough. The two bantams were still flailing, trying to push away the referee. And suddenly, out of the blue, a third yob hurtled into the ring and hit Loïc with a crashing blow to the head. He swayed and collapsed on to a chair. Women screamed, bottles shattered, the barman raced to the phone. Free from restraint, the two combatants were at it again; the big fellow was laughing as he watched them and François was attending to Loïc, who was coming round. Pervenche looked on from his bar stool. Then suddenly he felt his stomach knot. The blood was pounding in his ears, he wondered what had come over him. He saw only the face of the gloating thug. He left his stool, put down his glass and hurled himself at the man, who was standing sideways on. He thudded into him with tremendous violence. He felt his head hit a jaw, heard a howl and stumbled over an inert body in the midst of scattered tables and chairs. He stood up, saw startled people around him, forced his way through and went outside. He noticed François still squatting next to Loïc, a stunned expression on his face. Outside, the eyes fixed on him, although showing no hostility, paralysed Pervenche. He wanted to run, but didn't dare. His arms dangled, he saw stars. Eventually he regained his composure, crossed the road and dived into the first side street that would take him away from the bar. Then he stopped. He was sweating, gasping for breath. He started to take stock, to compliment himself, you really smacked that big guy. He edged to the corner of the street and chanced a look back at the scene. Le Nabec and Loïc were coming in his direction. They crossed the road and came to a halt on the pavement. One eye on the bar, Pervenche joined them.

'You're incredible!'

François couldn't believe it. Loïc, still somewhat dazed, insisted on thanking Pervenche.

'Our Breton honour is saved thanks to you. What a bastard that bloke was. When you come to Lorient, I'll repay you.'

The effects of the alcohol had evaporated, the music had disappeared. Pervenche decided not to go to Claire's after all. His head was aching, he discovered a lump high on his forehead. He would have liked to stay hidden where he was to get a look at his victim. But in fact he'd hardly paid attention to his face; he'd be unable to recognize him. Had he really hurt him? He felt the stupid pride of the victorious male. He took leave of his companions and steered a course towards his home port; it may not be Breton but it's well sheltered all the same. He turned around several times, which showed how safe he really felt.

By Friday the lump had gone. Pervenche sported an unblemished forehead, ready to receive the laurel wreath Le Nabec had woven for him the previous day. He had even sacrificed the fog-horn ritual to return to Pervenche's exploits; in the space of a few hours his adversary had grown by more than four stones in weight and seven inches in height.
All too soon the telephone broke the spell of a coronation which, all things considered, Paul thought justified.
'Is that Monsieur Pervenche?'
It was Armand's home help.
'Monsieur Pervenche? I'm calling on behalf of Monsieur Armand. He's just been taken into hospital, but don't worry, it's nothing serious, the doctor said he'd be home in a week.'
Panic-stricken for a second, Paul didn't think to ask any relevant questions. He simply asked her to confirm that Armand would be home the following weekend.
The news had ruined his day. His laurels were worthless. He was longing to recount his deeds to Armand. Now he felt strangely lost, as he always did on the rare occasions he had to spend a weekend alone: without Armand, that is.
Saturday morning and he was already counting how many hours there were between him and Monday. Two days, a desert. Somewhere a pianist tormented his instrument. Scales repeatedly interrupted came to him through the open window. Pervenche buried himself in his cushions,

winked at Arthur, slagged off Anne-Sophie and Claire. Especially Claire: he had called her to ask her to stay. Her parents were expecting her, Paul should have let her know sooner, she was sorry but . . . He had hung up on her. For some time now women had given him nothing but hassle. From the rectangular strip visible behind the roof opposite, he saw that the sky too was asking itself some questions. The branch of the tree, the branch the tree had assigned to his window, was forlorn: its leaves had decided to take off on lives of their own. They exerted themselves, brave yet indecisive, flying away then remorsefully returning, then waltzing, twisting, spiralling before finally landing with a skater's glide in the gutter; there a street sweeper would shortly cover them with a turd from a dog pleased to have urinated against the tree and defecated on the leaf, which is not within the capacities of just any dog. Old Pa Gautier – gazing blankly, nose to the pane, wiping with his fingertips the glass misted up by his heavy breath – repeated to himself, 'Isn't autumn just lovely.'

To drown out the anonymous pianist, Pervenche had put on some music. Pervenche was organizing himself, you have to organize yourself when there's nothing to do, otherwise it's impossible to cope. He couldn't manage to define the colour of the morning. The book he opened fell from his hands.

Having nothing better to do, he got up, performed his ablutions and succeeded in recovering all his clothes. His left shoe, hidden behind the fridge, took him some time.

He walked, blown by the wind, haunted by a sullen sobriety. He visited a few pavement cafés and with rash daring drank a coffee at the scene of Wednesday's exploits. At four o'clock he could have kicked himself: you idiot, what about Ella? He sprinted to the Square Jules-Ferry, sat next to a matronly lady engrossed in knitting. A horde of squealing children raced around the square. No Ella. Pervenche felt heart-broken, he would have liked to hear the small girl with a stutter. He allowed himself a few minutes to catch his breath, to while away the afternoon, to finalize his tactics for handling Claire. How could anyone drop in on their parents in Rouen when a dream lover was offering his services?

'I-it's Ella . . .'

Pervenche jumped. Ella was holding out her hand like a good little girl. Paul took the tiny fingers, held on briefly:

'Hello, Ella, how are you?'

'V-very well, sir.'

'Don't call me sir.'

'Yes, sir.'

'My name's Paul, will you call me Paul?'

'Yes, sir.'

'Yes Paul, try it.'

'Yes, P-Paul.'

'Very good. Aren't you playing with the ball today?'

'Yes, but I've lost it, I can't play any more . . .'

Paul was amazed by this combination of shyness and self-assurance. Or perhaps she wanted to show off to her friends watching from a distance.

'Sit down.'

She stuck her hands, urchin-like, into a pair of dungarees that were too short. He registered the deep shadow of her eyelashes, the round cheeks, the small, even teeth. He felt a sudden urge to take her on his knee, to tell her a story. He tried to arouse her curiosity.

'Do you know the story about the butterfly with the head of a horse?'

She hadn't heard, she'd shouted goodbye, goodbye Paul, and was running towards her friends whose 'Ella, Ella' had proved more persuasive than Paul's honeyed words. He watched her run. She lifted her knees high, pumped her arms; it wasn't exactly elegant or feminine, but it pointed to a love of running wild, and to a certain agility. She must beat her friends hollow. Pervenche felt proud.

Noise came from the Martins' flat. The Martins had visitors. From beneath the bedclothes, Pervenche made out muffled laughter, excited conversation, the chink of cutlery on plates and, occasionally rising above the general din like a trumpet solo, the voice of his future lover. He thought once more of Armand, of his photograph, of Claire, of Le Nabec. His horizon was one-dimensional. That didn't displease him. He swaddled his small world around him.

Sunday was even more of a pain in the neck. Little activity in the street, except for people at a loose end, others like him. He went to the cinema, was bored stiff, so forced himself to sit through a second performance, walked miles, devoted a whole hour to the square which was empty because Ella wasn't playing in it. Isn't that her, the little brunette over there? No. Too bad.

He chanced upon a florist's that was open, immediately scrapped the plans drawn up the day before, bought twenty roses, picked up a roll of adhesive tape from his flat and set off for Claire's. Good ideas cheered him up, gave his day-to-day life a glamorous façade and, in spite of everything, bolstered his self-esteem. Pervenche knows his stuff all right, a shrewd customer, sensitive too, a poet. He stuck the roses in place singly, decorating the surface of the door, filling the spaces between with the greenery that the florist had insisted on including. He folded in half and half again a large sheet of blank paper brought for the purpose and slipped it under the most beautiful bloom where it caught the eye, so that Claire would clutch it in a hand trembling with emotion, unfold it and find only emptiness. Pervenche calculated that the frustration which would follow the emotion could only add bite to the cocktail, that a question mark is never out of place in a declaration of love.

It would soon be eight; Claire would be arriving shortly. He went home whistling like a blackbird: Claire, problem solved, Armand, problem solved as of next weekend, what more could one ask? The Philadelphia orchestra was playing *Swan Lake*; poor creatures, Paul mused, attempting an entrechat or two. He observed his naked body. Flattered by the subdued glow of the bedside lamp, it seemed to possess an unexpected grace. Reflected in the window, he saw the skipping, slightly distorted by the imperfections in the glass, of a ballerina at her peak. He slowed the tempo a little, arms spread, thumb touching middle finger to give, so he thought, greater lightness to the expression of his hands. Legs together, feet pointed: as a ballet dancer he really looked the part. Pervenche needed no one else to be entertained.

He permitted himself a knowing glance in the bathroom mirror exposed by the open door, like a vertical pool; mirror, mirror on the wall, who is the fairest . . .? Pervenche could no longer discern the inspired look on his face of the night he had given birth to his photograph. There it was, lying on the desk. What was it waiting for, what was he waiting for? It wanted its corpse. Fine, then he would produce one for it. Stealthily he crept towards the mirror and suddenly pulled out a weapon. He moved closer until his face was pressed against the terrorized surface of the glass. He rolled his eyes, contorted his face, pulled a maniacal grin, gritted his teeth and fastened his fists on the weapon. He would strike, he would kill. Amused, he contemplated the features of the murderer at the very moment his fate is sealed. One of these days, he would photograph himself in the act of killing. Portrait of a killer, not bad, good idea. Yes, Claire must be putting the roses into her big vase, she'd phone him tomorrow. Pervenche ended his weekend as he had begun it, in bed, but steeped in new sensations: Ella loved him for certain, he had just killed, for certain, he had only to find the body. Roll on Saturday, goodnight Arthur, goodnight Petrushka, goodnight Anne-Sophie, goodnight Paul.

## — 5 —

It had rained heavily over the past few days. Pervenche no longer recognized the fields and forests, they spoke no more of summertime but of approaching winter. The clouds confined the landscape to downcast apprehension. The distant forests could have been shimmering in the sun, the banked lanes leading to fairytale castles, grass fires here and there could have warmed the heart. But no, the atmosphere remained grey and muggy, more rain was expected: put it down to the west winds.

Pervenche liked this sky. Armand had explained to him that there is nothing sadder for a photographer than a blue sky, as vacant as an ox's stare. He had been right to bring his camera; masterpieces greeted him with open arms, inviting him to forget the dark days he had just been through. One evening on his way back from Claire's he had decided to make a detour via the Rue Monte-à-regret. It had seemed more forbidding than usual, even dangerous. He had remembered his grimaces before the mirror, he shouldn't have acted the killer, it might bring bad luck. The very next morning, in fact, Armand had phoned, disheartened, he was at the end of the road, just waiting to croak . . . Paul had trouble cheering him up.

The narrow road that led to the village was bordered by flooded meadows. Pervenche was alive to the changing colours of this liquid plain criss-crossed by fences helpless to stop the reflected clouds scudding through it. He couldn't find a camera angle that satisfied him. But as he stepped back, he noticed in the distance the steeple and the roofs of the houses, in the opposite direction to the meadows. He paused for a few seconds, then made up his mind. It wasn't the thought of taking a possibly original photograph, but rather to prove to Armand that he was as off his rocker as him. He unlaced his shoes, removed his socks and trousers, hanging everything on the branch of an oak, climbed the fence and waded into the field. He was soon up to his knees in water. It wasn't unpleasant. He turned to face the village, aimed, shot. The foreground still didn't satisfy him. He was definitely having problems with his foregrounds. The sheet of water was too bare, it would make for a huge blank patch, he'd need a heap of corpses to fill it. No choice then, he had to go on. He went on. He removed his shirt and pullover, hung them on a barbed wire fence, moved forward; the water was up to his waist. With extreme care he climbed a final fence, deriding the barbed wire for looking as silly as a guard dog surprised in its sleep, and took three photographs. That was good, yes, the fences he had climbed zig-zagged across the foreground, gashing the clouds, running towards the row of trees by the roadside. Overshadowing everything, the village. The church spire plunged quivering into the heart of the lake. Pervenche too was quivering. He scrambled to the shore, dried himself as best he could and hurried to Armand's.

Life seemed sweet now that he was fully dried and dressed and could rub his hands over the flames in the fireplace. Armand and he had recovered from their surprise: Armand's at opening the door to a shivering, dripping figure, unable to tell if he was trying to smile or keep his teeth from chattering; Paul's at having the door opened to him by an old man. Armand had aged ten years; Paul realized he had aged mentally more than anything else. There he stood in the doorway, slightly hunched, wearing an old, brown dressing-gown torn at the elbow and fastened by a tatty braided cord, a dirty beret on his head. His slippers accentuated the thinness of his calves. He was unshaven. His spectacles magnified his blue eyes. They had looked at one another wordlessly and then he had taken Paul to warm himself, postponing the account of his decline.

Life seemed sweet to Paul as he bent over the hearth. He had refused to answer Armand's questions, considering it wiser to listen to him first and buck him up after. Life seemed sweet to Paul because, in the end, Armand's condition wasn't as hopeless as all that. He had been taken to hospital following a bad turn, just to be on the safe side. Admittedly, the doctors had confirmed that he wouldn't regain the use of his legs, that his condition in general wouldn't improve, but he could last out, no problem.

'Can you credit it, they say I can last out, but that's crazy, I can last like a vegetable, I can crawl, lick out my bowl, watch the telly, I can last out, but I don't *want* to last out, no way am I going on like this. I've already told you, you know it, as soon as I can pluck up courage, I'll blow my brains out. A worm's life, that's what's in store for me, and even then . . .'

Life seemed sweet to Paul. The fire was warming his belly and his heart. Armand was ranting beside him, good for him, it meant he was taking an interest in himself, in Paul, in life. He started to relate his adventures, the meadow, the brawl. Armand was clinging on to life, just look how excited he got at the story of the fight, how he laughed at the episode in the meadow. He sipped the grog Paul had made for him, listened to the singing of the log fire and forgot his legs.

'What about your bit of crumpet, you still together?'

Yeah, yeah, still together. Pervenche wasn't keen to talk about it, he felt as if he'd been caught in the act. Armand was all for variety, freedom, a high turnover. The older he got, in fact, the more impressive his tally grew. His eyes danced like the flames from the logs which broke in two and fell down on either side of the fire-irons.

'I've bedded a few tarts, I can tell you . . .'

It all came back, his Paris accent, his verve, his ribaldry, he was twenty-one, his legs didn't hurt, the future belonged to him.

'I've bedded seventy-nine women – not bad, is it? Mind you, it's going to be tough to make it eighty, I can't get it up. But I can eat pussy, though that would only make seventy-nine and a half. Not that I was particularly handsome, still, looks don't matter, what counts is being a smooth talker, and that I always was, there was no escape, but you're not very talkative, are you? Not like me, I really bullshitted them but they loved it, it made them laugh, and a bird that laughs is as good as in the bag. I remember in Ouessant, spent three months there once, fucked ten women, shore leave had been cancelled for the navy. My mates were playing at being lady-killers, but I wasn't taking any prisoners, chat them up and into bed, in a manner of speaking, that is, it wasn't all mod cons like now, out of the ten Breton birds I must have stuffed five in a field, not warm believe me, two in a hay-loft and three in bed, quietly does it so as not to get caught. In fact when I think about it, I didn't screw out of lust but just to chalk up another one, I actually used to make a notch each time in a school ruler I carried on me everywhere, it must be lying around somewhere, yes seventy-nine not counting the whores, 'cos when the urge took me I couldn't work or anything, terrible it was, so I went to see a whore and I calmed down for a couple of weeks. If I don't count the whores I can score two points for a virgin, seventy-nine including twelve virgins, there's a lot of crap talked about deflowering, the sob-stuff, the fuss, crap, so I can't screw any more, can't even play with myself, see for yourself, how daft I was though, how daft you are when you're young, the time I wasted screwing around, notching my ruler, mind you I was a gentleman, I wasn't a bastard with women, but they piss you off, birds are all right for a laugh in bed, but it stops there . . .'

Life seemed sweet to Pervenche. He conscientiously finished his grog, he was warm all over. Armand was warming to another of his favourite themes, poetry, which was closely related to the previous one because Valéry and Apollinaire had bought him three or four extra notches in his school ruler. It was darkening, the sky had still not come to a decision, the logs were fading slowly. Armand had begun to read out loud from *Les Rhénanes*. Gradually his voice, tinged by Apollinaire's false gaiety, had tapered off; he read to himself, descending alone into a world where shadows of scant faith vows make of no worth. He had slumped back in his armchair, the book on his knees, eyes closed. He sat up, gazed at Paul, to whom life now seemed a little less sweet although he didn't know why, and came to a decision, almost reluctantly:

'Look in the record cabinet, bottom left, you'll find an old LP.'

He added, slowly:

'I'm being silly, talking bullshit but, you know, I'm buggered, buggered. Put the record on for me, please, Schwarzkopf, she's in a class of her own.'

It was passages from *The Marriage of Figaro* sung by Elisabeth Schwarzkopf, an old scratchy record. With difficulty, Armand had left his armchair and sat stiffly at the table, resting his elbows on it and pushing back his beret. Paul put on the record. There was not a sound. Then suddenly the singer's voice soared into the room, enveloping everything in its white silk scarf.

*Deh vieni, non tardar, o gioia bella*
*Vieni, ove amore per goder t'appella*

She spoke to them of love, perfect love, she sang of the impatience of lovers, the happiness of longing, the bliss of the embrace. Paul looked around at the nondescript room pervaded by a smell of dust and old age – and filth. The whole world was hanging on the voice and the orchestra which burst into the evening drabness like a firework display. And in fact there was a firework display, on the wall, a photograph taken by Armand ages ago: tongues of light were falling towards a river where rejoicing silhouettes could be made out. There were other photos: kids chasing a soap bubble, clasped hands with the beauty of a cathedral, Provençal landscapes. Music, photographs, everything was exploding with joy, a joy too intense. The voice fell silent. The record kept turning, scratching, the clock reasserted its rights with authority, only a few embers glowed in the hearth. Pervenche turned to Armand to tell him how much he had enjoyed the music. Armand was blind to him: still leaning on the table, his chin resting on his hands, he was crying like a child, without shame, without restraint. His spectacles had slipped down to the tip of his nose, misted, useless. The tears streamed through his stubble, his shoulders heaved slightly with each sob. Pervenche would have liked to shake Armand, hug him, talk to him. He didn't. The shadowy presence of death illuminates sorrow. He stood, changed and prepared to leave. Armand hadn't moved. Paul went over to the record-player, put the record back on, opened the door, changed his mind and took advantage of the resumption of the music to go up to Armand's bedroom and pocket the revolver he knew was there. Armand was still crying. Closing the door, Paul saw his face. It was transfigured by the tears, its blind faith and innocence restored by the beguiling voice. *Deh vieni*, she was cheating on her lover, she was cheating on Armand who allowed himself to be ensnared by beauty when beauty was no longer his concern.

Paul tried to reason with himself. He was distraught about Armand, but then it was only natural that the man should go through periods of despondency. Yet he felt overwhelmed without really understanding the reasons. Perhaps he was moved by the encounter of old age with beauty, by the voice that promised love while stalking Armand like a harbinger of death. The scene had unsettled him. He thought of his photograph; the singing and the photo became bearers of dark premonitions. The revolver in his pocket did nothing to reassure him. The grey of the flooded meadows had turned to black, the clouds were skimming lower. Paul slowed his pace. Carried on the wind, no doubt from the village, came the distant sound of a brass band celebrating the dying flourishes of a church fête – a roll from a side drum, the thud of a bass drum, now and then the more fragile notes of the brass. On the road awash with shadows and apprehensions, Paul felt as if he were in a dream. Somewhere people were having fun, children were shouting and throwing streamers, their parents were trying their luck at tombola. Soon Pervenche could hear only the boom of the bass drum, the monotonous echo of a forbidden celebration.

The train brought him the comfort of its familiar creaking. There were few passengers. A girl near him was probably waiting for him to chat her up before taking her to his flat. Armand would have a fit at such apathy on Paul's part. But Paul wasn't looking at the girl. He was looking at himself in the train window; he wasn't making faces, he wasn't rolling his eyes, he could feel the weapon in his pocket. The train was going too fast, he wanted to cry.

## — 6 —

He devoted one evening to developing his film and another to printing and enlarging. The creative fever had deserted him. He dealt quickly with the routine tasks, avoiding as best he could the traps of the mirror. Redness and nakedness seemed neither necessary nor sufficient once one tried to get to grips with the mystery of genesis. He took special care over five photographs. He liked two of them, those that had raised his hopes, in fact. His expertise was growing. In normal light the chosen two lost something of their magic. They must be lacking a story, they could do with a few drowned bodies, there in the foreground. All the same, Pervenche finished on an optimistic note: these two photos were good, Armand would approve. With these two, the canal and the fog, and three or four others he was nursing in his magic box, he'd soon be able to exhibit. Armand had promised. Well, well, despite himself, Pervenche was smiling at the prospect, laughing to himself, or rather he was laughing up his sleeve, that sounded even better, Pervenche was laughing up his sleeve. His time would come.

And everything was going well. By Monday Armand had telephoned to apologize for his attack of depression and reassure him he was back on top of things. He was impatient to see the shots of the flooded meadows. He hoped Paul hadn't caught a cold. Till Sunday, then, without fail.

She was sporting a pony-tail which showed off two tender ears. Careful now, he checked himself from nibbling the shiny new earlaps, kept spick and span by a mother heedful of the neat appearance of her youngest little girl. He couldn't allow himself to. Later, perhaps.

She had come and sat next to him without a word, wearing a worried look.

'Hello, Ella.'

'H-hello.'

'Are you okay?'

No, she wasn't okay. He finally wormed out of her that she had been scolded at lunch for breaking her plate. It was a bitter pill to swallow. Where his words had failed, the lollipop brought by Pervenche was a hit: as the cares disappeared, there appeared a pink kitten's tongue. She took the matter very seriously, legs dangling and crossed, one hand on the bench, eyes riveted on the sweet. She spun out the pleasure, sucking but not crunching – crunching's silly – and didn't even turn her head when a friend called out to her, she had better things to do than play. Her sucking didn't halt her running commentary: yes she preferred l-lemon 'cos it tickles, and her daddy didn't b-buy her lollipops but her mummy did secretly when she got good marks and mummy gave her brother m-money but she didn't often give h-him money 'cos he didn't get good m-marks, but she d-did get good marks, she had stars and even pictures and when she had ten pictures she'd win a colouring-book but she'd rather have a scrapbook to stick the p-pictures in 'cos she always lost her coloured p-pencils and even her felt-tips but her mummy didn't b-buy her any felt-tips any more 'cos they made stains in her p-pockets and she'd been t-told off and it wasn't her fault and bother I've got a stain on my d-dress with my lolly, bother, bother, I'll get t-told off and . . .

Pervenche was no longer listening. He could hear her, he watched her showering attention on her lollipop, he tried to guess at what age she would lose this miraculous attraction of innocence and sensuality combined. No photograph could ever capture this intangible blend. Armand had tried to persuade him otherwise. For him, a photo was perfectly capable of baring someone's true face. He hadn't convinced

Paul. There was very little that photographs respected. They would betray Ella, they had betrayed Paul by inventing worlds that were not his, further along the canal.

When Pervenche came to his senses, the bird had flown. Just as a sparrow dumps ballast to take off more quickly, this bird had left the lolly-stick on the bench. Vacantly, Paul raised it to his lips and conceded he was in a bad way. The piece of wood fell under the bench. Something for the park-sweeper to look forward to this evening.

Well, she could have given me a kiss, Pervenche repeated to the passers-by he crossed on his way to a party that Frarçcis had promised would be lavish. When his immediate future appeared worthy of general interest, he enjoyed teasing those around him. She could have given me a kiss. An old man gave him a look of commiseration, a grocer hastily pulled down his shutters, a young girl giggled and blushed. Everyone was hurrying towards the miracle that was Saturday night: a meal with plenty to drink, a nice film with a happy ending, the cake taken round to the neighbours as an excuse for conversation in the best of taste about the economic situation, all of which was ennobled by the feeling of having earned, by virtue of a week's conscientious work, this modest reward. It does you good to relax now and again.

Paul woke up with his head in a vice. He should never have drunk so much. But the prospect of seeing Armand, the thrill of conquering a rather tame blonde and François' dexterity in refilling the glasses had encouraged him to go over the top. The fleeting flame of a match behind a tankard of beer which suddenly blazed with gold, the face of a girl, lips pouting gracefully, a bottle knocked over on the carpet, the thump of the hi-fi – that's all he could remember. François must have brought him home.

Twelve! He'd miss his train. He tried to get up. After two failed attempts, he abandoned the journey, dragged himself into bed and slept until five. He managed to find a payphone that was working and, between two bouts of retching, explained the situation to Armand. Armand was not amused. He was feeling low, he rebuked Paul for abandoning him, especially at this of all times. The accused put the coldness of the exchange down to his queasy stomach. He went back to bed.

What a night! On Monday the exploits of the revellers, embroidered and re-embroidered, set the office buzzing. Le Nabec wanted to know where and with whom Paul had disappeared for two hours; Paul, what Le Nabec had been up to during this time. It was the kind of Monday they loved, rich in memories and promise.

On Tuesday and Wednesday the music abated, the files took new heart. A little annoyed by Armand's attitude, Pervenche was waiting for Friday before calling him. He didn't have to wait that long. On Thursday at around ten the phone rang. When he heard the voice of the home help, Paul felt his world reel.

'Monsieur Pervenche? . . . Monsieur Armand's dead.'

Paul closed his eyes, opened them, opened them to see his colleagues, the office windows, Frigo leaning back in his chair.

'Where can I call you back?'

'Well, here. At Monsieur Armand's . . .'

Paul went down to the payphone, it was busy. He waited a few minutes, his head empty. As he dialled, it was a very strange feeling. He thought he was dreaming. It rang once, twice, he would hear the jovial voice of Armand, well then matey, what time you getting here? The home help answered. Armand had been found hanged on the stairs on Wednesday morning. That was it. She was sad, too, so anyway, she had to go now, she was sorry, if she could be of any assistance to Monsieur Pervenche, she would gladly . . .

Paul had not said a word. Armand had hanged himself. He had hanged himself. Hanged, hanging, hanged, to hang oneself – like the swinging of a body, the words came and went remorselessly. A grotesque tongue, obsolete arms, legs splayed for a final gratification. Paul had never believed in the orgasm of the beyond, but perhaps it was true, in fact? Armand was dead. Paul was suddenly waking up to the realization that their friendship hadn't been enough to stop Armand, that from here on he was alone, that he would face his weekends alone, hour by hour. He returned to his office, picked up his jacket and disappeared without a word.

Once outside he walked straight ahead. He barged into a young, effervescent woman who protested with a vehemence justified by being in the right. He stopped, went back to her, asked her if she intended to shut her face, stupid cow, and found himself none the wiser. It was windy, the shop shutters were rattling and spraying raindrops. Pervenche followed a very dignified gentleman with a trilby and an umbrella. Every two paces he spiked the pavement with his umbrella, every two paces he gave a short pull on the handle, just enough to make the tip come up almost horizontal. One, two, tap, one, two, and up in the air. Fascinated, Paul resented the traffic-light for stopping the show. He carried on walking, glaring angrily at people, fleeing the image of himself reflected here and there in the windows of parked cars. He was also fleeing an idea that was beginning to torture him: while he was sleeping off his hangover on Sunday, so pleased with himself, pleased at touching up a woman, Armand had been waiting for him in vain, sinking inexorably into depression. Paul's betrayal had snuffed out the small, already guttering flame his friend still clung to like a lifebelt. It had destroyed his last remaining illusions. If they'd spent the day together, Armand would have drawn enough strength to last out until the following Sunday. He had helped Paul so much over the years, he was entitled to count on some support in return for his loyalty.

Paul had arrived home without realizing it. He threw himself on his bed. He wasn't in pain, he felt drugged. He could hear Elisabeth Schwarzkopf. Armand had put on his record and stoked the fire. The heavy sky through the window was powerless against the voice and the flames which offered one last prayer to the old man. He had waited – to relish a little longer the music punctuated by the crackling logs, and also to give the telephone a chance to save him. And then he had climbed the stairs, he had climbed his cross, he had tied the rope to the banister, he had looked at the fire, he had admired the singer, he had straddled the rail. Pervenche did not move, did not breathe. Hands behind his head, staring at his photos and ribbons on the ceiling, he told himself that he hadn't telephoned, instead he'd related his exploits to the whole office and taken offence at his friend's disappointment. He counted the seconds, the minutes and the hours. They were the first in his life without Armand and they weighed strangely heavy on him. He was due to call the home help the next day. Before putting the phone down, she had added that there might be a service. The family of the dead man, eager for respectability, had in all probability made the necessary arrangements for a religious ceremony. The renegade would be back on the straight and narrow, despite himself.

The clouds had not moved since the last time: they were the same ones, come back to salute Armand. The meadows had begun to struggle free, the fences concealed their laughable pretentiousness, the church spire was now reflected only in a mixture of mud and regret.

There was a crowd outside the small church: the tearful family – it was now or never for displaying their affection for old Armand – and villagers with nothing better to do. The priest, irritated by a ceremony to which he judged, in all conscience, the deceased had no right, was smiling too much, joking perhaps, to show that he washed his hands of any sanctions the Almighty was moved to take. He himself had succumbed to the pressure of the good reputation of an influential family. Effusively playing down a death he did not hold with, but pleased at the high turnout, he opened the door – and the hostilities.

Lost in the restrained murmur of the faithful, Paul had threaded his way to a corner of the church. He wanted to be alone with Armand; it was difficult. Once the nave was full, the priest signalled the off. A hymn rose from the transept, surprising Pervenche by its strength and fervour. A small bouquet of carnations burst red, white and pink on the altar like the laughter of a child. The singing, the flowers, the stained-glass windows: so much beauty amidst so much despair overwhelmed Pervenche. So much beauty because of so much despair. The old stones covered in mould, the smoothness of the master of ceremonies, the rickety chairs rasping on the flagstones: he was aware of it all without paying attention to it. Two rows in front, a girl with a thick shock of hair was displaying a very nice bottom clad in tight-fitting red trousers. Beneath the cloth he noted the elastic of her panties making a victory sign. He pondered the probable colour of the article, decided on black, went for lace. Armand would be getting excited in his box, women would never leave him in peace. An old man next to her was lifting his head towards the vaulted ceiling; the skin at the back of his neck creased hideously. A respectable-looking man immediately in front of Pervenche made it plain he was just doing the done thing by planting his feet squarely, clasping hands behind back, the way he'd been taught.

At the back of the apse, to the left, a statue streamed with love. The inscription on the plinth left no scope for imagination: 'The Heart of Jesus'. A handsome lad, very clean, with a neatly trimmed beard, long combed hair and an expressionless gaze, wearing a long purple robe bedecked with gold, but barefoot for that hint of poverty, his left hand open, was pointing with his right index finger at his torso. On it, like a fly settled on a plate of soup, a gold-crowned heart was supposedly palpitating. A grotesque strawberry. Art and faith don't always make good bedfellows.

From one hymn to the next the ceremony progressed. From one hymn to the next Pervenche, by dint of mockery and rancour, suppressed his pain, delaying the moment when its tireless fingers would probe his guts. The priest inflicted a hypocritical sermon on a distracted congregation, the singing resumed and with it unstifled coughs and the raucous clearing of throats. Out of respect for the service, people would rather ruin the efforts of the choir than hold themselves back or make themselves conspicuous by disturbing the silence of the prayers.

They were well behaved, well brought up. They would never have permitted themselves the winks customary at weddings. They had only the deceased to deal with, but they were reluctant to attract the attention of death which was, after all, prowling nearby. Death endowed the service with an infinite, intimate frisson that added spice to the tedious passage of their afternoon.

Communion clarified the situation. When the priest beckoned, holding the host aloft above the chalice like a formal invitation, there was not a single taker. No one had said anything about a snack during the outing. Necks twisted to see whether someone might accept the sacrifice. In brandishing the host, the priest was levelling at Armand reproaches he didn't deserve. Finally, Pervenche took the plunge, more out of defiance than conviction. He hadn't been a church-goer for years. He crossed the nave, feeling curious looks focused on him. He closed his eyes and opened his mouth, to take communion in a most old-fashioned way. He didn't know that times had changed, that nowadays you shut your mouth and hold out your hand. But he wasn't there, he was far away in time and space, in the small church in his village; he was awaiting his turn to close his eyes and open his mouth. And in front of him, within reach of his hand, within reach of his kisses, her blond hair invited him to follow. He followed faithfully. Dust danced in the shafts of sunlight, the leaded windows cast blue and red splashes on the ground. She was already gone when he closed his eyes, closing them on her blond hair and her serious smile. Pervenche swallowed the host without further ado: the taste brought to life too many things long suppressed.

The choir had started singing a psalm. It would be the last one, you could tell from the sudden warmth of the choristers' voices. Soon they would be able to go home.

Finally opened, the doors flooded a wash of aquamarine light into the nave. The square outside glistened in the drizzle. Umbrellas went up, people waited for the coffin to be laid in the hearse. The faithful indulged in the pleasure, too long denied, of communication. Who's the woman over there? That is Monsieur Charcot, isn't it? A fine sermon, don't you think? So he hanged himself, then, astonishing, and I always thought...

The bells were not speaking of burial. They resounded, joyful and provocative; they mocked the low sky and the tears Pervenche was fighting back. The mourners, however, were not mocking the low sky. It augured nothing good. And anyway, they'd done their duty, they could go, and that Armand was a strange character, they only saw him once in a blue moon.

The family had crammed into a car. The hearse and the car had set off for the cemetery. Pervenche headed that way too. He hugged the walls of the houses to keep out of the rain. He passed a bar. A number of jobless men appeared a little less bored than most days: clustered at the windows, they were witnessing the end of a man who had worked. As he left the village, he noticed the bent silhouette of André. He followed him without joining him. He was thinking of his last evening with Armand, of the singer's voice, of *The Marriage of Figaro*. He was at Mozart's funeral, it was raining, the road was deserted, André replaced the small dog. Armand had listened to *The Marriage of Figaro*, he had celebrated his marriage with death.

André and Pervenche arrived at the cemetery too late. The coffin was in its place, the vault resealed. Two dogs were chasing around, barking. A boy let go of his father's hand to throw stones at them. Terrific, he already had a sense of order, discipline, propriety. Two cypresses bowed over the forsaken graves, these the most beautiful ones. As he left, Paul read a few inscriptions; their gold lettering traced the essentials of lives without substance, drawing a veil over love-life, storms and dreams. The dates prompted some mental arithmetic, one of the few satisfactions allowed by the place.

Armand's brother-in-law had spotted Paul. He invited him back to the house for a drink. Yes, it was his now, that small house where Paul had rediscovered life. Paul declined. It was over. Its photographs no longer had any point, its hearth would no longer be an invitation to travel, nor the wine to laughter. What was the point of going there? To take a piece of the rope, they say it brings luck? Unperturbed, the brother-in-law invited him and André to the café, where they earned the superstitious respect of the drinkers. The heir, who had calculated – you can never be too careful – how little Armand's estate would set him back in duty, was curbing an unbecoming joviality. He offered Paul his services, he was going back to Melun, he could drop him in Meaux. Paul accepted. He saw the little boy from the cemetery passing by the café. With an expression of conviction, he was listening to his father's arguments that a career in business is better than going into the civil service.

In the car the heater gave the two of them an encouragement that was quite superfluous. The conversation ranged from these Novembers you can't rely on any more to the evening's menu. In Meaux Paul changed his mind. He didn't want to take the train, he'd rather hitch-hike. The journey by train frightened him, he had too many fond memories of it.

Where the motorway turned off to Melun, the newly enriched next of kin abandoned him to his fate. He stationed himself under a bridge, just after the toll-booths. The rain was persistent, thorough. The darkness grew bolder. Opposite, a row of poplars swayed sadly, disheartened at having always to lean to the east. On the ground in the middle lane, a child's shoe told a story too important to be betrayed by a photograph.

The motorists sped away. Pervenche decided to go on. He walked from one bridge to the next, sticking out his thumb, tiring of waiting, moving on. In the distance to the right, he could see the lights of villages swallowed up by vast, windblown expanses. He walked on without pausing until he reached a service station. Shapes gesticulated, flags at the top of fragile poles proclaimed empty victories in the gusts. Some people scuttled about in the bad weather, others allowed themselves the comfort of a hot drink. Paul envied them, he envied their uneventful worries and pleasures. He suppressed the temptation to join them. He preferred his solitude. He wanted to feel remote from everything and everyone. The rain soaked his clothes but he wasn't cold, he was walking fast. A driver stopped, reversed, opened the door. Paul stammered that he was fine, thanks, he didn't have far to go. The driver needed no second bidding.

To avoid any repeat misadventure, Pervenche crossed the three lanes of the motorway and climbed over one of the two central crash-barriers. They made a space for a path of sorts, overgrown with grass, where he felt safe. He continued on his way as if crossing an unknown planet. On his left vehicles came at him, on his right they came past him, within arms' reach as they rushed headlong, overtaking, catching, following one another, like fanatical troops. Their headlights dazzled, projecting before him his disproportionate shadow, mutilated by the barriers. The rain was falling hard. Now and then he had time to catch sight of wan faces distorted by the drops running down the windscreens; he could imagine the music, the warm interior, the dozing passenger resting her own hand on the driver's. A body was swinging beside an open fire, Paul was raising his glass to the window in old André's cellar, Armand was sprinting to the tape: the images flashed past at breakneck speed, harnessed to the tempo of the cars.

A sound of unexpected braking jolted Paul. He saw a police car come to a stop fifty yards ahead. Without a second thought he broke from his cover and ran to the ditch on the far side, causing more cars to brake. Two police officers, shoulders hunched around their ears, stepped out of their vehicle and looked across at him, pointing at the crash-barriers. They made a helpless gesture and conferred. Then they ran for shelter and drove off. Paul slipped back into his secret garden.

He walked for a long time. Fatigue was creeping over him, the cold was chilling him to the bone. He regretted not taking the train. The roar of the engines and the swish of the tyres on the drenched road surface unflaggingly sounded the charge. He could hear the noise approaching from afar, swelling irresistibly, bursting as it reached him, then fading and leaving him even more alone. The spray thrown up by the wheels arched glistening in the darkness like gigantic scythes that cut short his breath. Armand was pointing out the silver blades, explaining how they could have photographed them. Advertising hoardings lit furtively by the cars displayed Paul's photograph. The light patch was no longer a void, a body was curled up in it. True enough, it was even more beautiful with a corpse in the foreground. Armand burst into the laughter Paul was so fond of, never mocking but full of love for others and for life. He had dragged himself up the stairs to die, he had followed his way of the cross. And Paul offered him his own, offered him his rain-sodden weariness. A pathetic offering! His own way of the cross was leading him to bed. He didn't have a gift for suffering in style. Armand was dead. What did he have left? What would become of him? He was spent. Despair swamped him like a black wave. He stopped and began to cry. Crying was all he was good for. Through his tears and the rain the headlights and taillights were exploding, rending the night with golden arrows and with blood. In serried ranks the vehicles surrounded him, bellowing. His feet sank into the grass and mud. He was trampling the ice-cold body of a dead man, trampling also his childhood that would be of no further use to him. He was frozen, even colder than the day when, streaming with water from the flooded meadows, he had rung at Armand's door. But this evening there was no fire in the hearth, no grog, no Armand, there was no way out. He straightened up and blinked, as if he were waking. A lull in the flow of traffic enabled him to reach the hard shoulder. He started jogging to fight his tiredness.

A car, broken down, was waiting for the downpour to end. He passed it. A window opened, a voice called out in poor French. It was a Dutchman. He invited Pervenche to rest. An hour later, a breakdown truck came and extricated them from their predicament. The Dutchman talked a lot, he wasn't short of things to say. Paul had recovered his senses. The biscuits, the thermos flask and the chatter of his host, the loan of a pullover – that was all it took for the well-being of the body to urge greater moderation on the heart and mind.

## — 7 —

The night had summoned the rain to officiate elsewhere. The sky slumbered, dark yet without sorrow. Its lack of tact rankled with Pervenche. As did the fact that he had slept well, undisturbed by dreams or startled awakenings. And so too did Anne-Sophie's scant show of interest in his misfortune. He could not will himself out of his bed. Cosseted by the snugness of the bedclothes, he made a leisurely assessment of the full extent of the damage. As his drowsiness dissipated, the contours of the new landscape of his life took shape, revealing ashes, parched rivers and devastated forests. He suddenly realized that he was an orphan, that revelry and reverie had abandoned him. He would have liked to indulge himself in lavish self-pity; he felt overcome by the fumes of meanness and aggression. He couldn't be cut out for an extraordinary destiny; he didn't have the makings of a hero. He had faced up to Armand's death – the end of the world, in fact – like the insurance clerk that he was. He had attended the service and had cried. He cut a very sad figure. Now he was going to get up, dress, return to work, earn the appreciation of his superiors, acknowledge his colleagues' condolences, exhibit excessive concentration over his files, and lunch as well as anyone else, or maybe even a little better because he had eaten nothing the previous evening. What else do you expect? Life reasserts itself, as it should. He would wipe the corner of his mouth with his paper napkin to look neat and proper. 'Pervenche? An excellent fellow, believe me.' He would drink a coffee to combat the lassitude that service sector employees have to cope with in the early afternoon, he would riffle, write, say 'Pervenche speaking', dictate, perhaps even think, take – who knows? – some initiative with Frigo's agreement in order to expedite a claim. Then in the evening, his shoulders all the broader for having served Magistrale well, he would visit Claire, she would give him a meal, he would give her an orgasm; tactfully she would ask no questions. And he would go home, make an offering of an obscene gesture at the Gautiers' door, think about the pert bottom of the young Martin girl, greet his three silent companions and slip between his sheets, just where he was now. It would be back to square one, nothing would have changed, nothing would have progressed, he would merely have added a bud to the lacklustre garland of his days, and a choice bud at that, because the day would have brought him nothing but satisfaction.

Pervenche leaped out of bed. He was going to be late arriving; that would be the last straw. He could already picture it: the stares fixed on the laggardly loss adjuster painfully distressed by an untimely death, his gait and bearing, yet to be suitably defined, but at once dignified and shaky. He started to run to work, then remembered he hadn't run for ages and that he ought to do something about it. He slowed almost to a halt to cross the footbridge: he climbed the steps as that day Armand had climbed his stairs, rope in hand. The incipient dawn cast a fragile light on the canal. Another photo I won't take, Paul thought. And at this instant of regret, he knew Armand had uttered the same thing to himself at the very moment of dying. He understood why Armand had chosen a spectacular death; he was sure Armand had left nothing to chance, not the lighting, the length of the rope, the composition, nor the depth of field. Armand had opted for a photogenic death, he had passed through the lens. Artist had become art, but, out of excessive egotism, the work remained unfinished. Like all works of art, Pervenche declared sententiously to some sparrows fluttering around the gutter. The thought must have caught their interest: Paul heard them arguing as he hurried away.

He arrived just on time and hid behind a file he could make neither head nor tail of, turning the same page twenty times without daring to lift his eyes. He was afraid that if he did so, he would meet the sympathetic gazes of his colleagues, have to face up to a smile of encouragement and be obliged to compose a countenance to match the circumstances. He considered he was acquitting himself not too badly, all in all. He left his desk to have a coffee but ran and locked himself in the toilet where he burst into tears. He had held up well during the morning; everything was going as he had imagined earlier in bed – no surprises, not a snag in the grey fabric of his new life. But he was now discovering that the greyness he had pictured with a sort of morbid, vindictive pleasure was something he would in fact have to live with. He was discovering that in future he would have to bottle everything up. He would no longer go down and telephone Armand to confide in him the worry that was clouding his day, he would no longer pack his bag on a Saturday or Sunday morning. His plans and regrets were denied the very thing that provided their justification: the thrill of confiding and conniving. For the past six or seven years he had lived each of the adventures, each of the events in his life twice, the first time when it happened and the second when he recounted it to Armand. Being shared, the second occasion was the more intense. But that was no longer to be. A section of wall had just collapsed, flattening the most exciting, the dearest parts of his existence.

The days passed with meticulous slowness. Pervenche passed through them with his head lowered and his back a little more hunched; he was shrinking within his grief like a discarded fruit. Paul could share nothing any more with Armand, except his grief: he guarded it jealously. Solitude was better suited to sharpening the pangs, but the perverse satisfaction he derived from this mortification caused him to question just how genuine his emotions were. Pain, bitterness, aggression, jealousy, uncertainty – this kaleidoscope cast things in shifting tones, presenting no anchorage for his life. And he took to wearing a soon familiar hair shirt, which he possibly expected to mollify the feeling of culpability he was desperate to elude.

That did not stop him paying the occasional visit to Claire. The prospect of a warm meal and a warm body had been enough to tear Pervenche away from worshipping a myth. The model employee was harmonizing his private with his professional life: conscientious and tidy. He would go far.

Afterwards he would slip away home to immerse himself in an atmosphere of memories and thwarted aspirations. He lectured himself, declared himself fit to square up to his affliction and come to terms with his inner disarray, rather than follow the sterile path mapped out for him by Claire and the others. He recognized the son of Armand. He recognized himself.

He crossed the Saint-Martin canal without concerning himself with the colour of the day; his instinct had deserted him. For all that, the sky struck him as noteworthy for a November sky: large grey and black clouds were fraying, revealing momentary patches of blue, the serene blue of a different season. The melancholy given off by the clouds and the sadness exhaled by the city professed no apparent justification other than highlighting these splashes of azure. He was still recovering from his surprise at the blue rents when someone tugged his sleeve. He forsook the heavens to find heaven at his feet:

'Hello. Hello Paul.'

Ella was smiling at him, Ella was giving him a subtle smile: guilty yet accusing. He didn't know what to say. The brother was waiting a little further off. Paul had shut the door on Ella, but had yet to decide whether it was for good or not: the sun had no place where the rain held sway. Pervenche had opted for the rain but now, dazzled by this unexpected brightness, he was elated. He had avoided the square on the previous two Saturdays, hadn't even tried to catch a distant glimpse of his tiny playmate. She was part of a world that Armand's death had wiped out.

'Will you bring me some sweets on Saturday?'

It was as if she had guessed Paul's torment. She was forcing his hand. Then within him, suddenly, the floodgates broke and a wave of gratitude, relief and joy washed over him. He caught Ella, who was being drawn schoolwards by her educational obligations and her brother, and kissed her on both cheeks, saying softly:

'What kind of sweets do you want?'

He waited on the pavement until the little lady had passed through the gates; he waved back at her. It was almost daylight; broad strips of blue were gaining ground on the clouds. A car grazed him, its radio blaring a song heard at Claire's. His step became jauntier. In the Rue de Lancry some chickens were already roasting outside a delicatessen. Pervenche stopped, to inhale the smell more fully. He recalled forgotten stories of barefoot children loitering by the fresh white loaves at the baker's. He felt like a small boy, but rich: no one would prevent him from buying a chicken that evening. The prospect almost made him laugh. The sun was about to rise; it was already lighting Paul Pervenche's life. He greeted this unfocused optimism, this sudden burst of spontaneous joy with the zest of a chicken whose life has been spared. He observed his less fortunate fellows behind the glass of the rotisserie: plump and golden, legs tamely folded. For the survivor salivating at the sight of them, they symbolized how hazardous is one's lot. There are losers and there are the rest; and he, Paul Pervenche, was going to celebrate his return to the land of the survivors by polishing off a loser.

The twenty minutes' travelling time were hardly enough to count the points in the new hand life had dealt him. Good job, nice good-looking girlfriend, a few good mates, not many but enough, a little sweetheart, but let's keep that quiet – a secret, the promise of some brilliant photos, a reasonably rosy future. It added up to something substantial, admittedly not spectacular, but substantial, attractive.

He had not left Armand out of this picture framed in the darkness by a spotlight. Far from it. But instead of devoting himself to barren hero-worship, he thought it more in keeping with his friend's character and vitality to fête rather than mourn him, to earn his approval rather than hark back to him – in short, to prove himself worthy of him.

The Rue des Petites-Ecuries left him in a state of euphoria; for all its garishness, he was not unduly perturbed. By the Rue Richer he had progressed to the next stage – congratulation. It was Armand who had pulled him from the depths of despair when he'd arrived in Paris in such a sorry state, Armand who had broken down, one by one, the barriers Paul had erected around himself. Armand had understood, known what to say, the right thing to do, Armand had restored him to life. Left alone, Paul would have gone under. Which is what he was doing now, once again, in the absence of support from an elder brother. Then suddenly, thanks to a small girl, a patch of blue sky and a crispy chicken, Paul had convinced himself he was going down the wrong road. The ease of his conversion worried him a little. But the essential fact remained – he had pulled through unaided. In the end he did have character, he had something of Armand's breed, definitely. From now on it was up to him, to transfigure the bland exterior of his existence, to explore its hidden riches. But he didn't have the luxury of exploring the riches of his affirmation: the Rue Lafayette was inviting him to don his loss adjuster's uniform. He did so with pleasure, surprising everyone with his drive and energy. Le Nabec was overjoyed that he could at last – having refrained from it since Armand's death – make the office thrill at five o'clock to the sound of a particularly good fog-horn performance.

So things resumed their course. Took their course, Pervenche corrected: he took it as axiomatic that he had changed direction, that everything was new from here on. One morning when he had broken off for a coffee and – in order to dispel the vague embarrassment that overtakes an employee when he grants himself a small treat during working hours – he was scanning the staff notice-board, shifting the still scalding cup back and forth from hand to hand, he came across a vacancy for a loss adjuster in Toulouse. Applications closed the next day. It seemed the perfect opportunity to turn the page for good. He thought it over carefully, talked it over with François and with Claire.

François encouraged him to go for it; Claire, a little more torn, intimated that, if Paul wished, it would be easy for her to obtain a transfer to Toulouse. Paul put in his application and from then on devoted much of his daydreaming to the south-west of France.

The only cloud in the picture hung over Ella. When he saw her, after his decision, he delayed telling her, then decided against it. Why spoil the last weeks of their love affair?

She was playing over there with her brother and other children. She was the smallest. Pervenche, suddenly fascinated by games with rules unknown to him, was dismayed to see that more often than not she was left on the sidelines, you're out, you're out, you can't play any more. And she, despite her disappointment, would watch the game continue, her face lighting up when another child's turn came to be out, only to darken again when she remembered she had lost, that she still had to wait her turn to be given a fresh chance. She had spotted Paul, stopped dead for two moments, looking at him, and had returned to the skylarking as if nothing had happened. She was out twice more. That did it. She thrust her hands in her pockets, dropped her head, didn't answer her brother who asked her what was wrong, turned her back on the cheats and came over to Paul. She stood there in front of him, head still lowered, without a word.

Pervenche had left nothing to chance. He had bought a bumper packet of sweets, assorted sweets, so as not to risk failure. She soon forgot her misfortunes, took her time picking out the biggest and, with no more ado, sat beside him. Her cheek swollen by a recalcitrant toffee, she could no longer close her mouth. Her legs swung free. Like a good girl she had rested her hands on her thighs, and was giving Paul a saucy look.

'Do you only come here on Saturdays? Don't you come in the evenings or on Wednesdays?'

'No, my mummy d-doesn't let me. Only S-saturdays. What about you?'

'Me?'

Taken aback, Pervenche explained that he came by now and again. But his mind was elsewhere; he was thinking that in having to confirm, as he had, the day of their rendezvous, he was somehow making their relationship official, publishing the banns of their forthcoming wedding. He enquired after her brother's name his age, his abilities at school, his qualities and his faults: there was no harm in knowing a bit more about the brother-in-law ... The first sweet had lasted quite a while. Now she began to unwrap a second one, just as big.

'Aren't you having one?'

'I don't like sweets.'

'Why have you g-got them, then?'

Precisely. Paul said he'd been given the packet and didn't know what to do with it.

'Do you want it?'

Her eyes opened wide. She nodded frantically.

'C-can I give some to my friends?'

'Of course ...'

'Thank you, Paul.'

She snatched her booty from him, jumped from the bench, raced away, braked like a cartoon character, came back to Paul, stretched her robin's beak towards him, gave the cheek he had offered a wet kiss, and was off again, singing. She never walked, she could only run, jump and dance. As he stood, Paul noticed the small handkerchief with which she had tried to wipe her hands. He picked it up, sniffed it and stuffed it into his pocket. It was blue – like a flower, like her eyes.

She was confident she could play without any danger of being left out. Which proved true. Unsettled by this first kiss, Paul spent long minutes watching the children play, admiring the cunning of the girl and the duplicity of the friends as they unwrapped a sweetpaper and decided that, no, no, this time she wasn't out but be careful in future. Big brother stood still a moment, staring at Paul from afar. Paul did not take kindly to such insolence. He rose and left without a backward glance at the children.

\*

Big brothers excepted, Pervenche was full to bursting with love. There was Ella, there was Claire, there was François, there were his insurance claims, some of them at least, and there was himself. He had been happy with himself for some time now. He was entertained at the prospect of this loss adjuster about to depart for pastures new where he would prove capable and thorough, where he would establish a home and family to be envied and await a well-deserved retirement.

Yet the walls he had thrown up around his certainties showed gaps in places. It ruffled him. Generally, he managed to cover these cracks with the protective paper of pretence, everything was just fine, wasn't it, why read too much into things. But at times nothing was safe from the scalpel. He dissected everything. Then the couple that was himself and Claire would wither – howling kids, a dog who received all the attention, a caravan, the story of his day at the office, over dinner. It was almost a month since Pervenche had applied for his transfer. He had assured Claire that he wanted her to join him in Toulouse. Since then, he spent the weekends with her and saw her almost every evening. They had been to Le Nabec's for dinner and had invited some of Claire's girlfriends. A real couple of lovebirds, a couple of senior citizens. When he left Claire's at night – he had made this token concession to the final throes of his independence – Paul found it hard to convince himself of his own happiness. As much as he enjoyed seeing Claire after a few days apart, he was happy to go home after a few hours in her company. It did not strike him as the ideal preparation for a life together. He was discovering boredom, a silky boredom, free of sharp edges, dotted with cajolery, sweet nothings and irritations. He was astounded to notice how fast the freshness of discovery took on a rancid taste. Shopping on Friday evenings, a film at the cinema, breakfast in bed, the Sunday outing, the lazy afternoon – he had embraced all this with the enthusiasm of a child making his first communion. Pervenche did not find it easy to forgive Claire when the simple repetition of these pleasures turned their rosy colour into grey. The future no longer seemed so radiant to him. All the less so because routine had crept into even their tender tussles and, with the dissatisfaction it heralded, so too had the desire to resort to various expedients.

No, at times Pervenche could not help but heave a sigh. He had given up photography, only temporarily, he promised in self-deception. In fact, he had the obscure feeling that making the break with photography would help prop up his still faltering serenity. The development and enlargement of photographs raised too many question marks not to endanger his good resolutions. He avoided thinking about it.

Jogging helped. He had, with a few friends from Magistrale, started running again, usually on Saturday mornings. The oxygen sucked in by his lungs soon expelled the fetid air of fantasizing that he censured in himself. Sport in the morning, Ella in the afternoon, Claire the rest of the time, François during the week – his timetable was taking good care of him. He knew what was in store.

Paul breathed in the night with pleasure. It was mild. The newly installed winter had favoured, this year, a smooth handover of office. It gave autumn time to pack its bags, to say goodbye, to soften a little. The damp, cool air bathed Pervenche's face. He had just taken abrupt leave of the extended Magistrale family gathered, as every year, around the Christmas tree. Bosses and staff mingled quite informally. The hope of an affair that would bring a promotion, or of a promotion that would permit some affairs, bolstered the credibility of the party. Behind their glasses and sly smiles everyone disguised their battle plan.

Elbowed by the dancers, harangued by the drinkers, Paul had turned tail and fled. Maybe Claire was in bed already, he would be able to surprise her in her sleep. He liked nothing better than to arrive like that, like a thief. He wouldn't wake her, he would lay bare the defenceless body beneath the sheets and caress it slowly. He would remain alone, with no need to talk or feign, just looking and touching.

His head was not clear enough for him to go back yet, to crouch over Claire. He walked. He walked and the force of habit drew him towards his own neighbourhood. He had the urge to see the Saint-Martin canal, and the square, and the canal side. He stopped on one of the footbridges, the air was cooler there. Cars passed now and then, marring the mournful stillness that emanated from the place. Leaning against the parapet like a captain against his rail, Pervenche watched the night draw in. He no longer really knew where his ship was taking him. In the end, the happiness, or what he called happiness, into which he had plunged over the past weeks, had no strength in depth. That's what true happiness is: happiness is not waiting for anything. Happiness and expectation have never made good bedfellows. The maxims he was airing rang in his ears like the encouragement shouted at the losing fighter by an ecstatic crowd. He left his perch, hesitated between his own bed and Claire's, and chose to keep walking. He wanted to see the Rue Monte-à-regret. He was in no danger, there was no fog. Everything was in place – the cobblestones, the street lamps, the patch of light, the arch he had leaned against. No fog, so no mystery; no mystery, so no good photograph. He mused, there, aware that these photographs had occupied too important a place in his life to be ditched overnight. Suddenly, he heard footfalls. Someone was coming from the far end of the street, on his pavement, aiming for the Quai de Jemmapes. Instinctively, he stepped back into the arched entrance and hid behind the door. The footsteps, slow and heavy, tolled. Pernickety, thought Pervenche, he's had steel tips put on his heels. The man was drawing closer. A sort of fear, apprehension, crept over Pervenche lurking in his hiding-place. A shadow floated across the pavement, distorted by the street lamp to the right. It lengthened and grew, and Pervenche saw him. A man, darkly dressed, hands in the pockets of his raincoat, walking with his head bowed. He drew closer and without warning Pervenche felt an explosion deep inside himself, in his gut. His head buzzed, sweat burned his eyes. The man had slowed, probably to look at something, on the ground or in his hand. For a fraction of a second, he had stopped in the centre of the patch of light. And the explosion which had panicked Pervenche was that of a revelation: he would kill this man, he had to kill him, there, at that very spot, and retake the photo.

Paul was motionless. He had not left his cover. He wanted to throw up. He could see Armand, hear his laugh. He realized that Armand had asked him to retake his photo. He had thought about it since, more for fun. He had imagined himself stabbing somebody. In front of a mirror he had set his face in the expression of a killer. But none of that counted. Tonight, in this doorway, he had just made his decision. Terrified, yet confident, he had just consented to the test set by Armand. Armand, too, had killed. He didn't know where or whom, but he knew. When Armand had said to him 'a corpse', he had looked him straight in the eye, in all seriousness. It was only afterwards that he had laughed. He had known then that he was going to die. But it was only now that Pervenche grasped the monstrosity of this last message, this hand outstretched to him one last time. And the monstrosity no longer frightened him. Now that he had accepted its inescapability, he felt stronger, ready to defy the world, to take his revenge. The man had continued on his way and disappeared around the corner of the street.

Images milled in Paul's head. Armand, the silhouette of the unknown man crumpled in the pool of light, photos that brought gasps of admiration, the face of Rimbaud pinned down on his poster, blond hair beside a river, the shade of dense foliage. He emerged from his lair, sidestepping, despite himself, the pale void and strode away. He held himself back from running.

# — 8 —

The office was humming smoothly, Magistrale was blossoming. Pervenche felt a new man. He could see things with greater detachment. That morning he had been called for interview. He had made a good impression on the head of the delegation from Toulouse. When the director had asked about the applicant's preferred starting date, Pervenche had suppressed a smile: in a month's time, that will be fine, just long enough to kill some punter and take a photo. He enjoyed saying terrible things, things that made his hair stand on end. Of course, he kept them to himself, but he thought them so vividly and so often that it was almost as if he said them aloud. In speaking them aloud he trivialized them, and in trivializing them he tamed them, they tamed him, and they grew accustomed to each other.

'In a month,' answered Pervenche, interested by the spectacle of his future boss, so concerned about details whose futility escaped him. Another one who took his work seriously, gave it his all and had stopped dreaming long ago.

Pervenche was not breathing the same air. While the man from Toulouse was explaining his approach to handling claims, Paul was miles away, taking stock. In a few days he had aged twenty years, grown older but much more discerning. He had acquired the composure that comes with the certainty of being on the right track. There was no room for disappointments or strokes of luck: such consolations followed only from the lack of imagination which makes you open a bottle of champagne to celebrate a piece of good news.

With a degree of commiseration he recalled the fairly rosy period he had just gone through. How could he have indulged in such honeyed pleasures and so much self-satisfaction? Nice little dinner parties, nice little films at the cinema, nice little walks – it's good to get some fresh air. And the haste with which he was burning yesterday's idols was by no means indecent, he decided: there were attenuating circumstances. True, he had groped around, even gone astray. Now, order had been restored, he knew where he was going.

He bore his secret within him. He was amazed by it. He was scarred by it. Just as a woman hides the fruit of forbidden love, he quelled his bouts of sickness, he calmed the over-excitement that gripped him in a cycle whose regularity had forced him into submission. Impatience and apprehension, the temptation, also, to forget everything, encouraged the muzak of his mind to take itself for a symphony.

It was not, in any case, the *Pastoral Symphony*; this particular twenty-fourth of December was doing its utmost to dampen the children's delight. It was shedding a freezing drizzle. The umbrellas, in the street, concealed gift-wrapped parcels, the bags laden with food promised indigestion, the vehicles stuck in the traffic jams awaited the Messiah in a concert of car horns.

Paul held tightly under his arm the gift that, after much hesitation, he had selected. It was almost six o'clock. He was hurrying towards the hospital where Bruno was expecting him.

Bruno was the hero of Pervenche's favourite insurance claim. He was nine and had been paralysed in both legs by an accident. Paul was handling the claim with ardour and application which were so out of the ordinary that his good conscience, he felt, entitled him to neglect all the other claims he considered of no interest.

Sickened by the parents who hassled him about when they would recover 'their' money, he had already visited the child twice. He had been struck by his courage and good spirits. Since then, they had written to each other regularly.

'Hey, a darts set. Fantastic.'

Pervenche let the little invalid hug him. He had known precisely what he was up to when he had chosen the darts set. He knew that Bruno would like it, that his parents would be constantly afraid for him but even more for themselves, that they would tear strips off him, and off one another, but that they would still be unable to confiscate the game from the child. He too would be able to live dangerously. Pervenche congratulated himself as he talked dart-throwing technique with Bruno, and discussed the best place to hang the board.

It was still raining, not that it bothered him much. He had plenty on his plate. Claire had gone to spend Christmas with the family. He had declined her invitation, as he had Le Nabec's, who was anxious about Paul being left on his own on Christmas Eve. Normally, Paul went to Armand's. This year he would celebrate solo. The solitude suited him. The world about him was wallowing in forced revelry, stomachs were being filled, glasses emptied, parcels unwrapped. Nevertheless, he was determined to mark the occasion. He lit two candles in his room, slipped under his plate a tea-towel that could have passed as a table-cloth, put on some music, opened a tin of mackerel in white wine, assumed that was more than Joseph had had, regretted all the same not treating himself to a chicken from the Rue de Lancry, and allowed himself a can of beer. His Christmas appealed to him. It had style – cultivation and moderation.

Shortly before midnight he went out. The Martins had guests, the television was helping the Gautiers to forget they existed. He went down towards the Seine, passed behind the Pompidou Centre, decided against the Left Bank, went back up the Rue Saint-Denis, through the red light district, coming face to face with desolation. There were women earning a living; there were men, shoulder to shoulder, hypnotized, who would have sold Christ to finger this pasty flesh. They didn't feel the cold, or their hunger; they lived only for the fever that consumed their loins. Paul walked on. He relished his night-time joy-rides; his pleasure was keener each time. He looked forward to them like looking forward to a first date. In fact, he still had a date: with himself. The bad weather didn't change anything, quite the opposite; to the enjoyment of walking it added the pleasure of knowing it led to a room, a bed, a refuge. He didn't ask himself what his outings swept him towards nor what they tore him from. He walked. Body and soul, obediently, resonated in unison.

He walked more quickly: he was being summoned, to the Rue Monte-à-regret. The silence, the livid light from the street lamps, the black hole of the doorway, a few exclamations of merry-making in the distance: all in all a night like any other. Having recovered from the inner turmoil of that other evening, Pervenche was reconnoitring the location. There could be no question of improvising. Hit-or-miss is no way to take an artistic photograph. Once *in situ*, he began first to calculate the trajectories. The difficulties of the operation suddenly became apparent to him. The victim had to occupy the centre spot of the patch of light. For Paul to be able to surprise him and strike, he had to approach along the same pavement, of course, and from the top end of the street, making for the canal. Paul could not visualize himself dragging a corpse by the feet to arrange the composition. He attempted a trial run. He walked away, then back on the correct pavement, bent his knees shortly before the patch and dropped to his haunches. He would have stretched out on the ground, but the rain persuaded him otherwise. He had to strike a yard before the patch, no more. If the man was walking at normal pace, the blow from behind would carry him across that distance, calculated Pervenche, who now had a clearer picture of the scene. There still remained the key problem: the weapon. Between Armand's revolver and the boy scout's knife he had unearthed in a cupboard there was a considered choice to make. He dismissed the revolver as too noisy. But the knife didn't inspire confidence either. The hour was crucial. He had noticed, further along, the scaffolding of a building site. He ventured in, stumbled through the rubble and unearthed an iron bar that was ideal, but no, too heavy. Finally, he took a length of wood almost as heavy, a spar, that suited his purpose. He carried it back into the entrance and hid it behind the large door, praying that no one would remove it. He gave himself a few moments to register that both the circumstances and the subject of his prayer were well chosen: *Heilige Nacht!* He cast a proprietorial eye over the place, walked away and back one last time, and felt a slight shudder as he passed the doorway where he had concealed the club. He would have to weight the blow carefully: heavy enough for the recipient not to recover, but not so heavy as to fell him on the spot. Come what may, he had to sprawl further forwards, in that damned patch of light. Okay, okay, that'll do. He didn't want to leave. He felt good right here. Around him Christmas was glorifying love for one's fellow man. And he was thinking of Armand; and of the photo he would take, to perfection.

He was ready. He had to wait for the opportune moment, and for a willing victim. Pervenche would conserve a tender memory of his Christmas Eve. When he got back home, everyone was asleep. He reproached his house guests for dropping off, Rimbaud in particular. He described to them his groundwork, detailed the technical difficulties of the execution and, when he knew they were wide awake, he disappeared into bed. He thought he had left nothing to chance. Of course, he remained at the mercy of last-minute hitches, but that did not worry him unduly. He could rely on his sense of initiative and his lucky star. He was off to Toulouse in a month: in January the fog would need little persuasion to fall. Anne-Sophie, no stranger to ambushes, remained pensive for quite some time.

Warmed by the satisfaction of leading a double life and covering his tracks with consummate skill, Pervenche put everything into leading a tranquil existence. His days at the office were no more than breathing spaces in which his quickening isolation paused before gathering even greater pace. The dark pleasure he felt at distancing himself from a flock he had gone bleatingly along with confirmed him in his convictions: where was there excitement or adventure without singularity? The mission entrusted to him was drawing him inexorably away from the ovine huddle. He observed the timorous tide of sheep with some condescension, but consented to blend in with them during his working hours.

He displayed care and even obstinacy in dealing with his claims, dictated flowery letters, surprised solicitors by his hard-nosed negotiating. He pushed Frigo, who was cool about the Rousseau settlement, and convinced him to go for shared liability: the precedents were categorical. And Pervenche revered precedent. It enabled him to avoid asking himself questions, to ignore exceptions and to shield himself from the very real tragedies that certain cases revealed to him. He revered nothing more than precedent, except perhaps photography. Precedent and photography: law and art, black and white – they got on famously within his scale of values. They had, to his mind, sufficient merits to be numbered among those things that are beyond question. He had made up his mind once and for all; that's how it was.

'Bloody hell, you've really got the bit between your teeth these days.'

Le Nabec was dumbfounded. It wasn't at all like Pervenche, who used to be more composed, more discreet, more retiring. This new image, attributed by his colleagues to his transfer to Toulouse, amused Pervenche. He delighted in pulling the wool over their eyes. No doubt about it, he did have the bit between his teeth.

# — 9 —

Paul had taken out the photo and pinned it beside the window: every evening he steeped himself in its unsavoury atmosphere, checked the denseness of the fog, peering out of the window to make a perfunctory comparison. Nothing doing, probably it was too cold. The sky stayed clear. He would turn on his television at the end of the news to listen, on edge somewhat, to the forecasts of the weathermen. With a venomous smile they predicted crystal clear days ahead. He didn't believe them. He drew the curtains before going to bed and, when he awoke, he lay there long enough to decide on the colour of the day. He had resumed his old obsessive habits, except that the colour of the forecast now assumed cardinal importance: what would be the colour of the day that would close with him taking his photograph? He had often dabbed his brushes in an over-extensive palette, but experience had led him to confine himself to just four colours whose designations he had embellished in order to give his ruminations a hint of esoteric chic. Pervenche went in for convoluted turns of phrase. He had come up with albuminous for those neutral days when nothing good or bad can happen, when one experiences nothing, those days whose sole raison d'être is to age one by a day; violaceous for those days cloaked in listlessness, when people were strait-jacketed in their hideousness and pettiness, when the sky closed; celadon for the days, in contrast, when girls displayed charms still hidden only yesterday, when emotion and sensuality coursed through the bloodstream like alcohol, when the air vibrated; lastly, peonin for the days he classed as social, days when he assumed his role as a man among men, attentive to others, eager for conversation, abounding with energy, at everyone's service. Magistrale had every cause for satisfaction with Pervenche when peonin was the order of the day, which did not happen that often. He had talked over his choice of colours with Armand, who had shown not a trace of interest.

Beneath the bedcovers, he lay in wait for the noises, the texture of the air, the feel of the light filtering under the curtains and spilling on to the carpet. Then he would take the plunge, reach a decision, get up, dress, drink his coffee and dash off to work, attending to the Gautiers' door or mat in passing, not looking up as he emerged into the street, but only stopping once he was on the footbridge. That's when the morning handed down its verdict – white, violet, green, red. Pervenche, his breath expelling little puffs of fog, had to bow to the decision taken by his neighbourhood. He was not often wrong; but, if need be, he happily owned up to his mistake, considering, justifiably, that the wind and its moods should be given a chance.

He lived a painful and pleasurable time. He lived intensely. He was ready, mentally and technically. He was awaiting the push from Providence. The weather forecast had promised a cooling in the temperature. The countdown began. Pervenche explained to Claire that he had a whole sequence of photos to take and that he wouldn't be able to see her for a few days. Le Nabec was surprised at the restlessness of his friend, who couldn't keep still. And it was true that Paul devoted the greater part of his time to scanning the sky over the building next door.

In three weeks he would be a Toulousain. He still hadn't said anything to Ella. He wouldn't say anything to her. One day he would disappear, she would remember him for a few months, then forget him.

He had a quick meal, bought some lollipops and followed the Quai de Jemmapes towards the Square Jules-Ferry. A cripple was waiting, who knows what for, balancing on his crutches. On the far side, large posters vaunted wealth and beauty to the poor and ugly who beheld them. Red lights on the canal competed with those at the adjacent junctions. Paul liked their reflections, shattered by the undisciplined water, at night when they denied or granted free passage to ghosts and madmen. On the footbridges diamond-shaped signs, half-red half-white, spoke a language which meant nothing to Paul. It was busy: gawpers, fascinated by the floats of sceptical anglers, pigeons skimming the water in imitation of swallows, men in cars, and a threatening sky. By the entrance to the Square Frédérick-Lemaître, a portly black man clung, with clasped hands, to the back of the bench on which he had fallen asleep. In prayer or despair? Even the bottle of red wine mounting guard between his legs offered no clue as to which. The Square Frédérick-Lemaître was given over entirely to the tunnel into which the canal disappeared. Entertainment was guaranteed by the lock, a little further up. Some regulars, and a fair number of stray tourists cursing the Arabs who monopolized the benches, were enquiring after their chances of sighting a barge. A notice stipulating that entry to the tunnel was prohibited to the general public sent a slight shiver of mystery up people's spines. Opposite, from behind metal gates, the Waterways and Canals Department kept a watchful eye, counting pieces of orange peel drifting very slowly, at the whim of the current, into the mouth of the tunnel. To them it was not prohibited. Pervenche liked his neighbourhood. He knew its smells, its noises and its colours. He had not yet dared to take a look at the Square Jules-Ferry. He had heard children's shouting coming from it. He tortured himself for a moment, then, when the last piece of peel had disappeared, he made his move.

She was already on the scene, chattering away with two girlfriends who, on noticing Paul, made themselves scarce.

Paul never tired of studying Ella's tiny face. Each time he discovered fresh reasons to be stirred. He noted what could have been rings under her eyes. He wasn't sure they were rings; it looked as if, in this part of her face, the skin was more delicate than elsewhere. It took on a bluish shade, like make-up intended to set off the sparkle of the eyes. These rings made her seem vulnerable and threatened. While she got stuck into her first lolly, having tucked the others away in her jacket pocket – see how good it is for p-putting my lollies – Pervenche blew the fringe that encroached on her forehead. He parted the hair on the curved brow and, by the grace of this parting, the eyes became larger, the cheeks pinker, the lips redder. With the tips of his fingers he put the finishing touches to the fringe. Ella was smiling, and sucking noisily.

'What's your name?'
'Paul. You know that.'
'I m-mean, what's your real name?'
'Oh, my real name. Pervenche.'
'What?'
'Pervenche, the same as a pervenche.'
'A what?'
'It's called a periwinkle too. Haven't you ever seen one? It's a flower, blue, a bit like your eyes, it grows in the country. Do you like flowers?'
'Yes, I do . . .'

They had a long talk about flowers. Night was already falling, grey and dark, while buttercups, poppies, pervenches, tulips and daisies wove rainbows fragile as smiles.

A love like this was his dream. He resented Claire for not being a child; he resented Ella for not being older.

Occasionally, he was annoyed by the inattention of the little girl absorbed by the leaf she wanted to squash by jumping off the bench, or by the strange shape her lolly made. Annoyed and angered – it's true, she simply never listened to him – Paul would ask a point-blank question to ensnare and corner the will o' the wisp against a wall of silence. Then, as her lord and master, he could treat himself to a gentle rebuke, show magnanimity by granting a pardon, and melt that much more. She did not turn her head or hear anything; she was too absorbed by her leaf or her sweet. But each time, echoing the crafty question, an answer was fired back, clean and sharp as a snapped branch, evoking coursing water and wide sky. Paul could have beaten himself. He made do with insults, reproaching himself for what afterwards he had no hesitation in calling blasphemy. Then he applauded his ability to captivate such a free spirit, to cage a breath of air. But he had no time to savour the obviousness of the conclusion which followed, that they were made for each other. She had already sprung in front of him, a triumphant look on her face:

'Did you see? Did you see?'

She had majestically flattened the hostile leaf. Well, then? What about her reward?

It was four, and she had to go. She explained to him that at four she took her five o'clock tea, that her daddy made her cross because he spoke so loud into the telephone that he wore it out, and that her mummy would tell her off because . . . He didn't catch the end. She had run after her brother. They soon disappeared into the fog.

There it was, and Pervenche, too absorbed in Ella, hadn't noticed. He didn't like that. Its unexpected, almost violent arrival troubled him. He would have preferred an unending crescendo, an imperceptible and inexorable infiltration, the better to savour the promise that at last he would be able to keep. Still, the fog was his. He went home and set about his preparations with a somewhat disappointing feverishness: he'd thought he'd be calmer but he was like an old man worried about missing the train. He switched on the radio to help put some heart into his work. He loaded the camera with a new film, checked that everything was working correctly and fixed the contraption to the tripod. Right, now for his togs. He had settled for an old, torn pair of trousers, grey pullover and a combat jacket he'd brought home from military service. Running shoes to move about in silence. Ella's handkerchief, naturally – he had to make sure everything possible was going for him. Feeling perky, he beavered about in his underpants; he had not quibbled about their colour.

The radio was churning out a string of paso dobles. Paul loved the paso doble. He could not resist the pleasure of taking a passing señorita by the waist, sweeping her across the room, arching the small of her back, feeling beneath his chest her rounded breasts. The orchestra told of sand and blood; the brass chimed in here and there to help the matador's concentration, but their false jollity and colourful brio only emphasized the imminence of death. Pervenche realized that he was dancing a funeral march; he cavorted on, dancing the dance of death and the birth of a photograph. He thought of Cocteau, for whom there is no hatred in a bullfight, just fear and love. Pervenche felt no fear, only a concern that he would be unable to overcome a technical difficulty: striking at the right moment, framing the shot exactly and choosing the right exposure. It also occurred to him that in some bullfights the bulls are spared, that in others the matadors are gored. Someone whispered in his ear that a photograph is not worth a kill, that a fake corpse would do perfectly well. He also heard Armand laugh. The photo by the window was quivering with impatience. Anne-Sophie had ensnared a fly. Rimbaud was guarding the gates of hell. Petrushka was sobbing unremittingly.

The hours ticked by, heavy and sweet. Half-past midnight, the witching hour. He crossed to the window one last time. Something was amiss, he knew it now. He opened the window and leaned out over the street. It was the fog. It had thickened; the halo of the street lamps was hardly visible. No way could he manage a photo in these conditions. Fucking fog. Pervenche almost screamed in anger. He reasoned with himself, and admitted it wouldn't do any good to lose his cool. The fog would eventually lift. All he had to do was to be vigilant and to be there at the right time. That's all.

He slept badly, getting up several times to check the state of play. The curtains, left undrawn, framed the rectangle of a milky glow. The fog dampened noises and colours. Tomorrow will be albuminous, the photographer teased himself. Even the branch of the tree nearby, his old companion, had left him in the lurch.

Sure enough, Sunday lapsed into albuminous gloom.

You couldn't see a thing; crossing the canal was increasingly perilous. Paul did as everyone else – he got bored and watched television. Still, one bright spot in the pea-souper: on the news they promised the outlook would improve the next day, so that France could resume work.

A celadon Monday, definitely a celadon Monday, Paul would have staked his life on it. The sky was sleek, affable almost. The street was celebrating its more or less restored visibility. His coffee tasted delicious and the footbridge confirmed celadon. There was still some fog but, disappointed at laying itself open to criticism, it had dressed itself up in all its finery. It enhanced, it glorified, it enthralled. It displeased no longer. Pervenche recognized it; it was the fog from his photo. Celadon, celadon: he used the fifteen minutes' respite granted by his haste to tail a pretty girl in the Rue Richer. He followed her into a café, took an espresso like her and then asked his neighbour to swap cups.

'Swap cups? What for?'

'To read your thoughts.'

On celadon days he could be quite witty, relatively speaking anyway. The girl with the coffee agreed to have her thoughts read; Paul tried to read into them things flattering to himself. She left him to his reading, wishing him a very pleasant goodbye. Paul awarded her top marks for the curve of her hips, promised himself he would be back for a coffee soon and arrived late at the office, where Frigo threw him a pointed look.

He forced himself to stay calm; no sense in overdoing things, wasting energy and concentration he would need this evening. At regular intervals he went over to the window and peered out: as long as the fog doesn't disappear! No, it was hanging on out there. As a section manager should, Frigo wanted to know what was exciting the curiosity of his loss adjuster. Paul stationed himself behind him, pointing towards the street with his nose:

'Just like London, don't you think?'

His aim was perfect. Frigo's face lit up with that comprehending smile which seals the mutual esteem held by two peerless beings. Frigo and England went back a long way. When Pervenche had first met him, he was afflicted with an anglophobia whose roots could no doubt be traced back to the death of Joan of Arc and which had since been fuelled by Waterloo, the Beatles and the latest hiding handed out by England to the French soccer team.

Then, two years ago, his wife had talked him into spending their holidays in England. The anglophobe had returned an anglophile, and the anglophile spared no effort to become an anglophone. What had happened? No one really knew. Sometimes, at a party where the drink flowed, he became expansive, talking of love at first sight or of a revelation. He had been fascinated by the rain on the lawns, which was more graceful then elsewhere, by the imperturbability of the drivers and by the colour of the sauces, the desserts and the legs of the English girls. He went overboard in his love for the Brits because he could not forgive himself for his erstwhile erring ways. From then on he dressed like a dandy – plenty of green, mauve and burgundy. He was no longer ashamed of his pale pink complexion, but poked fun at those with suntans. He had learned the rules of etiquette and taken to drinking tea. While his subordinates embarked for Brittany in the wake of Le Nabec, he embarked for his own scepter'd isle. He dunked his tea-bag in his plastic mug of hot water from the tap in the loo – it lacked a little distinction, okay, but if you must you must – and sipped at his decoction, not the better to savour it but because it went down badly. Tragically for him, he did not like tea. He had never inured himself to the wishy-washy aroma or the bitter taste of pee. He had tried everything – sugar, lemon, a 'cloud' of milk – to no avail; so he took it straight, trusting to the virtues of perseverance.

'Yes, just like London,' concurred Frigo, a little disappointed. He was expecting more. He would never have abandoned a file for so little; he might have done for one of those English fogs in a street where brick houses try to out-clone each other, a bobby on the beat, a phone box, an old lady pushed down the stairs, Hercule Poirot on the case ... Frigo and Pervenche, shoulder to shoulder and a thousand leagues apart, pursued their separate fantasies. The typewriters chattered behind them, the telephones called for help and files piled up. Le Nabec picked his nose, Blandine smiled and Calot cursed his pen, which had rolled under a cabinet. Mechanically, Paul registered this familiar hubbub; his imagination was working overtime. What colour would Tuesday be? When would he develop the photo? Next Sunday he would have to pack his bags for Toulouse. Ella accompanied a girl with long blond hair. Where had he put the revolver?

The trip to Brittany at five dispelled the usual moroseness of Monday evenings, too close to the previous weekend and too distant from the next. Pervenche could have sung, at the top of his voice, of the waves, the gulls, the ships, the high seas and the splendour of a vast horizon. The night and the fog had occupied the Rue Monte-à-regret; compliantly, they made the final adjustments to the lighting and the setting. Paul suggested a drink to François. There was already a scrum at the bar. It was the hour when the Republic plans its victories. Paul prepared for his with the help of three pastis that contorted his face in a grimace. Le Nabec talked of the week he was spending in Brittany at Easter:

'Coming along?'

'I'll be in Toulouse, you dickhead. Otherwise, of course I'd have come.'

One for the road, no grimaces this time, and they parted. Pervenche turned to watch his friend's slightly stooped silhouette melt into the dark. Soon another silhouette, perhaps slightly stooped, would emerge from the dark. Pervenche felt suddenly despondent – a bad omen. His solitude weighed heavily. Inside the bar, girls were laughing, men talking and clapping one another on the back and waiters working like crazy. Paul's and François' glasses still occupied centre stage next to the carafe of water. The sadness of these useless glasses, the taste of aniseed in his mouth and these people who had no need for him – it was a lot to take. Pervenche reacted: this was no time to be getting emotional. From the footbridge he glimpsed the stretch of canal embankment he would later be photographing. That encouraged him. He was no longer so alone: Armand was counting on him, so were the night and the pale void. He arrived home in a cheerful mood, laid out his equipment and clothes on the bed and, on the off chance, switched on the radio – no paso doble, too bad. Turning to the television, he watched a report on some distant war, was told that rain was on its way and dozed off during a heavy psychodrama. The crackle of the set woke him. He started and dashed to the window. It was not yet dawn, there was still fog. His alarm clock reassured him – quarter to midnight. Let's have you, you shower. On a Monday night at twelve he was unlikely to encounter many people, other than candidates for the afterlife. His vivacity reassured him too.

He set up his tripod and checked that everything was working. The footbridge was perfect – it was posing, showing off. The fog was fulfilling its duty to perfection. Okay, all set. The hardest bit was behind him. The hardest bit was behind him. He repeated it to himself two or three times, because suddenly he felt queasy. He had a lump in his throat, clammy hands; he was afraid. Fuck you, it's now or never. He goaded himself, squirmed free, caught himself by the scruff of the neck, kicked, struggled, and disappointed himself. Disappointed at disappointing himself, he finally stood his ground. Softly, he began humming a war chant. He slipped his arm round the door for the club, which he hoped fervently had disappeared. It was there. His fingers closed on the rough wood. Its presence in his hand put an end to his procrastination. He was ready. He placed the weapon beside the camera, against the doorpost of the entrance, and began his stake-out. It was chilly, one of these chills that numb you to the bone before you realize it. With his hands snug in his pockets and leaning against the old stonework, Pervenche saw himself as the Rimbaud in his room. He pricked up his ears, chanced a glance – nothing. There was nothing coming. The occasional car on the Quai de Jemmapes spoke to Paul of another world, a world he was preparing to leave behind, the world of the nobody and the never-has-been.

The roar of a motorbike had just faded into the distance. Pervenche was trying to guess the rider's route. Steps rang on the pavement twenty yards away. He had hardly time to glimpse the shape moving towards him. He grabbed the piece of wood and raised it, eyes on the exact spot where the victim had to lurch forward. His heart was racing. He found himself grotesque – both arms raised, face no doubt contorted – and he remembered the night when he had viewed in the mirror the mask of a killer. What did he look like? He was annoyed not to have a song or a tune in his head. In times of stress he usually hummed, but now the only music came from the click of heels on the pavement. The beat was too quick, the strides too short, the heels rang too clear. It was a woman. It could only be a woman. Pervenche was about to kill a woman. He stepped back, put down the club and saw a young woman walk past. She glided across the circle of light and she stopped. Paul was momentarily paralysed. Then he flung the club into its hiding-place and darted towards his camera. He heard the slam of a car door, the whirr of a starter and the revving of an engine.

Paul hovered between relief and rage. He would have gladly gone home, but he had ordained it would be tonight or never, so it would be tonight. He recovered his cudgel and twirled it a few times to warm himself, thinking of the passer-by. Was she attractive? Did she live here? Did he know her, perhaps? A man was coming, Paul could see his silhouette. He was approaching slowly. He must be wearing thick-soled shoes, his footsteps were hardly audible. Paul had resumed his stance, club aloft, but still no song on his lips. The victim's shadow preceded him, ushering him to the spot where he would fall. Paul clenched his hands on the wood and tensed his muscles. That's it, now. A voice had cried, 'Now!', he had heard it. He had heard but could see nothing. He was blinded by tears. He was crying from fear and revulsion. Armand was no longer laughing: Paul would never take the photo. He hurled his weapon away; it bounced off the cobbles and banged into a car door. It had made a terrible racket. Paul hid, watching the windows. Nothing moved. At the end of the street, the man turned round, stood still, then made a hasty get-away. Paul went and picked up the projectile and returned it to its place for the next time, doubting there would be one.

He made his way home without asking himself any questions. He knew the colour of Tuesday: violaceous, and violaceous the next day, and the day after. He had been afraid to kill, afraid of the consequences, afraid of waking up a murderer. Instead of which he would wake up a loss adjuster – punctual, a nobody, a never-has-been. Hardly to his credit. On top of that he'd lost Armand, the photographs and his rights to fantasy and folly. Now he was cold. To punish himself he went via the Rue Bichat, passing the Hôpital Saint-Louis. The gloomy building perforated the sky with thrusting towers and chimneys. Its endless façade left the night no chance. The odd light at a window, here and there, gave out a hint of brightness. Pervenche observed to himself that this particular brightness probably indicated either death or suffering.

He climbed the stairs to his room, thinking of Armand; he had just died for the second time. The first time Paul had only been a contributory factor, this time he knew he was entirely to blame. Since his dazzling revelation he had been putting on an act that now verged on second-rate melodrama. The curtain had fallen; once in Toulouse he would be on the mend.

Talking of curtains . . . he got up to draw his own. His window had nothing more to tell him.

The nobody, never-has-been loss adjuster climbed resolutely out of bed. No need for him to decide on the colour of the weather: violaceous, and for some time to come. A coffee, a quick buff of his shoes – talk about a shine, eh, Frigo – a kick of the spitefully closed door on the second floor left –

correction, right as you go down, decided the loss adjuster, a nobody maybe, but punctilious for sure – and he was submerged in the viscous tidal-race of those other nobodies, his blood-brothers. He stationed himself on the footbridge, watching the school in the Rue de Marseille: the hive was a-buzz, but he couldn't see the queen. She must have already gone in, her brother didn't like to hang about, he'd make a perfect nobody, with his conscientiousness and punctuality he might even land a fucking job at Magistrale.

Pervenche's forecast of a violaceous day was coming unstuck. A shy sun was peeping through the shreds of fog, languishing with the dark waters of the canal; a barge occupied the lock-keeper downstream and some onlookers upstream; a life-size labourer in blue overalls, lunch-bag slung across his shoulder, whistling, strode past the back of the white-collar worker slumped on his elbows. The morning was wavering, in fact, between peonin and celadon; there was movement and dynamism in the air but also a hint of tenderness and sentimentality, perhaps an imperceptible kiss that the spring was blowing from its fingertips. He conceded the day was peonin, but remained convinced that everyone else was wrong.

His rebelliousness broke out in the Rue des Petites-Ecuries. Pervenche lengthened his stride, he was late. Passing a fashion boutique, he stared at the elegant gentlemen and elegant ladies whose immobility did not prevent them smiling. They were waiting for it to wear off. One of the ladies had forgotten to put on her wig and her skirt, but she smiled all the same. Pervenche also saw the reflection of a nobody galloping after his superiors. He balked. Shit, just how spineless can you get, you bastard? Paul rushed into the Passage des Petites-Ecuries and swore: the bar was closed. He walked as far as the Rue d'Enghien and, as if Magistrale had set the police on him, dived into the *çay salonu*. There were few customers, he didn't know anyone except for the owner, who nodded to him. With Genghis he had discovered this place where the Turks came to whet their homesickness. They drank black tea or herbal teas flavoured with orange or apple, and they gambled. Time was forgotten. Paul sensed in himself the soul of an immigrant, in by the back door. He belonged here. He enquired after his two friends he had not seen since Christmas. He wandered about, then entered a supermarket to buy a bar of chocolate and steal twice as much. He slummed it, a nobody with the veneer of a could-have-been. Like the man at a loose end that he was, he ended up at the cinema, miserable at not being more excited by the spectacle of frenzied rumps and phalluses.

He did not fall asleep as quickly and peacefully as he had hoped. He had the fuzzy sensation that his bravura should not end here. He felt a little less ashamed of himself. All was not lost.

It was a lively session in Roupette's office. In the most correct of terms, Frigo had notified Paul that his presence was kindly requested in the departmental manager's office. The impromptu departure when Armand died, the concession of a day's leave to attend 'a cousin's' funeral and, to crown it all, the previous day's absence – it was the last straw. Pressed for an explanation, Pervenche offered none. He had been unable to come to work for personal reasons.

'Another cousin died?' Roupette saw red, which seemed obvious to Pervenche: the footbridge had promised him a predominantly peonin day, interspersed with discussions and transactions.

Roupette reminded Pervenche that he had bestowed a personal favour for his cousin's funeral, and look at the thanks he'd received. He was very sorry, but he had to take some action, if only as an example to the others. The action was a written warning. Did Pervenche wish to inform his union? He didn't have a union? Well, he could still contact one. No? Very well, as he wished. He could go.

'I've something to tell you.'

'What? Quick about it then,' Roupette urged him, having other fish to fry.

'I've thought it over carefully, I'm not going to Toulouse...'

Once back to his claims, Pervenche felt torn. He knew

what he was escaping by staying where he was – gloom, tacky pleasures, nights devoid of stars. He did not know what awaited him, but he felt as if he had been ensnared in a net. Either way, he hadn't betrayed Armand, that was the main thing.

— 10 —

He floundered in his attempt to draft the new set of instructions for his life. He wanted to forget the past, repudiate the future and take refuge in the everyday. It was not so simple. His usual haunts had lost their familiar, comforting aspect. He moved between the bluish glow of the street lamps and the glare of neon lights determined to afford no shadow. The shop signs branded the frontages with repeated lies. The tinted glass of the office windows darkened the sky, and the sun rose too late and disappeared too early for Paul to be able to confide his helplessness to it. At weekends, as he opened the curtains he would blink like a startled owl. He had forgotten what daylight was, could not adjust to it and resented it for granting the weak no relief from its harshness.

He had mapped out his rehabilitation. The methodical loss adjuster reckoned he could accomplish it by setting himself concrete, feasible targets. Like an accident victim learning to walk again – two steps, then four, then twenty – Pervenche was learning, in small doses, to live again. On Saturdays he'd see Ella, then perhaps he could take a few pictures, on Sundays lunch with Genghis but he'd promised Claire the afternoons, so much for the weekend, mustn't forget to remind François to count him in for Brittany at Easter, it'd be great if they could do some sailing, yes, he'd mention it to him on Monday and he'd book his holidays. He listed, ticked, deleted and each time he deleted he was drawing a line though a portion of his life whose insipidness had been planned and achieved on target.

That Sunday he ate with Genghis and a friend of his. It gave him the chance to add a more ambitious project to his collection: Genghis insisted that Paul should come and spend his holidays in Turkey. Summer filled the room and Paul was quick to accept.

The whole of July now pre-arranged, he rang at Claire's door with an easier conscience. He had brought photos and flowers, flowers for her and photos for himself, or was it the other way round? The attentions he gave Claire had lost their spontaneity – a whiff of calculation had crept in; they extolled the banality of being a couple. It had been a nice thought to take her flowers on a Sunday afternoon, she'd like it, and he'd be the first to benefit.

The previous day he had enlarged a few photographs, unenthusiastically. The flame had died, he had not even stripped. After much hesitation, he had made a new enlargement of his photograph, the one of the Rue Monte-à-regret. Just like the first time, he sensed the uneasiness it exuded; the red light again bloodied its contours. He had felt slightly more unhappy than before as he considered the void; he had been hoping for a miracle. There had been no miracle, the story of his photo remained unfinished. In the end, he did not show Claire his photographs, he was less and less keen to show them. His photography was for himself; the affair was too personal to be shared.

For want of an exciting topic of conversation he occupied himself with Claire, occupied himself with her body. He undressed her slowly and stroked her, without impatience but with the coolness of a technician. He indulged more and more in the pleasures of the aesthete, less and less in those of the lover; in so doing he talked less and less with her and more and more with himself. He had loved her, no doubt he still did, since he didn't tire of her body. But he no longer dreamed about her. Their embraces had acquired a routine perfection that he tried to escape by contrivance. He had explained to her that she was never more naked than when he stayed dressed, that the caresses he lavished on her exalted her body even more, that he was never closer to her than when he watched her, when he became the spectator of her pleasure. He had urged her to fondle herself. He had been unconvincing, she had refused. That had not discouraged him; if she had accepted, his certainty that he knew her well and his desire to remain in the driving-seat at all times would have been shaken. The skin was soft to his fingers. Shivers ran through Claire; she did not dare touch her friend. And as the shivers became more violent, Paul thought of Turkey: he had taken Ella, taken her in his arms, she was tired from walking so far. Claire, assuaged at last, had closed her eyes. Paul switched on the television, put some coffee on to warm, and returned to the bed. With his index finger he criss-crossed the burning body with lines whose point of convergence soon brought moans from Claire. She came once again, without violence. The coffee was boiling; Pervenche threw it in the sink and left.

He went out of his way to take the Rue Saint-Denis. Winter Sunday evenings suited his grubby excitement. Collar upturned, hands clenched in pockets, Pervenche compared his own plight with that of these men standing around. He had never pitied whores, their circumstances did not affect him. But he was sorry for these blokes, mostly immigrants. He recognized some of them, they must have their regular patch of pavement too. They were fantasizing from the bust or the face of a tart: she reminded them of the girl-back-home, the one who wasn't waiting for them any more.

Pervenche slowed to scrutinize the women at work; two or three were anxious to know: did he want to come up, love? Paul thought of the girl in the Rue Monte-à-regret, maybe it was the big blonde just there? He thought of the photo he'd botched, of his dormant claims and of Tuesday's rebellion. Was he capable of rebelling tonight? He took himself at his word: I'll screw the next one. The next one was a negress, fat and half-naked. Pervenche accosted her, asked, as one does, the price of a blow job and followed her into a passage. Without emotion and without repugnance he observed the sway of the thick hips, an ample-thighed woman if ever there was, but this one doesn't slither silently. He was pleased with himself. He hummed a rugby song. She drew him behind a staircase, squatted in front of him and waited for him to undo his flies. The woman – he would have preferred to have her kneel, it's more submissive – set to work. Surprised that, despite everything, she was getting results, Paul noted the bare bulb in the corridor: Anne-Sophie must have relatives around here. Below, the frizzy head was bobbing faster. She looked like Rosette, his mate from the army who was always shouting 'hallelujah'. She was bobbing and making a noise; Paul didn't like the noises of sex, he liked to see but not hear, a bit of music always smoothed things over, no music here, he wasn't going to start singing. He got a kick out of the spluttering of a moped. Hallelujah, things were coming to a head, say that again, what a joke, must definitely tell François. He shed his load with Claire's perfect body before his eyes, bathed in the glow of the bedside lamp, how her skin was burning . . . Pervenche paid off the glutton while she wiped her mouth with a tissue that joined its companions under the stairs.

Back home, he ignored the television. The news was on, but the weather forecast didn't matter any more. He resisted the desire to take a shower: he certainly wasn't going to do the whole bit of purifying the body after sin. He wasn't sure that his meagre extravagance would get him very far. He wasn't sure that he wasn't play-acting again.

The branch tapped at his window. It stood out against the sky, waving gently, saying goodbye to Paul or to someone else. The Martin girl had put on some music; he imitated her. He had the impression that since the other day Rimbaud had been unable to contain a smile whose irony irritated his host. Paul took it out on an apple. The first mouthful made him freeze: with the smell, with the taste, with the juice running down his throat, with the crunch of the bitten fruit, autumns had burst into his room – there was a sloping meadow, blond hair, a dress swirling.

Stunned one second, inundated with pleasure the next, Pervenche swallowed hurriedly, threw away the apple and opened a can of beer. That apple had proved too sweet and too cruel, he didn't feel in a Proustian mood. He drank some of his beer and thought, but not for long; he didn't like thinking, he preferred to dream. He recovered his apple, wiped it on his sleeve, polished it and devoured it, promising himself to consume the remaining seven or eight he could see on the fridge, convinced that only a fit of indigestion could put paid to his nostalgia.

The branch still tapped. It occurred to Paul that it only put in an appearance on the days he was unsettled. He drew the curtain.

He no longer worried about the colour of the days. He still lingered in the warmth of the bed after the clarion call of the alarm, still registered the tell-tale signs from the street, but without drawing any conclusion. He left at a carefully calculated time that permitted a five-minute halt on the footbridge. There, between sky and water, between peace and disgust, he was informed of the colour decided upon – over his dead body – by the canal, the walls, the trees and the clouds. He bowed to the judgement of his neighbourhood. After which, he loitered at the corner of the Rue de Marseille until he could exchange waves with Ella.

His sense of organization expressed itself with a vengeance in his insurance claims. One pile on the left, pending, one pile on the right, for filing – oh, the sweet smell of staleness and efficiency. There was a third pile – very small and very secret – of files lost. In one week he had handed three to Chantal-the-filer.

Exasperated by a claim one day, François had thrust the file at Chantal, a typist he happened to meet in the corridor.

'To hell with it!'

He was joking, she was not. He had never been able to lay hands on it again. So from time to time – in moderation, it's not wise to overdo it – Paul and François gave her a particularly daunting file and, just as water closes over a stone, so time erased from memory the ripples of this or that case. The victim would write or telephone: very sorry, but your file has been mislaid. Management got in on the act, the whole department hunted high and low, but the file was not to be found.

Paul was fascinated by Chantal. He phoned her then set off to bump into her, throwing Frigo off the scent by concealing among other files the one to be consigned to oblivion. No need for explanation or justification. Here, let me give you this, can you file it when you've got time? She would answer 'No problem' with the studious look of a departmental manager, take the folder and carry it away as if it held wafers for communion. The officiating sister walked off in her pleated skirt and flat shoes. Paul itched with curiosity. One day he had almost followed her; he could imagine her threading her away through the maze of unfamiliar corridors, producing a strange key from under her robes, pushing open a door and surveying the inner sanctum, the holy of holies. He had almost followed her, but had preferred to preserve the mystery. Somewhere on Magistrale premises files slept their last sleep; somewhere in France accident victims looked out for the postman, loss adjusters in other companies cursed those at Magistrale and garages demanded their due. The guardian of the secret contemplated her colleagues from afar; she too lived a double life, on the face of it a nobody, but in the shadows the queen.

Pervenche was without illusion. Losing files wasn't enough to make the problems they contained go away. Inevitably some day the calls from the victim or the garage would have to be returned and a settlement made without the file by piecing some facts together and coughing up. So what. As he got shot of the biggest nuisances, Pervenche felt the fleeting yet intense relief that comes from scratching an itch. He was persuading himself that his behaviour fostered the presence of the irrational in a computerized world, that he was watering a flower growing in concrete.

— I I —

'I'm going to d-die.'
She had announced the fact in a calm, determined voice. Paul could not help laughing. The rainfall in the morning had made him fear the worst, that their rendezvous would be cancelled. At the first sunny interval he had raced to the square, wandered around the bandstand and eventually sat on a dry patch of park bench. Ella soon appeared. She had ditched her brother and skipped up to Pervenche, halting in front of him and looking him straight in the eye.
'I'm going to d-die.'
'Why are you going to die?'
'Because I'm going to k-kill myself.'
'Well, in that case . . .'
The little girl was not joking. With a steely look on her face she took a dessert fork from her jacket pocket, where she normally stashed her lollipops. Its three prongs snarled ferociously. After the customary simpering, she unburdened her conscience. She had broken her brother's Walkman, after he had said she mustn't use it, of course; and she had still not confessed her misdeed to the rightful owner. It was no laughing matter. Paul agreed with her that death was the only way out. Courageously, she poked the weapon against her tummy. Her determination deflated like a soufflé.
'It hurts.'
She didn't die. They chatted for a while about anything and everything, like an elderly couple. A fleck of saliva formed at the corner of her lips when she talked a lot.

'Shall we go and see the tunnel?'
'What tunnel?'
'Just over there, you'll see, it's a magic tunnel.'

She ran off to tell her brother, who came to hear more. Paul had to soft-soap the future loss adjuster, future nobody. He even suggested her brother could join them, kicking himself for his rashness, but the boy was already into a football game. He gave the couple half an hour and went off. Hand in hand they stationed themselves beside the lock. The gloomy weather had deterred any idlers; there were only strays. The tunnel mouth yawned threateningly. Paul related that he had ventured inside, there were wonders and horrors, it was huge. There were also dragons and crocodiles that stopped explorers from passing, but not orange peel, that's why you should always take lots of oranges with you, and then far, far away it came out on the other side of the ocean, on a small island, with beaches and palm trees and a sweet-seller by the water's edge.

Ella had not let go of his hand. She had pressed against him.

'When are you going to take me?'

There and then. Pervenche would have swum with her into the tunnel there and then. But he didn't see the point of getting wet just to go as far as the Place de la Bastille where the tunnel re-emerged. Such petty considerations provided no excuse. He didn't have any oranges with him, his boat was being repaired; but they'd go away together, that was a promise.

They still had ten minutes. While he waited for the clock to strike twelve, he steered Cinderella towards the funfair caravan that stood at the entrance to the Square Jules-Ferry. She clapped her hands when she spotted the big wheel of fortune promising a prize at almost every turn. The red, orange and pink lights flashed colourfully, an accordion drummed up custom and some gigantic dolls showed their frills. Finally she won a bottle of sparkling wine every bit as good as champagne, according to the stallholder, and succeeded in swapping it for a water pistol. She told Paul it might come in useful inside the tunnel.

He accompanied her back towards the bandstand. The brother had also won, it showed in his mood. As he left he even uttered a 'goodbye' that went unheard by Paul, who was wrapped up in the smile of his fellow conspirator: her pistol gave her the strength to face the ordeal of confession.

As Pervenche took leave of Ella, his shoulders drooped under the loneliness. He found his room unappealing, Claire too. He opted for the *çay salonu*, which was packed with loners. All these hesitations in making his choices annoyed Paul. But what could he hope to achieve without greater resolve? His cop-out that night in the Rue Monte-à-regret had shaken his conviction that he possessed Armand's mettle. He stepped to one side to avoid a puddle, suppressing a smile of contempt: people who follow their fate through to the end don't deviate from their path to avoid a puddle. His self-respect wounded, he turned back and walked twice through the cold, ankle-deep water, much to the indifference of the passers-by, then hurried home to dry his feet.

Peonin – the footbridge was categorical. He was not taken in for a moment. Pervenche was steeped in violaceous hues once and for all, but he nodded his agreement anyway and descended from his oracle, just glimpsing Ella's pony-tail. On the off chance, he dropped into the bar where one morning a callipygous coffee-drinker had raised his hopes for a beautiful night. But she was not to be seen; no doubt she was pursuing elsewhere the apparition of the magnificent young man who had exchanged his cup for hers. Pervenche, who was beginning to take his fantasizing literally, was forced to halt. An ambulance had parked across the pavement; two nurses – spruce and pretty – climbed out. They opened the front nearside door and helped an old woman to extricate herself from the vehicle. Paul watched as the three of them shuffled away, chatting politely. Granny's faded violet dress blended perfectly with the white tunics. White hair, black stockings and felt slippers completed the picture. Paul was struck by the unstinting attentiveness of the two young women, by the love they put into their every gesture, by the love they put into taking the old lady to die a little further on.

Ella wanted to die, the old lady didn't – nobody was getting what they wanted. A young black boy was skipping around his mother while she wiped his little brother's nose. Paul felt unable to cope. He took refuge behind a mound of files: the dead did not ask such silly questions. That evening he had dinner at Claire's, then lay down beside her, stroking her and thinking of the negress from the Rue Saint-Denis. It coloured Claire's orgasm, which she experienced more deeply than usual. Her lover took no offence. Her sleep was probably feigned, to aid the escape of the thief, the thief who made off with the vision of a radiant body. The image became softer yet sharper as Paul reached the Rue Saint-Denis.

The negress had deserted her post, good job too; Paul comforted himself with the thought as he tagged behind a good-looking, bad-mouthed blonde. She discharged her client with an atrabilious tongue, drew his attention – since he too had the snuffles – to the difficulty of sucking when one has a cold, pocketed his offering and, from habit, inspected the paper handkerchief where snot and sperm were mingled.

It wasn't a patch on Armand's tales – enigmatic whores bedded in every port, brawls, ships' sirens, bivouacs in the jungle – but Pervenche was adapting, training. He was cutting his teeth. Little by little the violaceous was becoming muted. He had the feeling he was on course. Not tonight, though: Paul realized he had already missed the Rue du Château-d'Eau, he was almost at the Gare du Nord. He skirted the station, heading for the Quai de Valmy. He was almost there, in a narrow street leading to it, when he saw a shadow emerge from a building and advance towards him. It was not the kind of place you hang around; Paul nearly crossed over, but shrugged off the idea. The man came up to him, barred the way coldly and asked for a light. He looked less threatening than from a distance; he appeared embarrassed, in a hurry. Paul explained that he didn't smoke, then noticed that the man, who still stood squarely in his way, was not looking at him. Paul turned his head to hear a scraping noise and lifted his elbow in a reflex response. Something hard struck him behind the ear, stars burst before his eyes. Or candles? That's right, candles; the image burned into his mind even before the pain drilled into his head. He wanted to feel, he was afraid he was bleeding, but his assailant hit him again. He deflected the blow, taking it on the shoulder. He heard someone shout, 'Go on, go on' and wondered whether the guy was provoking him into fighting or egging on his partner. A violent blow, less painful than the first, hit him in the back.

He dropped to the ground, not that he really had to. Perhaps it was the instinct of the good actor, acquired through seeing staged fisticuffs on television, knock-out punches, fall guys biting the dust as if they enjoyed it. Something within him dictated his behaviour. He had just been attacked and struck; he had to fall. He could have stayed on his feet, even staggering, but that would have taken more fight than he had in him. He had a sore head. For a second he hoped that, seeing him at their feet, they would be satisfied and leave. Just the opposite. Like wild animals scenting blood they laid into him, one with the boot, the other with a cosh. Curled in a ball, his hands over his head, Pervenche regained hope for a moment; the blows were wide of the mark, his assailants were about to tire, he would escape with a few bruises. Then suddenly he felt fear, a growing fear. He had been involved in free-for-alls before, had been beaten up before, but this was different, there was something vicious about the ferocity of it. Paul started to shout, what a fool for not shouting earlier. He started to insult the two yobs. He wanted to scream at them that he didn't have any money; he wanted to raise himself on one elbow to explain more easily, but a boot caught him full in the face. He was aware of a muffled noise deep inside him, he told himself they'd broken something, he'd felt a small crack, it didn't hurt, just stunned him, knocked the heart out of him, he wanted only one thing, to go home and sleep, rest. His mouth became hot, a sticky heat, he was bleeding like a piglet. He still felt fear, but his anger was even greater; he rolled over, remembering that in westerns the hero always loses at the beginning but wins at the finish, and stood up more easily than he'd expected. His attackers stood facing him. One sniggered, his legs slightly flexed; the other appeared distant, his detached manner and staring eyes worried Paul more. Nothing happened, no one moved. Paul had taken out his handkerchief and was holding it to his nose with both hands. Tears misted his vision. His fear subsided: the Quai de Valmy wasn't far, there would be cars passing, maybe even pedestrians. The pounding of his heart was gradually slowing. He wished he felt hatred, it would have given him the strength of ten men. But he was merely angry, with no plans to defend himself; he felt pathetic, spent. His only thought was to get away, he'd have to see a doctor, his clothes must be a mess, he thought of the whore just now examining her handkerchief, shit, it was Ella's handkerchief he was holding to his nose, the bastards. The now searing pain soon brought him back to the narrow street. He had lost all sense of time: their confrontation could have lasted a minute or an hour. He thought he wasn't bleeding as much, that's all it needed for his spirits to perk up. All in all it had been a pretty good evening: Claire, the tart, the mugging in a sleazy part of town. They actually broke my nose: he'd have no end of things to tell them at the office, this was a real adventure. He was putting a brave face on things when the assailant on the right moved. Paul noted his white shoes, trainers probably, he must have got them dirty, serve him right. He advanced towards Paul, who retreated. There was only a yard between them. He slowly unzipped his jacket and reached into his inside pocket. Pervenche could not take his eyes off him; curiosity made him forget his misfortune. He took some time to accept that the man held a razor in his hand. The blade glinted for a split second; just like a second-rate crime novel, reflected Pervenche. But he did not reflect for long. He was not afraid any more, he was terrified. The hand holding the razor mesmerized him, the arm had swung away from the body and towards him as if in invitation. He noticed that the accomplice was no longer sniggering, he was mechanically tapping the palm of one hand with the cosh. Paul's back still hurt, the stabbing pain in his head was becoming sharper, his tears had dried with his blood, he gazed at the razor and the indifferent expression of his executioner. He told himself he was going to die, right there, without understanding a thing, his blood would flow in the gutter. He was going to die. And then he exploded, that was the feeling; a wave of rage and loathing swept him forward. He lashed out with his foot, connecting with his opponent's groin, feeling something soft. He saw him sink to his knees and made a dash for the canal. There was still the problem of the cosh, but he forgot the one he'd just disabled and ran past him, shrugging off a light blow to the shoulder. At last luck was on his side; the able-bodied thug had not had time to decide on a strategy. Torn between his mate's groaning and the desire to avenge him, he was too slow to act. Pervenche heard footsteps chasing after him, but he was already at the Quai de Valmy. A voice shouted:

'I'll get you, you fucker . . .'

Paul did not slow. He was still in the grip of fear, not knowing if he was still being pursued. He ran as hard as he could, breathing with difficulty because of the blood in his nose and mouth, choking with pain and panic. He went to Claire's; the memory of the naked body he had abandoned a short while ago, a longing to lie down, be tended and pampered made him forget his exhaustion. At last, he rang – twice, three times; Claire wasn't there. Something inside him caved in, the pain became more acute. The left shoulder of his jacket showed a four-inch slash. He lifted the flap; his shirt was drenched in blood. Before collapsing, the bastard had cut him, he might just as easily have got him in the throat. Where could he go? Not home. He made for the Place de la République, hugging the walls. By now the streets were almost empty. He knocked at Genghis's place. The door opened a fraction, then fully. Genghis shared a two-room flat with two other Turks. Action stations. Paul was laid out on the best bed, undressed and washed. He felt lifeless. The kettle was already announcing tea and on the walls the sun was shining in Istanbul and Bursa. The sound of Turkish sang in the patient's ears. Moustaches were bristling, Tamburlaine's warriors were stirring. They wanted to summon the troops there and then to mount a punitive expedition; all Paul had to do was to describe the two thugs and say where. He would not allow himself to burst into tears. He drank his tea and fell asleep listening to songs from home that the three migrant workers sitting to attention around his bed had put on – not too loud, so as not to disturb him.

The next day Paul had to relinquish, almost forcibly, the protection of his Ottoman guard. They had watched over him all night and wanted to keep him until he was fully recovered. Paul convinced them of the need for an X-ray. He had a fracture of the nose and a slight depression of the cheekbone. The cut on the arm needed stitches and the fracture a plaster cast; it was a kind of T-shaped cast that made him look like a crusader. He ached all over but the shooting pains had dulled.

Frigo, notified by Paul that he would be off work for a fortnight, informed Roupette. Roupette was positive it was a new form of rebellion. He swore he would keep a close eye on the wolf once he was back in the fold.

The wolf did not venture out of his lair. The colour-coding had vanished from among his concerns; he moved in a sort of whitish gelatine with hints of mauve. He spent his days and nights reliving the ambush. What did his assailants want? They hadn't uttered a word. None of the theories he came up with held water. Revenge for the big guy he'd thumped in the bar with François and Loïc? He would have joined in the fun. Junkies? They would have demanded his money. Pervenche was tempted to regard their intervention as divine retribution for his mediocrity. But he wavered between a feeling of persecution and one of injustice. Never had he felt so alone, so deserted. He'd been deserted by everyone; Armand had deserted him, and so had she, back then, so far away, the one whose voice woke him on nights when he was really low.

He paced in his bedsit, unable to concentrate on any music or television. He had given up reading long ago. So when night came, he opened the window, disregarding wind or rain, and stretched out on the parquet floor with his feet up on the radiator. February had bedecked itself with snow. It did not settle but melted, covering the pavements in brown slush. The cold entered the room, Paul felt the insistence of its kisses pressing on his skin, at the same time his feet subjected themselves to the scorching of the radiator. The sky was suffocating, an occasional snowflake carried on the wind landed on Pervenche's cheek or hand, as if to confide something he would not believe. The sounds of a piano floated up from the Martins' flat. Paul was convincing himself that the photo, still pinned beside the window, lacked nothing, he could be proud of it. His body shivered, his soul shivered and he refused to move his feet despite the excessive heat. The shadow of the branches followed its usual course whenever a car passed. He remained at the window for ages, watching the snow fall. The cast hampered him, mutilated his outlook, especially upwards. There was this white barrier, like a lid on his life.

The next day he went out. He took the negative to a photographic shop and ordered six poster-size prints. In the evening he visited Claire, dined with her, slept in her bed. He regretted cancelling his departure for Toulouse. He'd be there already, his mind would be fully occupied with organizing his new way of life, he'd already be getting to know his colleagues, his neighbours maybe, he'd be widening a social circle that, here, appeared to be shrinking daily.

On Saturday he could not resist the thrill of surprising Ella. It was no longer snowing; there were sporadic showers of hail that sensible citizens feared would turn to black ice.

Ella twice looked in his direction. The game was in full swing, she must be winning because she occupied the place of the queen in the left corner of the bandstand. Then the queen spurned her subjects. She approached the handsome prince and confided that she had not recognized him. Her surprise stopped there. It was just a few days before Carnival time and Paul's mask did not look particularly out of place. Somewhat miffed – what was the point if Ella didn't feel sorry for him? – he explained the difference between a mask and a cast, that a broken nose is very serious and very painful, and that it happened while he was risking his life exploring the tunnel for their journey, soon. The blue eyes opened wide. Yes, the dragon breathed fire, but it wasn't him who'd injured Paul, it was the phantom of the waterfall, yes there was a waterfall, with lots of whirlpools, really, and fish with pointed teeth, but luckily they were afraid of the torches that Ella would hold while Paul steered the boat. The expedition wasn't plain sailing by any means, but the troops' morale remained high.

'What about your girlfriend, does she know you're going?'

'My girlfriend? What girlfriend?'

Paul denied it profusely, childishly. Ella's question had caught him off guard; even worse, it had bruised his feelings. He would have liked his bride-to-be to display jealousy. But she obviously couldn't care less about his girlfriend. No jealousy, no love. The conclusion devastated Paul. He did not dare ask her the same question; he seethed with jealousy at the mere sight of the brother. Anyway, she was ready to journey with him, that was a good sign. A girlfriend who isn't jealous – there must be such a thing, mustn't there?

He discussed it that evening with Anne-Sophie. He wanted to confide his feelings to someone and she seemed best able to understand him. Her lack of goodwill exasperated him. He rummaged in his printing trays for two pairs of photographer's tongs, climbed on a chair and dislodged the uncouth individual. Nipped by the ends of the instrument, she didn't look so clever. Paul dropped her into a glass whose smooth sides discouraged her feeble attempts to escape, and opened the dialogue. Nothing doing. She refused to speak out on the contradictions between love and jealousy. Beside himself, Pervenche gripped the body with one pair of tongs and tore off a leg with the other. Anne-Sophie gesticulated less than expected. The winter was tempering her ardour. She resisted, Paul persisted. The legs came away after a brief struggle. Now equipped with four stumps, Anne-Sophie could make only a token show of protest. But she didn't lose heart and kept trying to haul her mutilated body up the invisible wall. She trailed the detached, curiously entwined legs like the tail of a kite, then slid back down. A little earlier she had amused Paul when, with three left legs and one right leg, she had begun a slow waltz, always to the right. Her two front legs were of little assistance to her. She was dragging herself along on an abdomen that served as a graveyard to quite a few flies, greedy cow. Paul was tempted to glue her legs back on, just to see, remembered that gluing four legs on a spider can't be done, delicately removed the left leg, sparing the right to give her a chance, and surreptitiously went and dumped the whole lot on the Gautiers' doormat. Adieu Anne-Sophie, we never quite got it together . . .

His enforced idleness gave him all manner of ideas: his room underwent a scene change. Rimbaud's was the only head not to roll. Everything else was either taken down or taught a lesson, face to the wall. Reversed and delighted at showing their underside, the ribbons streaked the ceiling with yellow, blue and white unblemished by pointless poetry or prose. The posters took possession of the room. The fog swirled, the six footbridges merged with a single night, their intangible threat welling up from the six pools of light.

He woke with a start: figures had materialized on the posters. Six corpses picked themselves up, chortling. It was Armand, six times over, now falling silent and lying down again. Armand was everywhere. Paul would call to him, then run away from him. It wasn't that late; Paul dressed and went out. His street, his whole neighbourhood sported a festive air which took him by surprise. The street lamps were enjoying a second childhood, the windows sang from every building, the cold, still air allowed the canal to believe it was the fourteenth of July, now and again a slight breeze stippled it, with goose-pimples. At the embankment Paul hesitated, then turned his back on the Rue Monte-à-regret to make his way towards his fellow men. They filled the bars and clogged the pavements. Hidden behind his mask, torn between the street and his room, Paul watched as others lived.

He walked past a bar, and back again; finally he pushed the door open. Faces stared in surprise. He pretended to be looking for someone; no one called out to him. As he left he collided with a couple discussing a show that was simply marvellous, despite what the reviewers had said. He willed himself to skirt the square as far as the bandstand; a puddle surrounded his bench, there was time for it to disappear by Saturday. A window on the far side caught his attention. Heavy red curtains, green plants, shadows gliding across the ceiling – must be a party, dancing maybe. The window danced too, in the canal; Paul had to admit that it formed the prettiest of pools. He returned home, feeling edgy. At the end of his street stood the entrance to the Hôpital Saint-Louis, crucified by the railings, dimly lit by a naked bulb, shunned by the canal – another one opting out of the festivities.

The fog from the posters had filled the street. Pervenche knew as soon as he woke up that the fog had returned, thin and distant. His uneasiness grew. It was as if he was being swept away by the current of an unknown river. His nose was no longer painful, his shoulder ached only a little. His plaster cast bothered him increasingly, he wanted to remove it but did not dare. The posters had him surrounded, cornered: his life accomplishment boiled down to one – possibly mediocre – photo.

He copped out, phoned Claire – he was hers for the evening – and killed time at the cinema. Claire looked beautiful. Why she was so radiant in his presence yet so lack-lustre in his memory he had never been able to explain. She pampered him, cooked him one of his favourite meals, suggested he could watch a film on television. He didn't feel in the mood for that, he wanted her. He told her so. He undressed her, feeling slightly more aroused than usual. He had stacked the cards in favour of a new form of worship. Soft music from the radio, soft glow from the bedside lamp.

His hands strayed over her for a long time before he leaned forward and whispered that he had a surprise for her. She smiled blankly. He rose to fetch from his raincoat pocket the dildo bought that afternoon. He had been thinking about it for ages. One evening he had mentioned it to Claire, jokingly. She hadn't said no, which surprised him. But he had delayed putting his plan into action, he was afraid she'd changed her mind. After the film he had entered a shop in the Rue Saint-Denis, his heart pounding like a virgin's. He was annoyed at himself for being so flustered over such a commonplace purchase. He had picked out a long, white porcelain object, thrust it into his pocket and walked out with his head down. But once in the street, he'd regained his confidence. The thing weighed down his pocket, banging against his thigh, exciting him. Now he was ready to get on with the job. She looked at the object, murmured, 'Goodness me,' then kissed him violently. He was completely thrown. That she should consent to give something a try seemed only natural to him; but the fact that she wanted and demanded to disturbed him. He thought he was forcing his fantasies on her, converting her to them; he was discovering she had her own and was waiting for him to fulfil them. He didn't know her, she eluded him, submitting to contrivances perhaps to enliven embraces that had become lifeless for her too. He ran the porcelain over Claire's stomach, face, breasts. It was like surf lapping a beach. The game carried on, with Paul feeling the stage fright of an actor in the wings. He was urging himself on, repeating to himself how ordinary this was, everyone does it, Claire's probably done it before anyway. The thing's hesitancy only lit more fires on his lover's skin. He finally made up his mind, if only gingerly, kissed her and, with his mouth to hers, tentatively inserted the dildo. His cast was coming away from his nose, it was the kind of detail that could blow everything. He straightened it, thinking what a first for Claire, a masked man with a dildo. She held her breath, arched, murmured some words he did not understand and, with her eyes closed, fell back. He sat upright, bolder now, still beside her, bending over her to feast his eyes on the body at last offered to him. She had spread her legs and was turning her head from side to side. Paul's hand became more persuasive, he experienced the intense sensation of shaping a body. The belly hollowed, the breasts swelled, the lips parted over clenched teeth. Convulsions shook her, he had to tighten his grip on the appliance. He watched her, pinned to her bed by an immaculate harpoon. He remembered the fish, in Corsica two years earlier, their outraged gesticulations on the end of the spear, the flashes of silver at the entrance to the under-water caves. Claire also gesticulated, the lamp bringing up flashes of amber from her curves. He watched, no longer part of it, it was no longer Claire, he was watching the body of a stranger as she whispered the rattle of death. At the finish she gave a cry and he swore that he loved her. His hand was out of control, she heard nothing. Very slowly, her features relaxed; she rested her hand on his, snuggled against him, her eyes closed, panting slightly. He was seized by infinite sadness, never had he felt so alone, yet he couldn't understand his loneliness; he didn't like it, he hadn't chosen it, it had come from realms of desolation to force itself on him. That's why he liked to leave her without experiencing an orgasm, still desiring her, with the vision of the abandoned body and with the satisfaction of having spoilt nothing. Maybe he was only in love with Claire's body: he tried to preserve its exultant appeal by totally denying the satisfaction of his own desire.

'What are you thinking about?'

Claire had opened her eyes and asked the question put by all worried lovers. Pervenche respected their silences. He had learned that women dread them. They are jealous of silence, it is the bearer of too many dreams. They're right, mused Paul after answering that he was thinking of nothing when in fact he was thinking of the essential – everything he had never told her. They're right, their fear is justified. Their intuition makes them ask the question just when you're furthest away, with another woman or with no one, with the wind or the evening, or just when you've come back and are standing there at the entrance to the bedroom, gazing at this rumpled female body, noticing an unexpected blemish, realizing you are bored with her, discovering your life is duller than expected. What are you thinking about? How should one answer? Who has ever confessed what his thoughts were – this fraying love, the vanished expectancy, rain clouding the dawn, the fading emotions, the forgotten songs?

Pervenche rejected the offer of a dialogue, he had been engaging in a two-part monologue for too long now. It was all he could do to agree to a dialogue of bodies, increasingly rarely at that. What could he have said to her? That one day he would take the photo he had to take? That he might have to kill her in the process? He pictured Claire's naked body on the uneven cobblestones; no, a body that was too neat or skin too naked would be out of place, the story wouldn't be true to life. Or perhaps he didn't love her enough to kill her?

'Nothing,' he repeated.

Confused, he rose, drank a glass of water in the kitchen and removed his shoes. The radio was playing an old Elvis hit, *Love me Tender*. Pervenche loved the song; he had always imagined dancing some day with the one girl worthy of it – her hair against his cheek, her brow slightly damp, her arms around his neck – whispering to her the words that stuck in his mind. *Love me tender, love me sweet,* he moved over to the window. Below, the fog had coated the street with a bluish sheen, muting the call of the street lamps. In the glass, Paul could see Claire, one hand mechanically stroking her flanks. *Never let me go*, Elvis was singing virtually unaccompanied. Never would Paul dance to this song, *never let me go*, then all at once his ears buzzed as if they had been covered by two sea-shells and his heart raced. The fog, Claire's hand now at her breasts, the melancholy song – everything was shouting at Paul it was time to leave. Persuading himself that Claire was asleep, he put his shoes back on and fetched his raincoat. He ran down the six flights.

He was swallowed by the night and immediately regained

his composure. It was more than composure, it was detachment. He felt good, on a high. His pace was quick but unhurried. A car with smashed windows caught his attention, he hoped it wasn't insured with Magistrale. Then it came back to him, just like that, without thinking, it was definitely ample-thighed and not dimple-thighed, yes, it was all coming back to him, school literature class, the sonnet they had to compose and Rondet's opening line that had them in fits, the ample-thighed women slithered silently by. My dear boy, said sir, that's no iambic hexameter, it doesn't scan. Talk about laugh. Beside him he saw the blond hair shaking with the giggles, hiding the face, just the hair, *Love me tender*, he could just about dance, with a bit of luck. A bar by a crossroads gave shelter to some taciturn blacks. Paul saw one of them – no more cheerful than the others – go through the motions of a dance by a juke-box.

In no time he had pulled on his combat jacket and retrieved his camera and tripod from the cupboard. He did not think it wise to change clothes but he did remove his cast. It would be foolish to run unnecessary risks. The fog seemed perfect, better than last time. He was afraid he'd forgotten Ella's handkerchief, was relieved to find it deep in one of his jacket pockets. In searching for it he had pricked his fingers on some pine-needles. They had been there for years, for ever. He recalled the walks in the forest, ducking under the low branches, the brown carpet of dried needles and cones.

His tripod stationed itself once more under the arch of the doorway, his lens readied itself for action. The club was still there. Pervenche took up his place. Ample-thighed women, how could he have forgotten? Rondet's face – and he'd thought he'd made the grade as a poet! Ella must learn poems at school, mustn't she? He'd ask her to recite some, that would be sweet. He'd forgotten all the poems he'd ever learned at school, just as well too; he retained in his memory some mysterious lines, fragments cut off from their contexts, he'd been meaning to buy the works of Rimbaud since God knows when, that was the smallest of courtesies if he wanted to talk to him now and again. The minutes passed pleasantly by; Paul let them take care of the night.

A car roared along the embankment and turned into the street. Hey, that's not allowed, it's one way. Paul was horrified; the insurer imagined an accident with terrible consequences. The headlights cut a broad, yellowish swathe across the entrance, highlighting stones in need of repointing and flooding the tripod. Paul panicked, stepped forwards to hide his props and realized he would have no time. He retreated hurriedly into the entrance, trying vainly to blend with the wall. He devised an emergency plan. Yes, he had been relieving himself, what of it? The camera outside? Yes, it was his, what of it? The car had stopped. Paul heard someone make heavy weather of parking, then the engine died and the headlights left his lair in darkness once more. Two car doors slamming noisily, one male voice speaking in the distance and silence returned.

That was close. Paul could have used a stiff drink to pull himself together. It was the first time he'd been disturbed like that in his hiding-place. He viewed it as a bad omen. Things were starting to drag too. And what if no one ventured along the Rue Monte-à-regret tonight? Would he ever encounter such favourable conditions again? And what if it was the same woman as last time, what would he do? His rising self-confidence began to sink. Hell, that car had really given him a fright. Okay, another half an hour, no more, after that, too bad, and on top of everything it was getting cold.

He was trying to make out the time by holding his wrist in the light from the street lamp when footfalls sounded some way off. Neither heavy nor soft. Neither a man nor a woman, Paul said to himself, just the job. Cautiously, he observed the approaching silhouette. He was not anxious, just alert, intent on getting the delicate exercise just right. The shadow soon lengthened on the pavement; Paul moved forward, raising the piece of wood. His mind was blank; afterwards he thought he'd been humming *Love me Tender* but he wasn't sure. The passer-by came into view in front of him, dressed in a sort of hooded overcoat. It could have been a monk. Paul hesitated for a fraction of a second before bringing his weapon down with all his might. It made an awful noise. He thought he'd broken the club, which had slipped out of his grasp. He assessed immediately that he'd struck at the right time and the right place, he'd done well to work it all out on the spot beforehand. The man bent double, sank to his knees and sprawled full-length across the pool of light. A job well done. Paul moved closer, swore, dashed to his camera. His foreground was perfectly placed. He took several shots, setting several different exposures. The first time he had been careless in failing to record the exposure selected as he went along. Whether that photo of his had been taken with a half-second or a two-second exposure, he hadn't the faintest. Tonight he was attentive to the minutest technical detail. He packed up his equipment, recovered the club and kept watch for a few moments. Nothing. To make his get-away, he kept to the wall and had to step over the body. He studied it. Yes, it was a man, what a relief. One trouser-leg had ridden up, revealing a glimpse of hairy calf and striped sock. The head could not be seen beneath the hood but it had adopted a strange position. The shoe was half-off one foot. The photographer was intrigued by the dust covering the shoe. Dust in the middle of winter, weird.

Pervenche would have loved to stay and survey his work. He was in no hurry to leave, he was taking in this shape, face to the ground, one leg bent, both arms raised as if in a last attempt to climb. Six feet away, he noticed a small black object, picked it up and slipped it into his pocket. He would throw it into the canal. A few coins had rolled into the gutter. That's right, he'd heard them, just after the fall, they had prolonged their owner's life with their crystal song.

Once on the Quai de Jemmapes, Paul slipped under the footbridge to drown the length of wood. To his relief, it did not float. He ran as far as the Avenue Richerand and, more silent than a redskin, climbed to the fourth floor.

Armand was waiting for him. His laugh pealed out in

the room, reverberated in the street, carried to the doorway in the Rue Monte-à-regret, circled the dark shape and finally vanished. Anne-Sophie was no longer available for comment, Rimbaud winked at him. Paul was convinced he'd caught a strange, knowing wink. He took no offence, removed the redundant posters, put them away with the combat jacket. He showered and mixed himself a stiff grog with plenty of rum, lemon and honey, just as Armand had taught him. He devoted painstaking attention to the details, indispensable when the soul is struggling. He made to blow his nose, damn this cold; his hand stopped in mid-air – a large red stain disfigured Ella's handkerchief. He had washed it after the attack the other day and hadn't taken it out in the Rue Monte-à-regret. His clothes weren't torn. So, how? He soaked it in the wash-basin, frantically scrubbing it with the soap. What if the stain didn't go, the eye of Cain, that sort of thing? The stain did go, the eye of Cain with it.

He went to bed, his apprehension growing. So far he had been completely absorbed in the action, in preparing and making even the smallest of his moves. Setting up the camera in the right spot, watching, striking, photographing, packing up the equipment, disposing of the weapon – each step had required utmost concentration and led to the execution of the next. Now he was home, he had erased all trace of the crime, taken a shower. It was over. Yet everything was beginning. Suddenly he felt helpless, as if part of him had been severed – the richest and most secret part. He had feared being hounded by remorse; he found himself deprived of the sweetness of expectation. The more he played back the day, the flatter it seemed. But, in the end, the main thing was the photo. Nothing else mattered – neither remorse, nor regret.

— 12 —

'Let's hear it then. I hope you slaughtered him.'
'What? Who?'
Paul jumped. Le Nabec's question had caught him off guard. He stammered out a few more words before collecting his wits.

That morning his alarm clock had asked him politely: did he wish to tear himself from his slumber? Did he wish to rise? In fact Pervenche had already been awake for some time; he had kept his eyes shut to fool everyone and also because he was in no rush to open them on the life of a murderer. As long as he had been wrapped up in taking his photo, the consequences had not troubled him. But insidiously, with the first noises from the street, the dawn had splintered his sleep with flint-sharp fragments of lucidity. Words echoed in his head – monstrosity, crime, tragedy. He hyperbolized in the hope of tiring the superlatives. At which point the fiendish monster, the heinous criminal, caught himself smiling, even emerging from the covers under which he had tried to smother the anguish of being alone with himself. It wasn't as bad as all that. He pictured the shape sprawled on the pavement. Perhaps he'd only knocked him out? And the photo, this time he'd really got his photo. He'd kept his word, shown himself worthy of Armand. What a carry-on though!

He had sat up and drawn the curtains. The street was still submerged in wisps of fog, the town was coming to life; below, some dickhead was somewhat stiffly flicking fluff off a brand-new suit. Madame Gautier was tugging on the lead to prevent her dog from urinating against a car. She cast a surly look towards the second-floor window where her pyjama-clad husband yawned pensively as he eyed a young piece of stuff, another towards the fourth-floor window where Pervenche was relieved that the world should continue to turn as if nothing had happened.

Although he had risen appropriately to the test of the first morning, Pervenche judged it nonetheless advisable to display a modicum of prudence in his handling of the inner man. The positive was gaining the upper hand over the negative, but this fragile victory called for precautions. The chief measure was soon taken: avoid brooding, avoid thinking. Paul had made his arrangements. In case of alarm, in the event the mind wanders, tell yourself immediately that the dead man was not necessarily dead but merely stunned, and even if he was, well he could have been only a nobody too, no one would miss him. His defence mechanism left something to be desired, but he had nothing better to offer in the short term. See to that later. He turned resolutely to his future: back to bed, a stroll, the cinema? He was in need of company. Probably a peonin day.

He washed thoroughly, dressed and went off to work neat as a new pin, not cheerful but almost. He jibbed at taking the footbridge, detoured, eventually plunged into a métro station, stopped in his tracks in front of a newspaper stand. What about the stop press? He checked his change, conceded that he was being ridiculous: what did he think he was going to learn? He changed his mind and jumped on a train. On this rare occasion when he was actually using public transport – what an eventful last few days – he appreciated the collusive indifference of a population engrossed in stories about old ladies being mugged and children abused. A hirsute forty-year-old, a fellow artist, indulged himself with *Petite Fleur* between Bonne-Nouvelle and Richelieu-Drouot. His battered sax did not compensate for his lack of talent. It would have been too much if he'd played *Love me Tender*. Pervenche gave him fifty francs, nothing less would do between colleagues.

He felt a slight lump in his throat as he entered the office but it seemed to be business as usual, everyone in their places, no one had been taking a walk along the Rue Monte-à-regret of a foggy night. Pervenche had thrown his mask away and, his nose as good as new, had asked Frigo if he could start back to work two days early. He savoured the familiar odour given off by the misfortune and money locked away in the files and opened one at random. It was then that Le Nabec had startled him.

'The bloke, who else? You didn't let him get away with it, did you, didn't you smash him up?'

'Oh, my nose, you mean?'

'What else do you think I'm talking about?'

'Nothing, nothing, my dear Le Nabec.'

Paul was reviving. He had already forgotten the attack on the Quai de Valmy, it was so distant. His epic adventure held the office spellbound until lunch. Clients who had the misconceived notion of phoning were told their file was mislaid but they would be notified as soon as possible. Frigo, a true gent, let things ride. The aura with which Pervenche felt cloaked seemed in fact justified. But he wisely displayed humility, covering up a superiority the others had no inkling of.

Little by little his inner defences became more robust. At times a shadow hovered overhead, only to be quickly driven off. He had played a tight game, erecting real fortifications behind which his days passed in accordance with rituals of uncompromising precision.

He would hoist the colours with an ever smaller risk of being contradicted by the footbridge, drink a bowl of coffee by his window, treat himself to a practical joke if the Gautiers' door permitted and reach his first staging-post at a healthy pace. There was something new to report here. He had discovered that the footbridge had two flights of fifteen steps on the left bank and, on the right, one of ten and one of fifteen. Astounded, he had double-checked. He didn't make an issue out of it, but now climbed the steps two by two, left foot forward to start. Which hardly left his imagination any scope for running away with him. He contemplated from on high the canal downstream, backside turned to the Rue Monte-à-regret: heart skipping a beat on grey days over a yellow coat or a red umbrella whose vivid splash chimed like birdsong; skipping a beat at times when a small yacht entered the lock, already setting sail for the isles where Paul would take Ella.

Ella was the next stage. The Rue de Marseille, the big red school-building that imprisoned his bride-to-be. Paul could hear the cries for help coming from the enclosed playground. A shade more miserable, he turned into the Rue Toudic, paused briefly outside a fishmonger's, took the Rue de Lancry and the Rue du Château-d'Eau and bowed his head in the vicinity of the magistrates' court, which often enabled him to avoid a dog turd. He had a soft spot for these shitting dogs that compel humans to greater modesty. When a distracted sole had irately purified itself by virtue of three or four tortuous scrapes, the pavement would resound with the contained yowls of some whelp swearing never again to turn his head for a passing girl, who wasn't much to look at anyway, and consoling himself with the thought that it was the left foot and that no one had laughed at his misfortune.

Paul, however, had avoided that trap and strode along first the Rue du Château-d'Eau and then the Rue des Petites-Ecuries. This was his favourite part of town, the Turkish quarter, where he sometimes encountered familiar faces. Then the Jewish quarter, the Rue Richer, the Rue de Provence and Magistrale applauded such a fine all-round performance.

This never-varying itinerary was enlivened by variations in the manner of its completion. A certain bend would be taken wide one day, hugging the wall the next; a certain crossroads negotiated on the left-hand or right-hand pavement. Some days strictly no stopping, whatever the colour of the traffic-lights. Such ruses, such anticipation to overcome the obstacles and what satisfaction in the event of success. Bad weather gave him a chance to pose: bareheaded, no raincoat, the guy who's got better things to do than worry about practicalities. Or instead, still scorning an umbrella, Paul would go to any lengths not to get wet, sticking close to the house front where a providential balcony afforded a much-needed dry spell, idling under shop awnings, taking a break in a doorway, sprinting across open ground. On rainy days Paul breathed more heavily. First because he would sometimes catch sight of Ella with her indomitable fringe beneath the hood of her buttercup-yellow raincoat. Also because his route generated tension, but a healthy, aerobic tension unsullied by any untoward melancholy. Finally because more than the other days, he gorged himself on images. The colours of signs, traffic-lights and clothing multiplied on the gleaming surface of the pavements, where cigarette packets, leaflets and scraps of paper watched the vanishing shadows of the passers-by. Paul did not see them, he recorded them, stored them, pitched them wholesale into his souvenirs-for-later, just as one throws into a drawer the photos by a friend that one has no time to look at.

Paul went to work, returned from work, dropped in on Claire, Ella, his Turkish friends. He had the impression he was living on the surface of his life, like a bird chasing its reflection in the mirror of the water. It had frozen over; the smooth, white, uniform layer concealed, if there were still any to conceal, the last dark ripples. He had dotted his route with markers to which he attributed the capital importance of trivial things. This down-to-the-ground life suited him: it led to nothing, was taking him nowhere. It strangled the song of his dreams.

It showed in his work: the meticulous loss adjuster buried himself in his claims. In fact, he sank without a trace.

Even on his way to the office – he nonetheless tried to dedicate the first half to his princess, the Turkish shops and the magistrates' court – a freshly revamped professional conscience disposed him to donning his white collar and shiny-elbowed jacket: must write to the barrister in the Ducloux case, start with Cher Maître capital C capital M to make amends for the delay, see Frigo about the Gamelot claim, he's going to hedge again, too bad, bloody hell I almost stepped in it, fucking dogs, well I'll have time for a quick coffee with François if I hurry, God, have I answered Boyer? That's three times he's asked me to refund his breakdown costs, he's going to hit the roof . . .

Even as he seated himself at his desk, while the others were still stretching, the victims of never-ending, highly contagious yawns, Pervenche would be raring to go. He laid a protective hand on the stack to the left, the claims he would deal with today. By the evening the stack would have shrunk by half. Tomorrow morning it would have doubled. Sisyphus cheated a bit, arranging it so that the claims deemed to be tedious did not budge from the bottom of the pile. They escaped from this exile weeks or sometimes months later, bristling with the aggressiveness expressed over the telephone or in a letter by some nonentity swearing he'd complain, it was daylight robbery.

Like a fair English maid sowing seed, Frigo scattered to the adjusters the morning crop. He distributed what were known as the 'declarations'. Everyone foraged through their batch in search of the dead or seriously injured party who would bring a ray of sunshine into their day: at last some exciting business that made a change from broken arms or dented bodywork. They laughed awhile at the guy who found himself condemned to a wheelchair for driving too fast, or who had dispatched wife and children to kingdom come. They laughed twice as loud at the description of his awakening in hospital: he hadn't sobered up, he was coming round, gleefully, my God we let our hair down last night, well oiled, I must still have been a bit pissed when I drove off, hey where am I? Gradually the haze in his mind would clear, the accident, the ambulances, a compassionate nurse lighting her lantern . . . They worked hard at Magistrale, but they knew how to let off steam.

Then the adjuster who had hit the jackpot – a basket case – called for silence, he needed to meditate. A basket case was quite something. It was the king of claims. A basket case could work out at three or four million francs – No, Calot, not old francs – more if it was a kid. You could make merry with people's misfortunes, but not with Magistrale money. The paralytic could sleep easy, he would be pampered and cosseted, sent letters, cash, advice, doctors, investigators, lawyers.

Not every day was a field-day. Generally Paul had to make do with grazes and squashed toes. Soon the trolleys would trundle round, loaded with trays overflowing with claims, claims pending that had been dragged from their hiding-place by a letter, a statement or an expert's report. It was these trolleys that fuelled Paul's stacks and carried away Paul's half-stacks, that set the pace, with their screeching wheels and squealing handles, for the good and bad moments of the loss adjuster's lot.

Flourishes were added to the rhythm by a cachou, by a sweet – bagatelles indispensable to the smooth running of the tertiary sector – by an immaculate turd, nine forty-five, important to have regular bowel movements in a sedentary job, by a cup of coffee, ten fifteen, by a walk around the department, fifteen hundred hours, digesting, digesting, by a tidy of one's desk, sixteen forty-five, by a spell in Brittany from seventeen hundred hours onwards.

Safe behind such safety barriers as these, Pervenche had no fears of growing old. He abandoned himself to the metrical pulse of this waterwheel, and the hours trickled by with a helping push from a chat with François, an absent-minded read of the latest rulings on motoring offences, or a much more diligent cleaning of his nails.

Pervenche had battened down the hatches at home too. No more sessions under the window with his nose in the stars. His television chorused with the Gautiers' set. He bought the TV guide like everyone else, took pleasure in saying to himself 'There's a good film on tonight'. He felt as if he was expected. He was discovering himself to be a natural as a box-watcher and would become somewhat sad when, to the sound of violins, the closing kiss left him alone in front of his set. If there was no film, he switched on anyway, you never know, listening to the news while he ate, news which did not interest him.

But no television tonight. Paul remained adamant. The

serenity that had followed from his new self-control entitled him to develop the photo. The excitement of the murderous night had evaporated, it all seemed to belong to another era. He took out the roll of film and ran through his usual repertoire of tricks. He hung up the negative to dry in the bathroom. A glance reassured him: it was good. He unearthed the posters from the cupboard and tore them up conscientiously, they were no longer of any use. He would have liked to throw the pieces into the canal at the spot where the club lay, as a farewell gesture. He had always been attracted by symbols. His still-convalescent serenity shied at a visit to the scene of the crime. The waste-bin took the place of the canal.

He had a good half-hour to wait. He didn't know what to do with it. He flattened his nose against the window, turned the television on, off again, took a beer from the fridge without being thirsty, stretched out on the bed in search of an interesting position, surreptitiously observed Rimbaud in the hope of surprising his conversations with Petrushka, brushed his teeth, washed his hands, mused over some flattery that he would have tried out on Claire if she'd had the clever idea to arrive just then – nothing succeeded in holding his attention. He vanquished the minutes by dissipating himself. At last the film was dry.

The artiste made his entrance, naked – to do things properly and to be more sensitive to a birth already marked by fate. Once again he ran through Armand's tips, these tricks of the trade not to be found in any book: use hard paper, not the hardest, number three, say, in order to bring out the contrasts muted by the fog, but at the same time – and this was the secret – dilute the developer to bring out a range of greys. Armand was craning over the tray beside him, see what I told you? It's coming up just right. When the outlines of the photo drew themselves in at the bottom of the tray, Paul's heart tightened. The silence screamed in his ears. Yes, there it was, the footbridge, the steps, the embankment and the shape in the foreground, in a halo of light, as it were, from the street lamp. Success. Paul made two enlargements, plus one standard print which was easy to carry. He left everything to dry on the tiling and lay down on his bed with a beer in his hand. He watched the shadows on the walls and ceiling. He endeavoured to go through the same motions, the same ceremonial as the first time, but he felt neither the jubilation nor the unease that had filled him then. Perhaps the shock of discovery could not be repeated, perhaps an absence harboured more threats than a presence, even if it were the presence of a corpse? He had sworn not to dwell on things, he dropped that line of thought. The light in the bathroom had forsaken its blood-tinged look, fostering only tenderness; Paul regretted he could not turn it to Claire's advantage.

He peeled off the photos; they were dry. In the white, unforgiving light of the kitchen they withstood criticism quite happily. Paul was pleased that the corpse didn't look too much like a corpse; it could just as well have been a large branch or some strange animal. The photo was open to all interpretations. Its author would have welcomed greater enthusiasm on his own part: however much he congratulated himself, he couldn't view it with uninhibited pleasure. He put it down to the wisdom of an artist who has achieved maturity. Jumping up and down for joy rarely begat a masterpiece. He put the two large prints in a drawer, the smaller one in his wallet to stay forever close to his heart. He then permitted his room to breathe again: Petrushka wiped away her tear to the jibes of Arthur, the ribbons unfurled their sophisms, Anne-Sophie's ghost returned to arouse in Paul something verging on remorse. The poor creature had had a difficult end, yet even under torture she hadn't confessed what she knew. Moved, her executioner organized a collection. A memorial plaque – a pretty rectangle of pink paper – was mounted above the web: 'Here lived Anne-Sophie, pride of Paul, scourge of the flies, passed away unseasonably one February'. Paul suspected that as soon as the good weather came muscidae and lepidoptera would have no compunction about covering the epitaph with swastika graffiti and appeals for remembrance. A buzzing delegation would demand a trial, the representatives of the rights of the fly would draw up a precise list of the charges against the accused, there would be demonstrations, medal-bedecked escapees from the web would arrive to give evidence, pushed in their wheelchairs by midges with raised fists.

Paul added insecticide to his shopping-list. He missed Anne-Sophie a little. But she had been given a grandiose end and, however shadowy her existence may have appeared, she had not disappeared from the collective memory, that was all that mattered. A work of art or a crime, that was all it took, no more no less, to pass down to posterity. The memorial plaque fluttered in the draught from a window not properly shut; it could have been a butterfly.

That same day, it must have been three o'clock, the telephone summoned Paul away from studying a claim. To be more exact, from studying his photograph concealed under the correspondence he was drafting. He had not felt happy since the morning. In the Rue de Marseille he had missed seeing Ella and had been splashed by a bus; Le Nabec had been out of sorts. Then he had pored over a distressing statement in the first file he'd opened: a lock-keeper in the north of France had fallen into the water in the middle of the night. His wife had been unable to pull him out. By the time she returned with help, it was too late. Paul's imagination had run riot with the photos he could have taken. There was no shortage of lurid details in the report by the constabulary, with the usual spelling mistakes. It was the adjuster's task to apportion liability, if any: superannuated installations, shoddy maintenance, staff shortages, human error by the deceased, slowness of the emergency services, the telephone company's failure to repair the line. After giving their particulars, those involved each related what they had seen, heard and done. They overdid the gloom to enhance their own intrepidness.

Paul had put the file to one side. Too complicated for today. He had dealt with the run of the mill stuff, but had been haunted by the lock-keeper trapped in the icy current. Perhaps at this very instant a loss adjuster, here or elsewhere, was studying the statements on a mysterious affair in the Rue Monte-à-regret; perhaps he was thinking of the superb photographs that would have been for the taking? The police had displayed concision: no witnesses, victim in no state to talk, someone thought they had heard something but was not sure. Family and friends had been interviewed: no, to their knowledge the victim had no enemies, he was a man with no problems or skeletons in the cupboard, they couldn't understand. Pervenche had taken the photo out in order to follow the course of the enquiries more closely, keeping one eye on Frigo. He revelled in this subterfuge, fabricating a chimpanzee out of people. Great photo though. If François had been in a good mood, he would have shown it to him.

Paul picked up the phone, annoyed at the distraction from his work. He was wanted at reception. Who by? Two police officers were asking at reception for Monsieur Pervenche.

Paul gently replaced the receiver, petrified. He prepared to assume a suitable expression but no one was paying any attention to him. Claims and typewriters occupied their minds more than Paul being asked for by two policemen. True, he was the only one to know. He looked at all these bowed crania. Some world-weary flowers in a blue vase on Blandine's desk recalled the song of the bees. Paul too. He saw the first bumblebee he'd ever caught, with cupped hands; it was drunk on the nectar of a hollyhock. He remembered his apprehension, his wanting to open his hands even though he'd been assured that bumblebees don't sting, the high-pitched, desperate buzzing, the insect colliding softly with its prison walls, while at Paul's feet other bumblebees gathered nectar with the same indifference as his colleagues around him.

He rose and crossed over to the window. The grey sky, the black building opposite – the scene was set for a gloomy denouement. Pervenche imagined himself opening the window, shinning down a drainpipe to the ground, slipping through the net, with flashing lights, sirens and loudspeakers calling on him to give himself up, he was surrounded. He would sneak across the border and go to ground in Turkey.

A second later, since an even heavier cloud had once more darkened the sky, Paul was going down the stairs, walking straight up to the police officers, holding out his wrists, alarmed to discover how much one could risk for a photograph.

The phone rang again. Must be getting impatient downstairs. Unless it was to say there'd been a mistake, that it wasn't him the police were after? It was Boyer, he still hadn't been refunded for his breakdown, things were dragging on and . . . Paul proferred the receiver to François.

'Can you field this? I've got to go to reception.'

'Give it here. But what's the matter with you, my love? You're as white as a sheet.'

'Me, white? No, nothing's the matter.'

Paul was a disappointment to himself. He had been convinced that nothing in his voice or attitude betrayed his inner turmoil. It upset him. In a loud, unwavering voice he informed Frigo he was going down to reception. He scarcely raised an eyebrow and did not look up from his reading. Pervenche stood for a few seconds beyond the glass door he had just closed behind him. François was wrestling with Boyer over the phone, Calot was wreathed in a satisfied smile – he had intercepted his pen by the skin of his teeth – Blandine was writing, the secretaries chatted over their typewriters, Frigo read. He felt tempted to poke out his tongue like Blandine or shout 'bloody job' like Calot. They were so far removed from him and suddenly he loved them all so very dearly. Through the glass he feasted his eyes on this cocoon in which he had lived, if anything, a happy life.

His chair, his pens, an open file, the closed drawer, the one where his photo slept – he almost went back for it, but what was the point? – like a clock that is stopped the moment its owner dies, his space had frozen in mid-flight.

He would never return. Someone would inherit his place while he, Pervenche, would provide delectation for a host of loss adjusters splitting their sides on reading such a novel statement. The murderer was perturbed by the idea: a night of fog and passion can't be summed up in a few sentences riddled with spelling mistakes, crossings-out and typos. He resolved to relate his story in the present tense: avoid the past tense at all costs, the police, as he witnessed every day, were not on the ball with past participles. Anyway, the present is more lively, one puts more life into it, perhaps they'd understand more easily the why and wherefores. And his grandfather always encouraged him to write essays in the present; he would relight his pipe, poke the coals in the hearth, scratch his neck. The window overlooked an orchard and, more distant, the river escorted by that double file of poplars. Yes, Paul would tell his tale in the present. It would surprise, it would shock, but that's how it would be.

But no way could he avoid the set phrases and jargon of the statement. A P/Sgt Dupont would have been deputizing for the o.i.c. of the section conducting the inquiry. The undersigned, Dupont Maurice, officer of the Judiciary Force, pursuant to articles 16, 28 and 75 to 78 of the Penal Code (Procedures), would report the following duties performed, acting in uniform and in accordance with the directions of his superiors. The above-stated person, that would be Pervenche. The above-stated person would be requested to state his details – surname, first name(s) (for females always give the maiden name followed, where applicable, by the married name), sex, date and place of birth, nationality, next of kin, full address and profession. After which the above-stated person could make his statement.

Perplexed, he went to face his destiny. He found the word rather apt. Redolent of tragedy, it finally spiced an adventure which, apart from the success of the photo, had not generated the sensations he felt entitled to expect. On the stairs an unaccustomed realism suddenly spoke to him of murder, arrest, trial, prison and vanished freedom. It shook him. It had never occurred to him that he was running any risks at all in his venture, other than making a success or hash of his photo, and proving or not his loyalty to Armand. Otherwise the social aspect of his act had not concerned him. He had taken precautions not to be seen, but more as a matter of form than out of conviction: no one would see him. No one had seen him. And now the investigators had tracked him down. What could he say to them? Paul guessed that he would be faced with the incomprehension of those who do not expect a work of art to turn their lives upside down.

As he opened the door to reception, he was not even sure his photo had turned his life upside down. He had no time to ponder further. With a jut of the chin the receptionist pointed out two men, hands behind their backs and noses uplifted towards pictures – works of art way beyond their comprehension, concluded Paul – meant to represent the aspirations and successes of a dynamic company.

'Monsieur Pervenche?'

'That's right.'

'Inspector Chédut. My colleague, Inspector Rateau.'

It was Inspector Chédut who took charge: youngish, good-looking, a Mediterranean accent that inspired confidence. The other one, older and with the standard-issue moustache, appeared absorbed in some knotty problem. Chédut was smiling at Paul, who admitted to disappointment. He would have preferred a cop more in keeping with the twilight world he was about to enter, someone colourless, transparent, unpleasant even, why not? It was not to be. The inspector got down to business:

'We have been told, by your management that is, that you are the person handling the Dumont case.'

'The Dumont case? That's right, why?'

'Well, I, that is we are conducting the investigation and would appreciate some information. I, we have taken the liberty of coming to you to save time. But, you understand, I, we . . .'

Paul did not understand anything any more. He could have flung his arms round Rateau and Chédut. How could he have had any doubts? Who could have seen him? Of course no one had seen or heard him. This all but official absolution confirmed Pervenche in a conviction he continued to cling to: the night of the Rue Monte-à-regret, the spread-eagled silhouette, the raised club – that was all beyond the pale, beyond the bounds of reality. What penalties could he incur for a crime that deserved none? The water had closed over the pebble, the ripples had faded, on the surface there floated the photo and the image of Armand.

'The Dumont case . . . Wait here, I'll only be a minute.' Pervenche flew up the stairs, deriding the person who had come down them just before with his head full of nonsense, burst into the office where no one had taken his place, where his pens and chair were taking a rest, where the nobodies were keeping their heads down and earning a crust. He grabbed the file and dashed out again. This whirlwind disturbed the prevailing calm: people were not used to exposure to gusting winds or gaping skies. Citizen Pervenche briefed the Republic in the person of its representatives. Stolen cars. The inspectors were trying to smash the ring and, judging by Rateau's kisser, it was proving an uphill but hardly uplifting task.

Conscious of having contributed in modest measure to the smooth running of the State, Pervenche remounted his wooden horse: the merry-go-round kept spinning, going fast and continually returning to its starting point. He dispatched post-haste a cheque to Boyer-the-barker, played a joke on Calot, who was having a hard time stepping into the shoes of a post-probationer, hummed some footling tunes, charmed Frigo with a 'I bet London's weekend weather's better than ours' and cleared his desk. Le Nabec was already collecting himself. Because the ship was sailing for three days, the Friday fog-horn was infused with even greater nostalgia.

In the street carnival lights and flags greeted the hero, brightening up what could have passed for dusk. But in the city there is no dusk, there is only day and night. Dusk, like dawn, reserves its splendours for the rats in the fields. The discovery filled Paul with a melancholy that had already soured the call of the gulls and the sirens and the cheers of the passengers. Brittany had been so vibrant this evening; he had envied François his homesickness, he would gladly have succumbed to an illness whose name chimed so sweetly.

Claire did not answer his ringing, even though he had told her he would drop by. He toured the neighbourhood, enjoying the attractions held by a stroll when no one knows it is a stepping-stone to an evening of tenderness, a chance to plan its stages and fine-tune the crucial moments. Paul thought it a smart move to buy a bottle of champagne. Claire loved it and it would induce in him greater boldness for his amorous experiments. His paradise was paved with good intentions. At the same time, but incognito, he would be toasting his return – almost – from prison. This abundance of joys brought a tear to his eye. It soon dried before the unrelenting door: Claire had disappeared, the ungrateful woman had left him in the company of his bottle and his porcelain. The threesome beat a retreat, one cursing, the others chinking in his pocket; from the footbridge the biggest of the three cast a provocative glance towards the corner of the Rue Monte-à-regret, whose magic had lost its youthful charm. That afternoon's red alert had straightened out Paul's ideas. It was all over, he had his photo, the rest would belong at best to his memories.

His doormat was graced by a letter. He recognized Claire's handwriting. He pulled a face as he picked it up, even more so as he read it. Things couldn't go on like that, she explained. For some time Paul had been different, he had a strange look and she was afraid of being a burden. She would really have liked to talk it over but he ran away from any discussion. She didn't know where she was any more, she suggested they didn't see each other for two weeks in order to get things in perspective and see where they were at. She loved him, didn't hold him to blame, maybe it was all her fault, she couldn't understand, she still cherished hopes of building something wonderful together, Love, Claire.

Paul was learning things: Claire had her own feelings and thoughts, she took initiatives, went her own way. Claire existed, and it rankled. She couldn't understand, nor could he. What was she counting on – his assurances on the imminence of their setting up house, the colour of the kitchen they would buy, the irreversible atrophy of his eccentricities, the withering of his secret gardens? Women were all the same, avid for security, calm and words of affection. They needed words whereas Paul felt strapped for words, he talked much better with his hands. He stowed the champagne in the fridge and on reflection reunited with it its hapless accomplice, to cool its ardour. He re-read the letter and resolved to reply forthwith. His pen soon lost its mightiness. He tore it all up and immersed himself in contemplation of his photograph. That's right, no statement, no file, no case of the Rue Monte-à-regret. Footbridge steps a bit too dark? No, it was okay, it was perfect. Two weeks, that wasn't the end of the world.

— 13 —

She was sulking, without the shadow of a doubt. Her hands tucked in the pockets of those blue dungarees that exposed her ankles, she could not make up her mind either to sit or to speak. Scowling, she kept her eyes lowered, withdrawing, Paul assumed, into preoccupations of the utmost importance.

In fact she kept her eyes lowered because she could not manage to tear them away from her new shoes, which were the source of her woes.

Paul had not paid attention to exhibit number one: a pair of sneakers that weren't so bad. She bridled: she had been instructed to put on these shoes that her mother – oh, they do look nice on you – had bought her without seeking her opinion. That was the rub. This crime of lese-majesty had annoyed the little thing much more than the shoes had displeased. Paul tried to cheer her up – nothing doing. He eventually made her see that once they were worn out she could choose a new pair. So they had to be worn out as quickly as possible. The ruse excited his playmate: from then on she scuffed her soles as she walked, kicking anything that didn't move, jumping higher and skipping faster. Since immobility was proscribed, they perambulated. The brother, from whom Paul deferentially begged permission, now evinced less suspicion: batteries for his Walkman here, a pen there – the gifts entrusted to the tiny go-between had smoothed the bumps along the way.

Paul and his kangaroo crossed the Rue Faubourg-du-Temple once again. The boundaries of their world were receding and now encompassed the Square Frédérick-Lemaître. Their hands clasped more tightly. Scared by these unknown lands, comforted by the cherished presence of the other, they explored regions where the streets, buildings and cars metamorphosed into forests, clearings and mountains. These were rife with tsetse flies and crocodiles on the riverbanks, from which they never strayed far.

There was activity on the river. A barge was sinking out of sight behind the lock-gates; the hissing of the water escaping in myriad cascades announced danger. The chasm was preparing to swallow the boat. This did not concern Ella unduly. Only one thing concerned her: the date of their departure. The captain had to explain that the snows were thawing with such ferocity that the rapids were impassable. The barge wasn't going far enough, it was mooring in a port where the crew would be plagued by mosquitoes, and leeches too, you know, they're a kind of eel that drinks your blood. Not until the weather was set fair, when the winds were favourable. The sun disappeared from the blue eyes and from Pervenche's heart. He hastened to steer her towards the wheel of fortune, giving her the packet of chewing-gum nestling in his pocket. Touched by the sad little face and the notes passing non-stop over the counter, the stallholder wangled it so that chance was pinned down. Ella opened her arms to a doll in flouncy petticoats and smothered it with kisses. Pervenche had never imagined that one day he would be jealous of a doll.

They returned to their home port; their bench was growing cold without them. With sudden inspiration Paul searched through his wallet and pulled out the photograph.

Ella put her little girl down, settled her comfortably and examined the photo: for a long, long time. She said nothing but turned to Paul with a look that had him on the run, a stern, piercing look. She had guessed everything, Paul was sure of it. He did not dare break the silence. The girl's friends were calling her over to the bandstand. She motioned to them without looking up.

'Is the man asleep?'

'What man?'

'The man in the photo.'

The music of her voice pierced the darkness engulfing the square. Paul had faced the ordeal of the police inspectors with greater confidence than this. He was convinced she had penetrated his secret, that she had asked the question to put him off the scent and reassure herself too. He stammered out that yes, the man was asleep, careful, her doll was going to fall. He had no grounds for pride with such cowardice, but he at least derived the satisfaction of noting how effective it was. He took a sudden interest in the colour of the dolly's eyes and made as if to examine them in detail. The plastic eyelids opened on irises of the blue of all dolls' irises, a faded, sickly blue, as sickly as the taste in Pervenche's mouth.

'Oh no, I've swallowed my g-gum. I yawned and swallowed my g-gum.'

A nasty business: it was the last piece and was calculated to keep her chewing until dinner. The diversion of the chewing-gum ended the torment to which Ella had subjected him.

The time had come to part. Ella went home, plus one doll and minus one stick of gum. Paul followed suit, deliciously smitten by the feeling of his entrails burning from the fire lit by the mute interrogation of the wide eyes, and by the admission of the increasing influence Ella exerted on his life with every week that passed. As soon as she had flitted away, his horizons shrivelled and decayed like a flower imprisoned in lifeless water. Paul then found himself up against the confines of a world he thought he had designed with greater foresight. His vision had been too narrow.

The first days of March were clothed in that dull grey robe he was fond of – perhaps because it set off the blue of Ella's eyes – but still they brought with them the echo of hesitant breezes. Strollers hummed to themselves; breathing the sharper air from the canal caused an inexplicable sinking of the spirits.

Claire's absence had sealed the shrinking of Pervenche's world. He was respecting her decision. To respect it even more, one downcast evening he took himself for a walk along the Rue Saint-Denis, kidding himself that the mouth to which he had consigned himself could pronounce the oracle. He returned to his room somewhat more downcast and more anxious too: the streets did not seem safe.

He knuckled under and consented to question certain tenets of his philosophy of everyday existence. Until now he had been looking for a sign, a message in every image that affected him. He assumed that it concealed a truth whose opacity he would overcome by sheer persistence, and that this truth was his, the truth of his dreams come true. One evening he had lingered, not far from home, over the butterflies of a ripped-up letter – a love letter, what else – that fluttered and died to the intermittent light of a shop sign. Someone had loved and suffered right here. A stretch of gutter, some scraps of paper, mediocrity transformed by flashes of jade and the surrounding night – that was his life, pathetic but brightened by billows of happiness each time he met innocence, violence and their perverse beauty. All of which was incompatible with the muddled exercises of analysis he sometimes set himself. He acknowledged that there is no relationship between what one sees and what one lives; it's only in heavy-handed novels that these connections are flushed out into the open. Denying himself this back door, he reverted to greater simplicity: feel before you think. From then on, like a true photographer, he found his excitement in the slope of a roof, the beginnings of rust on railings or a tattered poster. He recognized once and for all the importance of attention to detail and the flames that can be concealed behind an anonymous façade. He promised to laugh less at nobodies. Maybe they too were crying over the remnants of a farewell letter.

Pervenche had an urge to re-read Claire's love letter. His time in purgatory was nearing its end; he was keen to display good humour. For openers he would invite her for dinner at his place. She had been there only twice, not daring to drop in out of the blue. He would do the cooking and she could tidy the bloody cupboard where he squirrelled away anything that might come in useful and that he never used. He found the letter and noticed his combat jacket. He had rolled it into a ball on returning from that night, without troubling to examine it for stains. Which he now proceeded to do. No stains, great. But what's this, in the pocket? A cassette, oh shit! He'd forgotten it, he'd forgotten the black thing lying beside the coins, he'd forgotten to throw it away with the piece of wood. He'd do it. Tomorrow.

The next day he did not do it. He engaged in his 'premature wrinkly' activities, an expression he used on upbeat days (celadon – the hubbub of the city had promised) to make fun of himself, give himself a friendly slap on the back: lick of water on his face, flick of his comb, peep in the mirror, not bad if I say so myself, spot of coffee at the window just like all the local old-timers, half-glance at the Gautiers' dog, so it's Pa Gautier on fatigue today, let's be off, no let's not, he was early, he would miss Ella. How about listening to the cassette? You're on! Good idea. He put it on, tired quite soon of the violin clashing swords with an orchestra, stuck it in his pocket and dashed out. Now he was a bit late, he would miss Ella. He did miss her; he just glimpsed two white ankle-socks snapped up by the jail. He hadn't had time to throw away the cassette. Anyway, no point attracting attention by chucking it from the footbridge, the best thing to do would be to get rid of it at the same place as the club. He hoped that a cassette wouldn't float.

Le Nabec was at rock bottom. You couldn't get a word out of him. That was a good sign. Pervenche rubbed his hands at the sight of him and at the revelations in prospect. François had obviously been on a real bender the previous night.

He waited until his friend recovered to find out what he had escaped, because François invited him on all his thrashes. He had declined the offer, partying bored him nowadays. He despised himself after these binges: artificial euphoria was succeeded, on the way home, by even greater resentment. François' narrations were enough.

The atmosphere was not particularly conducive to work.

Paul hid behind the left-hand stack. Since Le Nabec could not surprise him, he happily immersed himself in the inspection of his photograph. He did not dare ask all and sundry whether someone happened to have a magnifying glass handy, insurers don't look into things that closely. So he scrutinized, peered, angled the photo, turned it. He could not make out the small black object he now had in his pocket. Perhaps the photo was under-exposed? He should reprint it a bit lighter, maybe the cassette would be clear, which reminded him, Claire, poor girl – don't forget to take her a present this evening, no expense spared. He could play the cassette before dumping it; what he'd heard that morning wasn't fantastic, but possibly the rest was better? The passer-by must have been listening to it when Paul clubbed him . . .

He extracted the cassette and placed it beside the photo after casting a wary glance at the outside world. Each was as black as the other. He checked the other side. Something was written on it. His chest tightened. He had been looking for a sign, a message – in a cherry dropped on a pavement or the flight of a pigeon – and here he was, discovering more than a message; it was an appeal. He was discovering that his victim had listened to music, had lived. It had a strange impact on him. For a whole month he had taken not the slightest interest in what the silhouette that had crumpled at his feet might represent; that didn't concern him. There was Armand, him and the photo. The silhouette was part of the photo. And now a cassette, a snatch of music and a word were casting their flickering glow – like a candle at the bottom of a shaft – on the walls of another's life. He would form some idea of what the guy was like, as good a way as any of making acquaintance. It would be weird if they had tastes in common. A budding affection brought a lump to the criminal's throat. He did not regret what he had done. Far from it. It was simply that the microcosm in which he moved had just been enriched, thanks to a cassette, by a presence which he was undertaking to unmask. He possessed few friends – make that no friends, behold Le Nabec with his head buried in his hands – he had room and time for a dear stranger.

He felt joyful, curious and joyful. His programme for the coming days was going to be exciting, what with Ella, Claire and Whatsit. Hang on, what was that? There was a name on the cassette, two letters and a name: M C FLEURIAULT, in impersonal capitals. So he was called Fleuriault, funny name, M Christian Fleuriault or M Cricri, or M Claude. Anyway, bugger the name. Pervenche wanted to focus solely on his tastes in music, on the feelings of the man; he wanted to know what his cudgel-blow had interrupted. He asked himself briefly if there wasn't something morbid about this curiosity, did not reply, but put away his treasure. He felt upbeat. A truly celadon day, everything hunky-dory.

François had surfaced. He was recounting last night, which had been short and sharp. His wife had refused to open the door. He had slept on the mat, the neighbours had to step over him to go to work. He was over the moon. Paul did not enquire into the details, François' escapades were getting into a rut, they didn't make him laugh, in fact he found them rather sad. There was no Breton show at five, the fog-horn was hoarse.

Pervenche had organized himself a princely evening. He bought an enormous bunch of roses which he left at Claire's door. He attached a note with which he was not dissatisfied: he was giving ground, but not too much, inviting Claire to spend the coming weekend out of town, anywhere, let's just go. He returned home, taunting the canal by showing it the cassette. Two taps on the Gautiers' door and he darted away on tiptoe to socialize with his new-found friend.

He stayed on tiptoe: listening to the cassette made him feel he was breaking and entering a temporarily vacated house. There was no instant infatuation. Paul listened once and then a second time to the same side. Nothing but classical stuff. Somewhat disappointed by his friend, Pervenche decided it was a mistake to rush things. The other side could wait. A sensible argument. At the third listening Paul noted a passage, an operatic aria or something like that, someone, male or female, was singing. He liked it. So the guy had taste. Paul listened again. He liked the passage more and more, and his friend also. He must have been an interesting bloke to talk to. Young or old? In love, or not? The quest fascinated him. What if he took the cassette along this weekend? He'd play it to Claire. She knew her music, she would put him in the picture. The weekend menu was looking positively mouth-watering. The only cloud in the sky was Ella, he wouldn't see her. Try and talk to her tomorrow morning before school, make loads of promises and hope to be forgiven.

He waylaid Ella in the Rue de Marseille. Her crestfallen mien touched him. He upped the ante: the Saturday after he would take her to a pâtisserie, that was a promise.

'A pâtisserie? Mmmhh!'

Paul stuck out his chest. These little twits with their satchels on their backs couldn't take Ella to a pâtisserie, could they? He didn't like them. They were a bit too close to her for comfort. One of these days he'd clout one of them, for sure.

No sooner had he dug his first file out of the left-hand stack than the phone interrupted him. A chirpy Claire thanked him for the flowers. After a short hesitation she added that she was pleased to be seeing him again. So was he, he told her. The cassette, Claire, Ella, soon Brittany – Pervenche was beside himself. The footbridge made no mistake: celadon, peonin, peonin, celadon. So many colours spot on. What a week, fucking hell. This was living.

The cassette slowly yielded its secrets to Paul. On Friday evening he caved in. He put on the other side, which was in fact side A. He had vowed to postpone the pleasure in order to relish it all the more. He gave in, delighting in his weakness. He settled comfortably into his armchair, facing the window and with his back to the music. March had forgotten it was due to bring in spring.

Paul jumped. A voice had suddenly spoken behind him, a girl's voice, talking to him. He turned round in alarm: it was the cassette. 'The day you know my ennui': he had caught the last few words. A silence followed. Paul was recovering as best he could from his fright when the clear notes of an acoustic guitar made his body thrill: *Love me Tender*, it was *Love me Tender*! Elvis lent confirmation. Paul saw Claire's bedroom, his reflection in the window, the fog in the street; he heard himself humming *Love me sweet* under the arch of the doorway. He could not think straight enough to decide whether it was awful or wonderful. And here was someone who'd decided to stop believing in coincidences. He stopped the tape and rewound. What was the voice saying?

He had to repeat the operation several times. He was so agitated that he could not concentrate single-mindedly on what he was listening to. Gradually he calmed down. In fact the girl was not talking, she was reciting a poem, four lines which Paul was unable to identify despite an appeal for help, which Rimbaud cold-shouldered.

> *Oh this reveals my delight,*
> *As it perchance reveals me.*
> *Will you then confess your plight,*
> *The day you know my ennui?*

Pervenche was devastated. He replayed the poem over and over, not tiring of it or really knowing what he was doing. This changed everything. Nothing he had heard so far or had yet to hear originated from his victim. It was a girl who was revealing herself on the tape, trying to share her sighs, her hopes, her despair. The silhouette in the Rue Monte-à-regret was no more than the recipient of this cry. It was a cry of love. Pervenche was not alone in the house he thought deserted. There were a boy and a girl looking for one another. The originality of their relationship heightened his regard for the man, something or other must have made him worthy of the cassette. Paul felt a growing desire to get to know him better. The cassette would not lead him far, a pity.

He could not help thinking that Claire had never surprised him, that with Claire originality was loth to express itself.

\*

Unoriginally, she rang at his door that Saturday morning.

'Where are we going?'

Her smile warmed his heart. She was complying with Paul's predilections from the outset. They would go where he wanted. He hadn't given it too much thought. Off the top of his head he suggested Loches. He had read in a dictionary that it was a small town just south of the Loire noteworthy for its historic buildings. A touch of culture would not be amiss on such a promising weekend.

They had the roads to themselves. A uniformly grey sky blended as best it could with the brown of the fields and the forests and the green of the pastures. It intensified the languid torpor of the ponds of the Sologne as they drove by. They ate lunch at an authentic country auberge. The log fire made them drowsy, the wine decorated the silence with garlands of over-blown colours, Claire pressed her leg against her companion's. In the car music took the place of the fire and the wine. With one exception Claire succeeded in unmasking the musicians disguised on side B of the cassette. Paul was keeping the first side for himself. He noted down the names and the works. Claire was surprising him, he wasn't expecting her to be so knowledgeable. He eyed her attractive profile. Why did she keep quiet about her talents, why didn't she put together tapes for him? Why didn't she make him unhappy?

It was an impressive line-up. Beethoven, Mahler, Mozart, Schubert and Verdi, a concerto for violin, an opera, a trio, a symphony – Paul would buy the lot. He wouldn't make do with the extracts on the cassette, he wanted to learn, to compare with the rest of the work, to understand what had motivated the choice of this or that passage. Claire was stumped by just one piece, the one that intrigued Paul so much. She listened to it three times, declared that it was a counter-tenor and patiently explained the mysteries of castrati and counter-tenors. Fascinated, the philistine listened to his teacher and then listened once more to the voice and the strings which transported him to realms he had never imagined, realms whose rulers must have mislaid the keys. She thought it was Vivaldi but could not swear to it. She would find out. Paul took back his cassette and rested his hand on the neck of his driver. The firm warm skin, the parted lips, the untrustworthy grey sky, the lurking spring – it all proved too much for male patience. The climax was scheduled for after dinner, in some cosy bedroom. But you had to know how to cut corners and improvise, especially when the setting was not congenial.

They turned off the main road and jolted along a winding dirt-track that led them towards a forest. The track petered out in a field. The hills beyond, dotted with copses, arched their backs while the forest deployed its dense barrier in front of them. Paul reached over and switched off the ignition; the engine left them alone in the world. He kissed Claire on the neck, the lips; his hands wandered feverishly. He asked her to undress, yes here in the car. She kept her panties on, she had her period. Paul conceived a feeling of vexation but did not tire of exploring the body offered to him.

Abruptly he said 'Come on' and opened the door. She looked at him in disbelief.

'Put on your coat and come with me. Yes, like that.'

She obeyed. Paul took her by the shoulders. They entered the forest. A path covered in dry leaves meandered through the pallid late-afternoon light. A raw chill whipped up the blood. Paul's needed no whipping. They left the path. Paul opened the white coat. Claire had never seemed so naked to him. She was shivering; trembling, he pulled her to him and caressed her violently. He forced her to lie down, then lay on top of her. She was no longer cold, she murmured that she loved him. He tore off the panties without really knowing what he was doing. He looked away as she removed her tampon. He could not stomach any blemishes on the occasion, it was as bad as a scratched record. For a few seconds he remained propped on one elbow, staring into the undergrowth, thinking only of the cold water she had just involuntarily poured on his excitement. She had taken off her coat so as not to dirty it. He looked at her, so naked and so white against the moss and the fawn bed of leaves, the goose flesh outlining her breasts more boldly. He plied her with caresses that were also a massage; he felt beneath his lips her icy skin, beneath his hand her burning pudenda. His head was spinning. He took the dildo from his pocket, heard Claire saying 'Why? Why?' He ignored it, set to, his mouth pressed to Claire's. His hand became frenzied, no, not frenzied, relentless; out of the corner of his eye he could glimpse the object as it disappeared and reappeared, smeared in blood. Claire was moaning, she began to cry out, whether in pain or pleasure he did not know. He did not let up, he was wielding his club in the darkness, could hear the sound of the blow, it was Claire who crumpled, it was Claire he was stabbing until she lay still, it was Claire screaming 'I want you, please, please'; he threw aside the white phallus, unzipped himself in clumsy haste, plunged into her like an animal, they were both animals and that excited him even more, he raised himself on his arms, she was biting her lip, she started to cry out again. They came together, something that had not happened to them for a long time. She came with cries of pleasure and of joy at knowing that she and Paul were making a fresh start, that everything would be fine from now on. He came with moans of pleasure and because he knew it was all over; the golden harrow had crumbled, ashes and dust pervaded the wood.

She put her arms around his neck, murmured 'My darling'. He did not dare return her look. The dildo lay nearby. The blood had painted vivid streaks on its milky shaft; the leaves sticking to it tamed the impetuousness of the white and red. Correction, albuminous and peonin. Paul noticed a leaf slightly paler than the rest. A red stripe decorated it for bravery in the cut and thrust of action.

The cassette also contained an extract from *Dido and Aeneas*, by Purcell. Claire had the record. Earlier she had sung him the last words: 'Remember me but, oh, forget my fate.' Paul would remember Claire, she would be part of the cassette, together with the murdered shadow and the unknown girl.

They stood up. Claire wrapped herself shiveringly, amorously in her coat; Paul's arm placed itself shamefully on her shoulder. Through the branches he saw the white and red stain, he thought of a death cap mushroom, it had the shape and poison of one. Something had just come to an end, it was a little colder, a little darker. The warmth inside the car dulled the sadness that assailed him. Claire removed the coat, revealing as she searched for her clothes a supposedly perfect body. A furrow which had never before caught his eye cut the body in two, causing the abdomen to bulge. It looked like a gigantic ant. The ant flashed Paul a trusting smile. He did not notice, he was viewing the distorted abdomen and all it foreshadowed – pregnancies, country weekends at the in-laws', butchered promises. The dust refused to settle. The blood had dried on his fingers.

Paul resumed his act. He took Claire to a restaurant where he played unconvincingly his role of traitor. She was no longer smiling. She had guessed it was the parting of their ways. They returned to Paris that evening.

She had cautiously placed her hand on Paul's, withdrawing it to change gear. Gear changes loathe lovers. There was a hold-up, an accident. Blue and orange flashing lights punctured the night, diffracting on the rain-spattered windscreen. They saw two cars in the ditch. Tied to the aerial of the first were the shreds of a wedding bow, stirring gently. Claire's hand did not move from the gear lever again.

She dropped Paul at his place, waited for a word, a sign. He kissed her on the corner of the mouth and promised to phone. The tail-lights disappeared. Paul did not really understand what was happening to him. He was not sure he was in command of his own decisions. He remembered the furrow across the abdomen. He grabbed his bag and went up to his room.

It wasn't that late. His widowhood was already getting him down. He abandoned the cassette; he suddenly wanted to talk about the summer. Genghis would be playing cards like every Turk in town on a Saturday, cards or backgammon, it's all the same. Every weekend Paul spent a while in one or other of the *çay salonu* frequented by his mates. They had reluctantly renounced the idea of a punitive expedition but always demanded to escort him back home.

In winter especially Paul loved the warmth emanating from these bars where kettles on makeshift burners clouded in steam the video machine which enabled turbans, minarets, scimitars and veiled women to recall to the workers of Strasbourg-Saint-Denis a history of bygone glory. Music and newspapers helped them to regain a bit of their soul, a piece of their homeland. Paul was jealous of a misery which lasted only eleven months and was redeemed by the twelfth. Eleven months to prepare, to dream and to remember.

Genghis called to him from the back of the room. A chair was vacated for him, a luxury on evenings when the card-tables were besieged. Holding his piping hot tea, Paul slipped into a mood of well-being nurtured by the clamour of voices, the wail of a *saz*, the whistling of a kettle.

— 14 —

Splitting up with Claire had created a bigger vacuum than he'd imagined. He concentrated on offsetting this absence by the presence of strangers who crossed his path. The guy with the cassette already featured prominently in his fantasies – him and his woman and their love story. And a bizarre love story at that. Very odd. Hints of hopes and promises, nothing more. Like all the best love stories, in fact. When he was not working on the tape, he exercised elsewhere – on his way to and from work. He worked hard at reading the minds of those who found favour with him, scripting scenes and weaving plots. He would put words into the mouth of some bird he was trailing, mesmerized by the first rays of the sun entwining themselves around her legs. He would put himself in the shoes of some schoolboy racing with his slapdash homework to a dreary lesson. He was hoping to hone his powers of observation, his intuition, his imagination. He could not afford any mistakes in his detective work on the cassette. He was starting to unravel what made the girl – and thereby the boyfriend – tick. He was on the right track. He just had to keep on his toes, no slacking, be methodical, disciplined.

Side A of the cassette was slowly unveiling the girl's delights and sorrows. Paul had still not listened to it all: one new piece of music a day. Whereas he gorged himself on side B. The further he delved, the more he envied his victim the knowledge of such a woman and the arousal of such subtle feelings within her. He envied him while lamenting the limitations of his own imagination. His exercises must be badly thought out, he was getting nowhere. He was stuck at the body sprawled in the darkness; there were insufficient clues to build up a picture of his life. The girl was beginning to reveal herself on the tape. But the victim refused to emerge from the shadows. Apart from the coins, the cassette, which he must have been listening to – Paul had just decided to buy a Walkman to get deeper under the character's skin – the stripy socks and the hairy legs, there was not a thing to point him in the right direction. So, like an aimless drunk, he continued to soak up the music, although he avoided the part where Dido wept at Claire's leaving. He was sorry the girl hadn't included *The Marriage of Figaro*.

*Deh vieni, non tardar, o gioia bella* – then he could have listened to his whole life on the cassette: Armand, Claire, the girl and the shadow. And himself everywhere, because the more he listened, the more he felt implicated. It was as if the cassette was revealing to him his own tastes.

The pâtissière had motioned them towards a corner table. Two old dears next to them remarked: 'You naughty pair, mind you watch your young figures.' She had crossed her legs in a rather adult posture and was putting on a virtuous air totally at odds with the avid stare she was directing at the cakes piled on her plate. Paul had taken only one. He preferred to feast on the little face, watching for the clouds and sunny spells that transformed it from one second to the next. Almost a young girl, still a babe, princess then clown – he never tired of this river with its unexpected reflections. She was his river, the one flanked by poplars that had lulled his childhood. He nearly made a hurtful comment, just to see the clouds pass over her cheeks. He recollected a time when he mercilessly teased dogs and cats solely for the pleasure of comforting them and cheering them up afterwards.

Ella was wolfing the cakes as fast as her one-way chatter allowed: her father – Paul was delighted that father had replaced daddy – had said that if she didn't work hard, he'd have more to say, but her t-teacher had said she'd soon have her scrap-book, she'd show it to him, and she would take it and all her pictures on the b-boat, but she would find lots more pictures in the big port they were going to...

With the fairer weather, the journey was drawing near. The organizer was beginning to give it some serious thought: what if he did go off for a few days with Ella? A long weekend? Her parents wouldn't object. He'd have to see them. If it came to it, he could take the brother too. The trip would lose some of its appeal, but it would be better than nothing. Or else just snatch her! Disappear with Ella, not say a word to anyone. It could all be sorted out afterwards. It was worth bearing in mind. Ella had also been pondering: she wouldn't eat the chocolate éclair. An orange-juice washed down the cakes whose fate she had already sealed.

They approached the jetty where their boat would soon be tugging at its moorings. The lock-gates were dappled with green, blue, white and multi-coloured patches, tattered plastic bags, rags, a jumble of objects hanging here, there and everywhere like relics, mortal remains or offerings placed there by grateful sailors. Paul talked about the expedition. By way of thanks he requested a song from his sea-nymph. She sang a sad nursery rhyme.

'Your turn.'

'What?'

'N-now you sing a song.'

Highly embarrassed, he sang in a low voice, alarmed that other people might hear him, overjoyed to see Ella smile. As he sang, he thought of Claire, who had capitulated on the spot when faced with a rival she did not even know, of the Rue Monte-à-regret, of the cassette, of the songs on it which tortured him without his knowing why. Where was Ella taking him? Where was he leading her? He held her hand again, dismissed the pointless questions and escorted her back to her brother.

Paul worked harder: he wasted less time peering into his drawer at the photo that was waiting for him. He wasted a great deal of time laughing with François about the fishmonger whose son had run over a paterfamilias. Le Nabec, who was handling the claim, had obtained proof of a deliberate false declaration by the fishmonger. In order to reduce his premium (so he bragged to the prettier of his two secretaries, who took an interest for once in what he was saying – he would have preferred her to show an interest in the jaunts he invited her on) the good man had stated that no one apart from himself drove the car. In fact the real driver was the son. Insurance contract null and void, article L.113.8 of the Insurance Code. It was the loss adjuster's dream, along with basket cases. And they all drooled at the prospect of not only total physical invalidity but an invalid contract to boot. So L.113.8 it was: letter to Bordeaux advising that Magistrale would not pay a sou and that it was up to the swindler to indemnify the victim. Better reckon on a million francs, two maybe.

Le Nabec was laughing fit to burst. He was tempted to phone Bordeaux to ask the price of a lobster. He was talked out of it. The laughter died down, then was rekindled by a final spark of humour – that's put him in his plaice, another shopkeeper who's had his chips . . .

Paul was groaning at a batch of mail badly typed by a real dog of a secretary when the phone rang. A lady called Madame Ribaud, no doubt far from a dog, who owned a gallery on the Left Bank and who was devoting an exhibition to aspiring young photographers, wished to meet him. Would Monsieur Pervenche care to drop by on Monday evening? It would be better to talk face to face. Having recovered from his surprise, he was about to voice the questions milling in his head when she excused herself, she was rather busy. She was counting on him. She rang off without further ado.

Paul kept the handset pressed to his ear for some time; the piercing tone did not prevent him from fantasizing wildly. What if she offered to show his work? What if his photographic career finally took off? But who was she anyway? How had she heard of him? Paul hovered between euphoria and apprehension. The way things were going, his destiny was at last coming alive.

That was all it needed to spur him on: his enquiries wouldn't mark time any longer, the dead man would have to come clean. With the imminent official recognition of his photograph as a work of art he could not be satisfied with guesswork. Having obtained Frigo's permission to finish early, he thumbed through a directory and jotted down the address of one of the tabloids. His audacity went to his head; he left work as blissfully as someone setting out to meet a friend off a train. Surname, first names, date of birth, profession, address, marital status – his imagination was already running riot over the guy's curriculum vitae. It was more restrained at the newspaper offices, where he was shunted from one department to the other. Eventually a Cerberus enquired after his wishes. The back number of the eighth of February? The ninth too? What for? To look at? He knew full well it was to look at, but to look at what? Paul became tangled and tongue-tied. The man would not let go. Pervenche's patience snapped and he confessed the true reason for his visit: it was for wiping his arse, he needed the back numbers from the eighth and ninth of February to wipe his arse today, the eleventh of April, satisfied? He would have thumped the jobsworth if he'd been sure of finding his own way out. He gave him a moral thumping and held him in sheer contempt.

The detective was stymied already; the wind in his sails was no longer as fresh. He walked into a bar, sorry he was not wearing a hat. He would have tipped it on the back of his head, leaned against the bar with a match in his very white teeth, ordered a bourbon, make that a double, a dame would have accosted him, I can help you honey, I can help you find what you're looking for. He would have laid his hand on her rump, given her a kiss, with the match, like real cowboys do. He would have ducked the punch thrown by that son of a bitch there, because he would have seen him coming in the mirror. Then he would have gone off with the dame to where they had to go. No hat, no bourbon – he made do with a coffee. He drank a second one because the dame had not shown and because he had an idea. He recalled seeing newspapers at the

Pompidou Centre. They probably kept back numbers. His sails billowed again.

Early that Saturday Pervenche was questioning with exquisite politeness the lady who appeared to reign over the newspaper corner. Beginning of February? No, we don't have them any longer. She took pity on Pervenche; he obviously had set his heart on his newspaper. She asked him to wait a second before presenting him with a small box. It was a microfilm: all the January and February issues of the paper requested. She pointed out a row of white cubbyholes; all he had to do was take a seat in one of the booths and read the instructions.

Paul chose an end booth. It was like being in a sort of phone box: he was preparing to phone the beyond. He took the roll of microfilm out of its orange box. Somewhere in his hand were ten or twenty lines that had caught the attention of readers wrapped up in their own troubles. For one it would be a fight among hooligans, for another the settling of a gang-land score: it's no great loss, it's getting dangerous to walk the streets though. Somewhere in his hand was a name, a life. Paul took his time; he read the instructions at length while keeping an eye on the other booths, most of which were occupied. This wasn't the moment for a Nosy Parker to come spying over his shoulder. He inserted the spool and used the handle to unwind the film, as instructed. He had only to turn the handle one way or the other to make time go forwards or backwards. One aged rapidly in the microfilm booths at the Pompidou Centre.

The pages of the newspaper scrolled across the screen. He stiffened: they were black, the letters white. He was projecting a negative, it looked like a funeral announcement. It was he who spied over his neighbours' shoulders: all okay there – black letters on white pages. He checked the box. The label 'negative' proved he was not dreaming. He persevered with his obituaries, reading was no problem. He was dreading finding a photograph of the victim or of the Rue Monte-à-regret, especially of the street. He panicked at the idea of viewing a negative the same as his own, the one he'd worked on in the bathroom, the same as his own but carelessly framed and lit, lacking feeling, lacking love.

January in thirty seconds, now for February. The sixth, seventh, there was the eighth. Paul rewound to read his stars for the seventh, deciding he would only go on to the eighth if the horoscope was good: 'Nothing will upset your plans, initiatives or hopes. But take steps to prepare for the end of the month, which will be very busy yet propitious for all sorts of developments. You can make your mark if you wish.' Spot on. For fun he had a go at picking out his victim's sign. He settled on Gemini: 'Following a hectic afternoon, you will find some peace in the evening. If you can accurately calculate the risks and chances, you will avoid disappointment.' Paul chuckled: the guy had miscalculated. But he'd certainly found his peace.

February the eighth and Paul had not made the front page. He took it well. Some hostages and a couple of child-killers had stolen the headlines. He cranked the handle and went through the pages with a fine tooth-comb. Page two, singers and writers shooting their mouths off, a crossword and funeral announcements, real ones this time. Page three, adverts and news in brief. Paul studied the screen: a few sordid stories, a man murdered near the Halles, no that wasn't it. Page four, games, competitions, the weather, bloody inane these papers. Page five, more short news items, more sordid stories. Paul was becoming agitated. These hacks wrote on any old thing: a cat stuck on a roof, a girl missing, but nothing on anything important. Page six, a feature article, some claptrap about hospitals and the latest novel by F. S. Paul had not read a thing for months: the opportunity beckoned, so did the mystery serial. A summary enabled amnesiacs to pick up the thread: 'While celebrating her birthday, Hélène learns that her sister has been rushed to hospital in Boulogne in a critical condition, having taken an overdose in a suicide attempt. (Paul was grateful for the explanation, the summary was for amnesiacs and idiots too.) She dies without regaining consciousness. Already very tired, Lord Campbell takes to his bed as soon as he returns home.'

Life was not a bed of roses for everyone. Pervenche could not resist the temptation to find out more.

'Farewell, dearest sister, my companion in misfortune, with whom I dreamed so much. You will never again share anything with me, not fame nor the social whirl. You will never see the skyscrapers of New York, but neither will you have to struggle to wrest paltry favours from the gods or from mortals. She started. John had taken her by the arm.' Paul could have wept, but the funeral oration reminded him of the work he had to do.

Page seven, politics and the game with the ten deliberate mistakes, much of a muchness really. Paul soon spotted them, his perceptiveness bucked him up. Page eight, racing. Page nine, more snippets of news! Nothing out of the ordinary, just a legless parachutist who wanted to help others like himself. Paul browsed through the article. Page ten, comic strips; page eleven, sport; pages twelve to fifteen, small ads. Page sixteen, the arts and books. Unsmiling, Paul made sure that the photography column carried no mention of the affair in the Rue Monte-à-regret. Page seventeen, cinema and theatre; page eighteen, the complete listings of films and plays, really cultural this paper, but what about the short news items? Page nineteen, television reviews; and page twenty, the TV programmes.

He was overcome with disbelief. He examined the newspaper from back to front and from front to back once more – nothing. Impossible. He scrolled through the issues from the ninth then the tenth. Nothing. Impossible. A murder always excites the interest of the population and the Establishment alike. Impossible.

He returned to the counter, requested the spools of two newspapers likely to do him justice and scoured them from end to end. No dead, no wounded. Had he simply stunned him? Had the guy feigned unconsciousness to save his skin? Paul heard the ominous crunch, recalled the violence of his blow and the weight of his weapon. He hadn't been dreaming, a silhouette had fallen at his feet and he had photographed it. Something inside him told him the devil was abroad.

Paul handed back the two boxes and, since it was not yet time for Ella, headed for the tourism section. He wanted to gen up on Turkey and his neighbourhood, and acquaint himself with the secrets of the tunnel. That might come in useful. He began with a scholarly work on the tenth arrondissement of Paris. He soon forgot his uncertainties, Turkey and the tunnel. His photograph was set, give or take a bit, on the site of the Montfaucon gibbet. There was the justification, if any were needed, for the uneasiness his photo had inspired.

Sixteen uprights joined by thick wooden crossbeams from which were suspended iron chains four feet long. Those who were hanged had time to get acquainted: they were left until the skeleton disintegrated completely. In the middle of the structure was a mass grave for the victims of the scaffold and of the other instruments of torture in the city. Pervenche was spellbound. His torture victim had ended up in the mass grave, that's why he was no longer to be found. The condemned – Pervenche was discovering the joys of culture, those gasps of breath that well the chest when one succeeds in rising above mediocrity – the condemned arrived on foot or in a tumbrel, stopping outside a convent in the Rue Saint-Denis where the nuns served them three pieces of bread and a glass of wine. Things had changed on the Rue Saint-Denis; now it was the tortured who gave to the sisters of mercy. And the monk who accompanied them returned with the escort to Châtelet: a hearty meal and a call-out fee rewarded his services.

His thirst for knowledge assuaged at last, Pervenche joined Ella. For a moment he was afraid that he would not see her, that her brother would maintain he'd never had a sister. Despite the fine weather and the brisk wind his neighbourhood was not reassuring. It was overshadowed by the gibbets: not satisfied with playing host to the Montfaucon gallows, the locality had also seen the smaller but no less persuasive gallows of Montigny. Paul thought he could detect a whiff of the terrible stench which, when the wind blew from the north-east, beset the whole city.

She babbled and babbled. There was a hole in her left

shoe, she'd got three stars at school, she was getting a Walkman for her birthday. Paul let himself be carried by the rise and fall of the fluty voice and by the sun, like a feather on the breeze. He had his Walkman to buy too. He'd do it later. All the same, it was funny that not a single paper mentioned the incident. The theory that the body had disappeared into the grave at the gibbet, attractive as it may be, didn't hold water. The detective was stumped but not disheartened. He had an idea at the back of his mind. He took Ella to the wheel of fortune; chance was implacable. When she left him, he watched her trotting along beside her brother. His cassette, his work, François, his Turkish mates – there was his life. But his life stood still for two hours each week. It hung on two big blue eyes and a slightly protruding upper lip, on a hand held in his. He went off to buy his Walkman. He shut himself away in a Sunday of music, with the added piquancy of the possibilities – more far-fetched by the hour – raised by Madame Ribaud's call.

Monday. An April Monday, peonin with a violaceous streak according to the footbridge. A wave to Ella, nothing to report on the way to work, nothing to relate to himself, a quick coffee with Le Nabec, an impressive stack on the left side of his desk. On Monday Pervenche resumed his enquiries with a vengeance. He went downstairs to the payphone, scouted around – no one, perfect – and dialled the number of the tenth arrondissement police station. In the calm voice of someone in the trade – assertive but respectful – he explained his problem to a civil servant whom he was terribly sorry to be troubling so early in the morning. His name was Bernard, Christophe Bernard, he was an investigator at Magistrale, the insurers of course, you may well be one of our clients? No? A pity. So he was the inspector looking into an attack that had occurred in February, in the Rue Monte-à-regret. What about it? Well, would the superintendent believe that the insured who had been so savagely attacked on the night of the seventh had lost his memory and even his mind? He remembered nothing.

What about it? Well, he, the inspector, Monsieur Bernard, was trying to round up information on the circumstances, any witnesses, etc. The night of the seventh of February, you say? Correct. In the Rue Monte-à-regret? Ten out of ten. The silence made Pervenche afraid he'd overdone it. The policeman came back on the line. Paul heard him turning pages as he commented on what he found: the fourth, a hit and run, nothing on the fifth or on the sixth or seventh either. Nothing. Pervenche thanked him. His mind was a blank.

He had run out of ammunition. The shadow remained a shadow, while he had the impression he was overstepping the limits of his dreams. There was nothing for it but to accept the irrational, to believe in the unreality of a night in February. What his body still felt deep inside, movements, sensations embedded in him like roots filling him with dread, those few minutes that had turned his life upside down, what his camera had captured – his mind questioned all this because there was no ending and every story has to have an ending. Because the canvas of the story was torn and there was nothing behind it. Buried in his files, Paul spent a long time studying the photograph and the dark shape in the light from the street lamp. He ran his finger over it but felt only the glazed paper.

Perhaps Madame Ribaud didn't exist? Perhaps the invitation was a dream? As Pervenche neared the gallery he imagined the worst in order to prepare for the best. Whatever happened, he would cope.

The gallery director, a less attractive woman than he had hoped, gave him a dizzily warm reception. She was very pleased to meet Paul. She had heard so much about him from Armand. Of course! Armand was an old friend of hers. It was he who had been so insistent about the quality of Paul's photographs. That was shortly before he died. He had assured her that there were some worth showing. Torn between the pain caused by Armand's death and the pleasure of recalling his inveterate eccentricities, she suddenly added that he had set a condition. He had stipulated, quite mysteriously, that Paul needed four or five months before he was ready. That was why she had not telephoned earlier. With a look of amusement she eyed Paul. Was he ready? Yes? Well then, she was waiting to see his three best photos.

Pervenche could only stammer: 'Now? You mean now?' He ran out of the gallery, overawed by the exhibition – an exhibition exclusively for highly talented young photographers, his patron had stressed – and even more so by Armand's intercession. He had never doubted Paul or his photo; he had foreseen how long it would take. And he had got it right. Paul felt his presence, closer than ever.

He returned to the gallery one hour later with his portfolio under his arm. He had selected one photo of the flooded meadows, one of old André raising his glass in the dusty light from the cellar window and, naturally, the photo from the Rue Monte-à-regret. Madame Ribaud examined them and complimented him. Perhaps she wasn't bad to look at after all. They spoke of Armand and of photography. She urged him to call in whenever he wished. She would need the prints for two weeks.

Confident now of his talent, he immersed himself in music until late into the night. He listened to the cassette, noting the nostalgia and sadness that ran through the entire selection. He played side A again:

> *Oh this reveals my delight,*
> *As it perchance reveals me.*
> *Will you then confess your plight,*
> *The day you know my ennui?*

It was him the now familiar voice was addressing, he was convinced of it. He played the beginning of the tape over and over. Delight, plight, ennui – the words swirled within him, striking chords that left him paralysed. He heard Elvis, *Love me Tender*, he saw the silhouette, the noise then the silence. Of course he'd killed a man. The songs spooled past. He allowed himself a new one. Here was a man's voice, deep and gravelly, saying terrible things to him. It was in English; he translated as best he could as he listened. There was talk of friendship, love and death, a blue raincoat torn at the shoulder, a rose between the teeth, a brother and a killer, a sleeping enemy and his woman who was free. Paul's memory told him his victim had been wearing a blue coat, with a tear at the shoulder. His enemy was sleeping, his woman was waiting.

The notes of the guitar and the words permeated him, distilling a poison which he gulped in long draughts. He whispered in time with the singer *my brother, my killer*. By the canal a shadow was melting away, a body sinking into the grave at the gibbet; with a last jerk, an arm broke free of the darkness proffering a small, black object. Paul was singing among the rotting corpses, the north wind made the chains creak, the hanged indulged in a last ride on the swings.

The silhouette vanished. Paul told himself that the man had just died a second death. But his death had been sweet because he had fulfilled his mission by handing to its rightful recipient the message he bore. Paul tightened his grasp on the cassette. The poison was coursing in his bloodstream. The realization struck him: in dogging the messenger's footsteps he had gone astray. What did his name or destiny matter? His path had crossed Paul's just long enough for a photo, for a cassette.

Paul played the song once more. He revelled in the mordant gratification of the tones and inflexions of a voice whose still-distant echo bewitched him like lank, umber seaweed undulating in limpid waters. He was surprised that so much sorrow could obscure so much happiness. He was listening to a song and he heard a girl, saw her face floating in the fog. He remembered the conversations with Armand, or rather Armand's disquisitions, because once the agenda turned to questions of aesthetics, there was no reining his friend in. Beauty, love, death – nothing else exists, nothing else is worth the risks of art. Each element in this trinity finds its justification and its fulfilment only in the presence, however covert, of the other two. At which point art verges on perfection. And life verges on a masterpiece. Armand declaimed his well-polished lines as much for the emotion of reciting his articles of faith as to convince Paul. His interlocutor nevertheless suspected him of borrowing his most persuasive quotes from little-known authors. Paul also remembered his last sight of Armand in tears at the call of Mozart, love and beauty. Pervenche had been right to put the record on again and leave him alone with his trinity. It must have been that evening when he took his decision, when he chose to hang himself, chose to erase the borders separating art from reality.

On Wednesday evening Paul joined François in their usual bar. The trip to Brittany was drawing near, there were things to discuss. The matter could only be settled properly over a drink or two. After the details had been finalized, François declined to accompany his friend to the gallery: he had to meet some mates for a mammoth piss-up. Paul rebuked him, things became heated. One of them couldn't care less about galleries and photos, the other didn't give a shit about Brittany and in fact hadn't the slightest inclination to waste his time there. In three minutes their words destroyed five years of friendship. François was the first to leave. Paul did not even notice, absorbed as he was in contemplation of the froth coating the sides of the glass he turned in his hands.

The ground was crumbling beneath his feet. He didn't care. From now on he could concentrate on the essentials – the cassette, Ella, his photo. Le Nabec and company could go to hell. In the end, what did the two of them have in common? Not a thing. The friendship couldn't have been founded on anything substantial if it had keeled over in the first squall. It was no great loss.

So he was alone and proud of it when he entered the gallery. No petits fours, no speeches, but punctilious expressions and an almost worshipful attentiveness. He greeted the director, mingled with the visitors and inspected the rival exhibits. He liked many of them, which troubled him: would his hold their own in such sophisticated company? He forced himself to take an objective look at his photos, his photo. He did not recognize it, they'd changed it: too dark, the footbridge steps foundered in a sort of mush, the corpse resembled a sack of rubbish and, worst of all, the fog had lost all its mystery. Instead of the golden rain there was a greyish gel. Paul felt ashamed. How could he have taken pride in this crap? He was dashing out when Madame Ribaud caught his arm:

'So, what do you think? Your photos are a hit, you realize. Several people have remarked on them.'

'Can I change one of them?'

'Change one? But why?'

'I must change one. I'll bring it tomorrow.'

Leaving her speechless, he rushed home and locked himself in his bathroom. Back to square one. Nothing had changed in eight months. He had stripped; the mirror returned the peonin contours of his body. In the tray the canal bank, the cobblestones and the fog were meticulously asserting themselves. Nothing had changed. Armand had died, a stranger too. In the other room the counter-tenor and the cellos were oblivious to the passage of time. Paul groped around to make sure that the refuse collectors had actually removed the blood and feathers of the bird. He repeated to himself ample-thighed, ample-thighed, ample-thighed women. A hideous thing, a woman with big thighs. That's it, it was ready. Stop-bath, fixer, wash, tiles, normal light – and the uneasiness. Paul was choked by the same uneasiness, the same diffuse anxiety. There was no comparison between the two photos: one without a corpse but with the golden rain, the tonal range of greys and the veiled threat, the other with an indistinct corpse and nothing else.

Paul looked at his photo for a long time. He wanted to accustom himself to the uneasiness, to defy it. The cassette and the photo were made for one another: the counter-tenor's voice sounded as if it came from the centre of the footbridge, where the steps vanished. A voice without tremolos, level, unruffled, neutral. Just like the setting of the photo. And, like the setting, it commanded expectation. But what was expected of Paul? Hadn't he done enough? Had he killed for nothing?

He picked up the botched film, the one where his victim lay prostrate. He unrolled it, opened the window and struck a match. The cassette had ended, the radio had taken over. There's some beautiful stuff on the radio: a woman was singing *I cried for you, I'll die for you*, in other words, Paul brooded, I'll die for nothing. The film flared, casting a furtive light into the window of the young Martin bird, then the Gautiers'. Writhing in agony, it wasted away near a drainpipe. The stranger died a third death. He'll have a job getting over that, reckoned Pervenche, revived by a swig of beer.

The following day he scorned the canteen to make the switch. The gallery-owner enquired what on earth had got into him the previous day. She hung up the photo Paul had brought, stepped back, screwed up her eyes.

'You're right, this one's better. A beautiful photo.'

'Yes,' Paul replied, in no mood for discussing his work.

With an air of casualness, he made some unlikely excuse and fled.

Pervenche did not discover what life was like in Brittany. He cloistered himself in his bedsit, he had plenty to do. First think. Think then decide. She was called Fleuriault, what more could one hope for when one's name was Pervenche? But who Fleuriault? The first name was a problem: Claude, Carole, Corinne, Chantal? His list didn't carry much conviction. What about the M? Madame? Mademoiselle? No, there'd be Mme or Mlle, no, it was a double-barrelled first name, beginning with an M as in Marie. Marie-who? Had to be Marie-Claude or Marie-Carole. He'd cracked it. With the surname and the first name in the bag Paul had the keys to the castle. Now he could listen to the tape; he could understand better . . .

Dido and her lamentations filled the room. Claire's favourite. Claire began with a C too. He'd forgotten her. Now there she was, finally daring, forcing his hand. Paul suddenly missed her discreet, loyal presence, the undying flame of her feelings that had consumed her like a cancer. He missed too the twilight zones into which her life sometimes vanished, her unexplained absences that he never tried to elucidate, her lips and her caresses. She should have hung on, refused to obey. They just hadn't got it together.

He pulled himself together. He set about making up a crazy tape containing twenty times over, alternately, the two pieces that moved him so much: the counter-tenor and *The Blue Raincoat*. Sitting in his armchair facing the dwindling light, he listened to his cassettes, starting with the girl's, Marie-C's. He wasn't used to the first name yet. Despite his attentiveness and concentration he nearly turned round again at the sound of the lovely voice: 'As it perchance reveals me . . .' Had she written these four lines for him? Or stolen them? He was no longer eavesdropping on a conversation between a girl and a murdered stranger. He was conversing with Marie-C, she was asking him passionate questions, he would give passionate answers. 'The day you know my ennui': the intonation of the voice called him to witness their complicity, their common aspirations. He reproached himself – it did all seem far-fetched – but he was lapping it up as he put on his crazy cassette. The counter-tenor then the deep voice of the Englishman. Latin, English, Latin, English. Two voices, two scores, two texts poles apart yet more alike than two peas in a pod: the same strange sadness, the same overture to something murky and disturbing yet sublime. The singer was telling of broken finger-nails, burning loins, the sails of a ship burning down to paper. The counter-tenor was dialoguing with the strings: at the end of the passage the cellos quivered in a decrescendo like a fading storm. Like a dying orgasm the voice continued to inflame wild thoughts: Paul and Marie-C were running headlong into the flooded meadows, the sprays of water glistening in the sun.

— 15 —

Pervenche was untroubled by the morose atmosphere at the office. François had started work without a word, saying, 'fine' to Calot when asked about his trip to Brittany. A claim soon forced Paul to consult the Magistrale file index. Begin at the beginning. If Marie-C were insured by the company, it would make life easier. He drew a blank: no Fleuriaults among Magistrale's clients. Never say die; strike while the iron's hot. The phone-book proved more cooperative: three Fleuriaults but no Marie-C or even Marie. The plot thickened. To keep his morale up Paul decided, very conveniently, that she was still young and lived with her parents, which didn't help much but was better than nothing. Having made a note of the numbers and addresses, he returned to his labours, side-tracked by umpteen calculations of the best approach and his chances of success.

He waited until evening to call, choosing his ground – the local post office at the corner of the Rue Léon Jouhaux. It was from here that he used to phone Armand. It smelled of old age and polished wood. Evidently out-of-date forms lay waiting for a glorious end; the two booths were huddled at one end. Paul occupied the one on the left, stepping in left foot first to clinch success, and dialled the first number. The phone rang in a flat where a girl was maybe listening to a counter-tenor and dreaming of Prince Charming. She couldn't have heard. Paul dialled the second number while pondering the next move if he failed in his telephone quest.

'Madame Fleuriault speaking.'

Paul stopped pondering. His spiel was prepared.

'Good evening, Madame. Could I speak to Marie, please?'

'Marie-Ciel? She isn't home yet. Who shall I say called?'

'It's Pierre. I'll ring back later. Goodbye.'

Paul all but hung up on her. He wanted to be alone with his elation. It had been as simple as that. Marie-Ciel. What a strange name, what a delightful name. As original and beautiful as the cassette. She lived in the Rue Jouffroy. Not so good. At work he had located the three addresses on a city map; the Rue Jouffroy was a long hike. Still, he'd ferreted her out in five minutes, that was a good omen. To set his mind at rest he tried the third number. A man answered: there's no Marie here. He returned to the attack with the first number, still silence. In his head there was no silence: the celebrations were in full swing, the crowds were cheering, a radiant Marie-Ciel opened the door to him, her hair as blond and her eyes as jet as he had imagined.

Aware that the music encouraged fantasizing rather than level-headedness, he prudently postponed all further decisions on his battle plan until the following day.

He spent several days on it. The urgency of the operation faded. There was one slight wrinkle: what if Marie-Ciel didn't match up to expectations? From then on when he thought of her, he glossed over the details and, above all, avoided idealizing her figure. He tried his best not to bias his judgement, to give it space where it would be able to reach a calm, considered and objective verdict when the time came. It didn't matter whether she was blonde or brunette, tall or petite. His only fear was that he wouldn't find her attractive. Then he remembered the beauty of the cassette: how could she not attract him when her tastes already held him captive? He scoffed at himself – he'd be wetting his knickers next – plucked a file from the left-hand stack and immersed himself in some unappetizing claim.

Things had been patched up with François on the surface. They spoke normally to one another and cracked the occasional joke. Deep down, they both realized that something had broken down, irretrievably.

\*

In the elegant hubbub which befits a gallery worthy of the name, in the midst of the reflective contortions of viewers grimacing at an ill-adjusted spotlight, Pervenche was discreetly checking in a glass-panelled door that his reflection really did match that of an artist. Reassured, he wandered here and there, especially there, near his photos, on the lookout for the eulogies promised by Madame Ribaud.

'Your photographs are a real hit,' she had complimented him. 'Especially the one of the fog. You must have an exhibition to yourself here. I would be so pleased to have Armand with us again, thanks to you: one can feel his influence on your style.'

She had released his arm to hook into that of a tall woman with a hat. Paul had spotted two middle-aged couples who were taking their visit very seriously. Convinced that more haste meant more speed, the ladies had drawn ahead and were chattering in front of Paul's photos. He moved closer, in the belief that nice things were being said about him. The blonde turned to her husband:

'Darling, do come and see this one. It's fabulous.'

Darling came, saw and struck a pose; he was at pains to primp his undisputed authority and expertise with hieratical gravitas. His wife grew impatient:

'Don't you think it's super? It has fantastic atmosphere...'

Darling was apparently still lost in thought; then his face brightened fleetingly:

'Atmosphere, atmosphere, do I look like someone who goes in for atmosphere!'

'Sorry? What's the matter? I didn't say anything wrong, surely.'

'Neither did I. "Do I look like someone who goes in for atmosphere" is a famous line of Arletty's in a famous film by Marcel Carné, *Hôtel du Nord*.'

'So what?'

'This photo was taken exactly where the film was shot, that's what. I think it's the Quai de Jemmapes. You're right, it is a nice piece, but the chap has plagiarized. He must have liked the film and that's what gave him the idea for the photograph...'

That's not true, I've never even heard of the film, let alone seen it. What a load of bullshit. I conceived it all, it's my photo, not Carné's or Arletty's, or even Armand's. Pervenche was choking with indignation. The unspoken protests scrambled for expression. The old fart. Another clueless jerk. Paul was on the brink of ripping up the photo before his eyes, flattening him and spitting in his face for good measure. Instead he hesitated. The best thing was calmly to explain the origin of his masterpiece. Yes, that was the best way. By the time he'd decided, there was no one left: his admirer and the film buff had scarpered.

Paul chewed over his anger, subduing it by painstakingly recapitulating the praise which had hailed his work. All said and done, the outcome was more than positive, no point in quibbling. Once more unto the records, citizen. He left carrying a bag full of LPs and hopes. He had managed to obtain those that Claire had named and especially, thanks to a knowledgeable shop assistant, the mysterious Vivaldi. It was still daylight, the hour when the city tires of all the bustle. The air carried the smell of cooking, applause escaping from a television set via a window left ajar, the barking of a dog followed quickly by that of its mistress – scenes which force folk to admit that, in the end, they're not that hard done by, the neighbours not that unpleasant, life not that miserable.

In passing, Pervenche cast a covert glance towards a pharmacy. He had noticed that pharmacists, with their sharp eye for business, often dressed their shop windows with mirrors bearing manufacturers' logos into which the passing punter could gaze and discover he was off-colour. Paul wasn't worried about his colour. His attention was on his appearance. He had been happy with the artist reflected in the glass panelled door at the gallery just now. Which was rare. His reflections almost always disappointed him; he never wore the air he credited himself with. One day as he was going to work – in a sullen but superior mood, with a rather arrogant expression and a swagger – he had come face to face in front of a bar with a little guy dressed like him, but with a mincing gait: a nobody, a real non-starter.

It was him, it was his own reflection in the plate glass. Appalled, he had stopped dead, looked himself in the eye and fashioned an appearance worthy of his aspirations: hair spruce and sporty, jacket straightened, shoulders back, supercilious fixed grin. Just as everything at last seemed to fit, he had noticed that behind the glass customers were slapping their thighs as they watched him pull himself together. Arrogance gave way to sheepishness as he swore in future to consult his reflections only with the utmost caution. The pharmacy window was kind to him: it offered him an artist in love, a love soon to be gratified. Perfect. So why did he come to grief so often? Why did his reflection betray him so consistently? At the moment of the crime, had he worn the killer's mask he had rehearsed in the mirror this winter? The question seemed all the more crucial now, only a matter of days before consummating his love for Marie-Ciel. He could not afford any mistakes: the artist in love could seduce her only if he looked like an artist in love. He observed himself uncompromisingly, not knowing which of Pervenche and his reflection was observing the other, which was endeavouring to imitate the other. He had never dared try his hand at self-portraits for fear of betraying himself; yet nowadays he only felt safe in the mornings, in the bathroom, when shaving-foam and toothpaste concealed his expression like a curtain drawn on a stage set assumed to be perfect. He shaved only with great reluctance, aghast at the thought that a pharmacy mirror might not see the same thing as Marie-Ciel. He had been avoiding mirrors, preferring plate glass shop fronts which, with the help of his self-deception, reflected an evasive and therefore palatable image. But this evening he had taken risks now rewarded by the endorsement of the pharmacy window. Things were looking good. He continued on his way. He was vaguely conscious that his tribulations with his image raised sizeable problems, of which he had an inkling and in front of which he cowered like a dog before a cathedral. This inability to get to the root of a problem sometimes made him despair. By living on sensations alone, he had amputated himself. He did not dwell on this reproach. On the only occasion he had forced himself to sit and think, his ramblings had terrified him. He had ended up with two solutions to the enigma of his reflection: either smash the mirror, or take a photograph of which he would be the author, object and subject but never a viewer. Although unachievable, the ploy had left an unpleasant taste in his mouth.

Moving from one reflection to the next, the amorous artist arrived at the Avenue Richerand. He had a date with Marie-Ciel. The records would provide an elegant prelude to their meeting, which Paul had planned for the following Monday. He had taken a week's holiday to accomplish his mission and had already inspected the lie of the land. She lived in a smart apartment building, on the sixth floor. He had ventured an ear to the door, without success.

He listened to the whole cassette, religiously, to distraction. He put himself in Marie-Ciel's place: why had she liked this record, chosen this extract? She had always chosen the best passage. Never had Paul felt so much in collusion with someone. Even with Armand. He probably admired him too much. Whereas now he was communing intimately with a stranger who was no longer a stranger; he did not doubt that they shared the same sensations at the same moments. Vivaldi's spell came to an end. When he put on the record, he was seized by the fear of not recognizing his piece. The first side did nothing for him. The second, *Nisi Dominus*, was ecstasy. He'd found it! It was the fourth movement, the *largo*. The rest was beautiful, but the *largo* was like a fresh discovery. In order to understand it better, to understand Marie-Ciel better, he began to study the notes accompanying the record. They informed him that 'a particularly explicit instruction is given for the setting of *Cum dederit*, where the drowsiness of "beloved sleep" is suggested by a slow siciliano movement over a drone bass marked "tasto solo"'. Vivaldi specifies that the strings 'play "con piombi", i.e. with lead mutes ... Following the normal Italian practice of this period the bass-line of the string orchestra is augmented in certain numbers with a bassoon and the continuo section consists of organ and chittarone, also used separately on occasion.' Paul rested the pages on his knee. He had launched into his reading on a D-sharp, he was finishing on an E-flat. He possessed the awareness of having greatly edified himself without the certainty of being any the less of an ignoramus. The counter-tenor had disclosed not one of his secrets; he was luring Paul and Marie-Ciel into ambiguous regions where explanatory notes are out of bounds and the logic of truth is banished. The throbbing strings teased out caresses and confessions; the voice sent darts of pain and pleasure soaring over charred cities. Pervenche could no longer resist this threatening tenderness: it recalled the spells cast by his photo, it foretold luxurious embraces.

On Fridays the staff of Magistrale had taken to winding down. A ray of sunshine had only to hint at the weekend to put paid to the legitimate hopes of clients clamouring for compensation. The clients Paul was dealing with this particular Friday – the one he was delighting in looking upon as his last as a bachelor – were harder done by than most. Professionally Pervenche was having a bad day because emotionally he was having a good one. That morning on his way to work he had sacrificed some of the details of his rituals and the images that meshed to form the canvas of his existence. He was even beginning to take liberties with decreeing the colour of the day. Peonin: whatever the footbridge may say, he stuck to peonin, but tinged with pink, it was a shade more tender and sensual. His walk to the office was becoming a full-blown pursuit of Marie-Ciel, punctuated by surreptitious glances into a pharmacy and other windows. An artist in love? An artist in love, confirmed the butcher's in the Rue Richer.

He made it through his off-day by dint of imagination and grit. Shamefaced, he answered a letter from Bruno, who had just come out of hospital. He had not seen him since Christmas and promised to call by as soon as he could. The darts were a really super present: Bruno was still full of praise for the projectiles which had brightened his days in hospital and darkened those of the nurses.

Great, a good job done, what's the time? Ha, ten thirty, not to worry, it'll soon be lunch-time. Why not take a look at the menu to whet the appetite, that'll kill ten minutes. Paul resorted to the tricks of the trade: repeatedly consulting his watch, which only made it slow, exchanging a few bland words with François, counting the number of revolutions completed by Calot's pen plus the seconds he wasted picking it up, dividing the total by the number of files that remained unprocessed in the meantime. He made out to a client telephoning from Nice that his file was being fetched, asking him to hold when by a miracle the file was open on his desk, solely to punish him for enjoying such a mild climate. He viewed unenthusiastically the weekend he had to see through before beginning his quest for the Holy Grail Ella, naturally, a quick visit to the Turks, a lot of music: take your time.

He took his time, rising late after pretending to sleep. Then he listened constantly to the two cassettes on his Walkman. On his way to see Ella he crossed both footbridges straddling the canal between the Avenue Richerand and the square, trying to catch a glimpse of his sweetheart. The trees and the caravan were in the way; he did not see her, only the black vault of the tunnel steeped in deathly torpor. In the absence of Ella, Paul did his circuit of the neighbourhood, returning towards the Square Frédérick-Lemaître. At the Pompidou Centre he had read the life-history of this nineteenth-century actor and retained nothing except that he had his statue here, and his square. He resented the fact that he snubbed the statue opposite, whose plinth declared: la Grisette 1830. They must have known one another; the innocent thing had applauded him and admired him still. As he approached, Pervenche noticed that Frédérick was pretending to look elsewhere but in fact his eyes were riveted on la Grisette: he was ogling her like mad. That changed everything. She was the provocative one, the actor didn't dare. For decades he had languished, covering his desire. An artist in love who had become the past master of the sideways glance. With the tunnel and his hapless colleague, the evil omens started to rattle Pervenche. Fortunately, his Walkman quickly brought him back to the reality of imminent bliss.

Ella was the picture of unhappiness. She came up to him without skipping, greeted him without laughing. To cheer her up he made a joke:

'You look awful today.'

'Do you m-mean it?'

'Of course I do.'

She did not answer but turned her head away. Her silence worried him; he leaned forwards to see large tears forming at the tips of her eyelashes. She never cried; he had seen her pick herself up after painful tumbles, pull a face, then rub her knees and elbows without shedding a tear. And now with his bloody silly remarks he was making both of them unhappy. He sat her on his knee and talked of the voyage. The sight of the sudden smile despite the tear trickling down her cheek made him wax lyrical. He had repainted the boat white, with blue clouds. What colours did she want the sails? Pink and green? Okay, at least they'd be visible for miles. He played her his tape and was moved by the grave expression that came over her face as she listened to *The Blue Raincoat*. She put her hands to her head to press the earphones tighter. When it was over, she handed the Walkman back, her head full of vivid music.

'It's nice,' she said, 'but it's sad as well.'

He would never grow used to this blend of mysteriousness and transparency or to these lightning adult flashes. No one else could understand Paul, see into him and disarm him as she did. Unless he was making it up? Was he crediting her with feelings and powers she did not possess? He observed her covertly to try and surprise the truth. The truth was she was hungry. They took advantage of a new game of football to escape the brother's surveillance and scurry to the pâtisserie, where they bought cakes which they ate on their bench with the satisfaction of unpunished rascals. She was laughing less and day-dreaming more than other days; several times she was lost in the clouds. Then Paul tweaked her nose, she jumped, a flicker of humour made her eyes sparkle and they resumed their discussion. When she left him, Paul on impulse clasped her to him with all his might.

The atmosphere in the *çay salonu* warmed his heart. He felt that his friends were lavishing on him the same attention as the night of the attack. Yet he was in no danger, everything was fine. He was among the last to leave and returned the next day for the whole afternoon. The bar was awash with sea and sun, the holidays were approaching, plans were taking shape. Pervenche was elated. The holidays were approaching for him too. They started the following day in the Rue Jouffroy; there would be sea and sun. The music demolished the objections he no longer raised anyway; he had turned it up full blast, it went right through him. Once home, he left the lights off and mingled with the shadows gliding across his walls; he began to dance, to sing with them, with the voice, with the girl. He was chilly, he was rocking himself in his arms, he was rocking her in his arms, he started to cry, he had never felt so happy yet so unhappy, he had never danced and sung so feverishly, he was shivering and shouting, 'Tomorrow, tomorrow.' Someone was knocking at the door. To his surprise it was the young Martin girl. If he didn't mind her saying so, he was preventing the household from sleeping and her father had been banging on the ceiling for the last half-hour. She had volunteered to beg him for mercy on her father's behalf. She stared at him, torn between mockery and consternation. Paul packed up and went to bed. The countdown was running.

## — 16 —

The apartment building was struggling to wake up. From the faint sounds and odours reaching through the doors Paul could imagine the breakfasts being gulped down with no appetite, the rush to get ready, the desultory attention paid to the day's news. It was seven o'clock. Pervenche had not thought it necessary to arrive earlier. He had decided against entering the café opposite, which was ideally placed for keeping watch on the entrance to the building. The exit, actually. He was unconcerned: he'd recognize her at first glance. But in the end he thought it best, on this day of celebration, to be meticulous. So he had stationed himself on the sixth-floor landing, off which there were four apartments. A stone would prevent the stairwell door from closing completely behind him at each alert, and through the crack he could scrutinize whoever was calling the lift. It was unlikely that on a Monday morning there would be any takers for the stairs.

It worked like a charm. As soon as the tumble of a lock announced a visitor, he retreated to his hiding-place and put his eye to the crack. It reminded him of his friend Anne-Sophie. The minutes passed. There wasn't much to get his teeth into: a schoolboy with his hair plastered down, a Japanese with a briefcase who used the privacy of the corridor to do a few stretching exercises, a mother taking her little girl to the crèche, she must be late, she was impatiently prodding the button for the lethargic lift. Once the coast was clear, Paul slipped into the corridor to get a better feel for the sounds. The Fleuriaults' door creaked.

Paul just had time to hide; his heart was racing. He heard the hum of the ascending lift. He peeked. A man, fiftyish, was lighting a cigarette. Her father. Pleasant-looking, admittedly, but he marked him down for not oiling his hinges. He consulted his watch and tried to suppress his rising anxiety. What if she didn't go to work? What if she wasn't there? Eight twenty: he gave himself another twenty minutes before phoning. He needed only ten. The door gave the same creak, light footfalls glided across the corridor carpet and he saw her.

She was standing in profile: black hair cut fairly short, jeans and a white blouse accentuating the slenderness of her figure. Despite commendable efforts and eye-strain, Paul was unable to assess her face. It didn't matter, the first impression was a good one, no surprises, she was living up to expectations. These encouraging thoughts spurred him in his breakneck dash down the six flights in pursuit of Marie-Ciel. He came running out of the building, braked on the pavement, sighted her to the left and gave chase. They walked a while. She was airy, her heels clicking cheerfully in the morning, her bag swinging in time with her hips. He was fired with the desire to overtake her, turn round and finally face her; but told himself that there was no point in rushing things, that Eurydice had found such haste nail-biting. She walked into a métro station – Brochant, the most beautiful station in the city, on the Châtillon-Montrouge line, the most beautiful line in the world. On the platform he contented himself with the profile still. In the carriage the gates of paradise were at last opened to him. She had sat beside a newspaper obscuring a bespectacled reader, opposite a nodding old man. Pervenche wormed in to snatch the vacant seat from a mother-to-be. He did not hear the recriminations, he did not see the incensed looks of the pregnant female or the disapproving glances of those beside him who were far too outraged to think of giving up their own seats. He had ears only for the music on his Walkman, eyes only for Marie-Ciel.

For a fraction of a second Paul felt a pang of disappointment, but so short-lived that he paid no heed; he was already fascinated by the heady charm of the marriage of blue and black. Her eyes weren't really blue, more green, violet even; mostly celadon with a hint of violaceous, like the balmiest days. Against the dark background of her hair the limpid eyes were full of sorrow. Paul was struck by this melancholy; he wanted to see in it hope rather than suffering. Her boyfriend had been dead for three months, the memories were palling; slowly she was beginning to dream again. So many contradictions between her dynamic, jaunty manner in the street just now and this blank face.

The counter-tenor was confirming for Pervenche the strangeness of his world, which was Marie-Ciel's too. He almost started to sing and shout that he would help her forget, that this was a new beginning.

They left the métro at Montparnasse. The ballerina resumed her movements to the beat of the songs that were intoxicating Paul. She turned into a courtyard, took one of the staircases and disappeared. Paul noted the firm's name. His head was spinning slightly from the music, which he had just turned off, and from Marie-Ciel. He would have liked to step back and assess the situation. No way. Boy had finally met girl, he would get to know her, they would fall in love. The idiotic clichés made his day. He was nearing his goal, but it had been a long haul since Armand's death. He no longer knew what he had been chasing after since then: a photo, a girl? He had killed for it, abandoned Claire, François, a part of himself. The success of his photo and Marie-Ciel's charms justified every one of his actions. Yet a shadow hung over the photo, the shadow of a work unfinished. He had failed to make the most of the necessary prostrate shape in the foreground, miscalculated the tonal range of the greys and blacks. Perhaps the film was to blame? Yes, he should have opted for something slower, a twenty-two or even a twenty-one DIN. Slower film, longer exposure: that would have enhanced the slight blur effect, would have been more suggestive of the imperceptible golden rain. The compliments on the photo without the corpse did not disguise the feeling that something was missing. A shadow hung over the girl too. Paul could recollect now his fleeting disappointment as he sat down facing her. Why, when immediately afterwards he had decided she matched his expectations?

He entered a bar, ordered a coffee and looked up the phone number of the firm where Marie-Ciel worked. He asked for Mademoiselle Fleuriault and was asked to hold. He hung up. His last remaining doubts vanished; there was no mistaken identity.

He kicked his heels outside the courtyard from eleven-thirty until one, in vain. He spent the afternoon at the cinema and resumed sentry duty at four thirty. She appeared an hour later. In the métro she noticed the man with the Walkman sitting next to her. Her gaze flitted over him: hadn't she seen him somewhere before? Paul quivered at the contact of her eyes and of her arm against his. Sitting so close, could she hear what he was listening to? He lifted one of the earphones a fraction: the counter-tenor escaped, pirouetted and was lost in the slam of the closing doors and the gallop of the wheels along the rails.

The following day Paul sat at a table outside the café in the Rue Jouffroy. Marie-Ciel had changed neither her dress nor her gait. The excitement of discovery gave way to a more critical scrutiny. She was slim, fairly tall, her walk hinted at a great energy. Her hands, resting on her bag, met with Pervenche's approval: less witchlike than those of Frigo's mistress – on her visits to the anglophile she had so often caused a stir among the loss adjusters and prevented them from finishing a delicately-worded letter – perhaps because they were unvarnished, but displaying intelligent lasciviousness. And he was weighing his words. From Miromesnil to Montparnasse his eyes stayed fixed on the miraculous meeting of her jaw and her neck, below the ear, where the shadows and curves lift a corner of the veil over a woman's mystery. He was burning to place his lips there and whisper: it's me.

She did not hide her surprise that evening when he sat opposite her: she raised her eyebrows a flicker and a crease appeared on her forehead, as fleeting as Paul's disappointment the previous day. Then she took shelter again behind her melancholy. Pervenche wavered: today, tomorrow? There was no shortage of arguments for acting immediately. He hadn't lost his nerve, had he? How could be bump off the boyfriend yet not dare speak to her. Still, he postponed the decisive words until the next station. His confidence was boosted by the window against which he was being squashed by the nobody next to him: the artist was obviously in love, and the lover obviously an artist. The same glance took in the reflection of Marie-Ciel. With a reflex sweep of the hand, she flicked her hair to uncover an ear and the pure and oh so arousing line of the neck. Pervenche hastily turned from the window for a direct view. Their eyes met and Paul took the plunge. He removed his earphones.

'Have you noticed I've been following you since yesterday? Don't be alarmed, I just thought that in this day and age a bodyguard can come in useful.'

This was not the gambit he'd rehearsed, he'd played it by ear. She smiled anyway, but remained silent, which he took for a sign of encouragement. Encouraged, he kept talking, talking all kinds of nonsense, spurred on by his attentive and occasionally amused listener. He who in the past had accorded scarcely any importance to a look or smile from a girl was now intoxicating himself with her eyes and her mouth. She certainly had an uncanny charm, shot with sparks of vulgarity which one could not swear to having seen but which made her more accessible, more vulnerable.

Finally, she answered one of Paul's questions. He listened yet heard nothing; while she spoke he recited with her '*Oh this reveals my delight, As it perchance reveals me . . .*' He woke up with a start, asked her to repeat what she'd said and recognized the voice. In fact, it did not quite match the voice on the cassette; it seemed more silken, more sensual. In the end, it was the same voice, but even better. And that was that. He played out his bodyguard act, escorting her home. Was her name Jane, by any chance? No? Ah, Marie-Ciel. Well, too bad; anyhow, Marie-Ciel was a nice name too. Her laughter rang out in the street and in Pervenche's heart.

\*

They fell into a routine. When she came out of her apartment or office, he would catch her up and report for duty. They talked of everything except themselves, laughed at the slightest excuse. Since the pattern never varied, Paul was able to fill in the time. He hung about at the *çay salonu* where a few Turks without jobs played cards with others, newly-arrived and without papers. He went to the gallery to collect his photos; the exhibition was over. Madame Ribaud heaped compliments upon him yet again. She would call him in September about a second exhibition. She had really liked the photo of the fog. Now what was it that Armand had said about it? She had forgotten. Oh yes, that something was missing. It was true; that was her feeling too.

'I'm going to take it again. This time there'll be nothing missing.'

Paul surprised himself by speaking without thinking. It was hard to imagine how he could take it again. Another killing? Try using a fake corpse? The conviction and motivation weren't there. He'd talk it over with Marie-Ciel, he'd show her his photo. She would decide.

On Friday evening, outside her door, he explained that his holidays were coming to an end and that spending the holidays as a bodyguard had been great. He urged caution and ventured to be of service at eventide. By starting work earlier, he could leave at five thirty and catch her at Montparnasse. His pomposity made her giggle. She was delighted to accept. He held out his hand and the touch of her fingers was solace for the inanity of his words. He took with him a hint of her perfume, walked slowly so that it did not waft away. Back in his room, the songs and the photo were electrified by the intrusion of her fragrance. Paul sniffed at his right shoulder, from which it rose. Her fingers in his hand, her shoulder against his, her body in his arms: believing in miracles, Paul fell into a blissful sleep.

She was sitting on a bench facing the bandstand, watching her friends at play. Paul saw her shake her head when asked to join in. She came to him without a word. There was nothing the matter, she answered Paul's concern about her listlessness. This time he did not succeed in making her laugh. She even declined to sneak off to the pâtisserie. Without warning she stretched out on the bench and rested her head on Paul's knees: she was tired, she wanted to sleep.

Feeling moved, awkward, Paul placed his hand on her forehead; she didn't have a temperature. He stroked her face, delved into her hair which ran through his fingers like black sand. The rings under her eyes were the colour of an elaborate make-up. Some sparrows were hatching a plot under the next bench. But his sparrow did not move. With her ankles demurely crossed and her hands thrust into her dungaree pockets, she was fast asleep. Paul held his breath for fear of waking her; his hand continued singing a silent lullaby. He was overwhelmed by the child's confidence, it was the first time someone had trusted in him body and soul. It went on for a long time. And then she stirred, opened her misted, startled eyes and smiled at Pervenche. The clouds had disappeared. At that instant he was struck by her likeness to Marie-Ciel. The black hair, the blue eyes – although they were very different blues, light in Ella's case, unnatural in Marie-Ciel's – were enough to establish far-reaching similarities between them. He prepared to talk to her about her boyfriend so that she would question him on his girlfriend. Today he was as eager to raise the topic as he had been anxious, the first time, to avoid it. He wanted to describe Marie-Ciel, confide to her that they looked very much alike. He derived an ambiguous pleasure from this fusion of his feelings for the little girl and the young woman.

But she chimed in first:
'It's nice today . . .'
'So?'
'So c-can we set off?'
'The sails are almost painted. We can go in two weeks. Have you packed?'
'No . . .' she confessed guiltily. 'Tell me a story.'
'A story? But I don't know any stories.'

'Yes you do. But not the one about the t-tunnel.'

How could he refuse a plea from Ella? Paul embarked on a tale whose ending he had forgotten.

'The man had come from far away, you could see it from the sadness in his eyes. Yet there was no dust on his shoes, only faded flowers on his tunic. He spoke and the child listened. These figs had been abandoned and I gathered them up. Take them. He asked for a place to sleep and was offered the dunes stalked by Time. The child showed him the way. The wind streamed his hair and swept into the waves the words he called from the crest of the dune to his parents huddled together at their garden gate. His father took a few paces and picked up a flower fallen from the tunic. He had never seen anything like it. When he raised it to his lips . . .'

Ella had fallen asleep again. Paul fell silent. He ran the tip of his index finger over the curves of her upper lip, around her chin and slowly along the line of the jaw, near her ear: yes, it was as tantalizing as with Marie-Ciel. He would have liked to take her in his arms, take her home with him. It was her brother who took her home with him, after yanking her arm mercilessly. Paul refrained from the well-deserved slap. She walked off, only half-awake. Just as she was about to cross the street, Paul ran up to her, claiming she hadn't said goodbye. He lifted her up, squeezed her tight and kissed her as if he would never see her again. That was the premonition he had had as he watched her depart, frail and sulky; it tormented him late into the night until he finally put it out of his mind thanks to the counter-tenor, *The Blue Raincoat*, warm fingers in his and the bouquet of perfume.

Back at the office Paul discovered what boredom was. In all the time he had been dealing with claims, he had never thought twice about how interesting his work was. He just did it, more conscientiously than not. It enabled him to earn a living, occupy his mind and wait it out until the following weekend. Things had changed with Armand's death. The weekends had lost some of their sparkle and

Paul had withdrawn into his claims. There he forgot the emptiness around him, filling it by giving inordinate attention to the trivia with which he had studded his existence. Next there had been the photo, its execution, the crime and then the cassette. Now he was no longer seeking; he had found. There was no vacuum in his life, Armand's memory was no longer painful. The blond hair – back then, back home – seemed far away, belonging to another life. The work which once had helped him bury himself was now preventing him from spreading his wings.

He could not understand how he had been able to tolerate for all these years the hell of these hostile stacks of claims, the absurdity of these vacuous letters – 'you will be aware that', 'we shall be contacting you in due course', formulae which meant nothing but entitled a file to change stacks. Yes, we're trying to locate your file, bear with me a moment, I'll put you on hold, dickhead, you can listen to Vivaldi while I finish my nails, are you still there? I'm afraid your file's been mislaid, yes if you could call back, in a fortnight, say. And hey presto, another file moves to the right-hand stack. Not to mention the scholarly showing-off when he felt on form – pettifogging over this or that article of the Civil Code, without a second thought for the Cameroonian about to receive a letter duly informing him that the purported claimant had affirmed a reciprocally binding contract giving valid consideration. Or the paralysis which sometimes seized him, his despair at all the claims, the downcast faces around him. The letter crossed out, screwed up, tossed at the waste-paper basket, missed, so go and pick it up and try again; got it! Now left-handed. All these solitary, shifty games, forever misleading, the professional quizzical look, a file open, the phone off the hook but no caller. The desperately boring training seminars with the optimistic animateur moving the discussion on, 'Now tell me...', when his rabbiting had already lured the imagination towards warmer climes.

The days weighed him down; so did the files. Having been reprimanded by Roupette no doubt, Frigo rebuked Pervenche for being behind, that is, for having such a big stack on the left. He entrusted three files in one go to Chantal-the-filer, admiring yet again the solemnity she brought to her job; he switched from left to right a whole load of cases whose victims could wait. He was then free to devote himself to Marie-Ciel, his nose poised on his pen. He no longer asked any questions about her beauty or charm: she was the one, and that was more than enough. That Monday he had invited her for a drink; she had impressed him by ordering a cocktail, which forced him to rethink quickly and swap the coffee he had in mind for a pastis which François would have loved. She confessed to enjoying an aperitif after work, why not? He had invited her for a meal on Friday: not on, she was going away for the weekend with her parents. Thursday then? Okay, oh no, I can't, I've promised to go to a concert by a friend. But everything had sorted itself out: they would go to the concert together, and afterwards for a meal.

> *Will you then confess your plight,*
> *The day you know my ennui?*

Her voice was his constant companion – hers and the one on the cassette. Paul took his Walkman to the office and paid frequent visits to the gents where, wedged comfortably on the seat in the dark, he honoured his trysts. Frigo's intrigued looks did not perturb him. His conscience was clear: the left-hand stack was shrinking fast.

Falling out with Le Nabec had not only put an end to the Breton's five o'clock performance, much to Frigo's relief. It also deprived him of the sole unspoilt treat open to an idler at this place of work: the joy of meeting a fellow idler, that ineffable communion which unites two beings in the same inertia. How receptive one becomes to one's neighbour's woes. What a serious, even lofty tone the discussion takes on. All those expressions of healthy concern.

Paul could see the bowed head across the desk. No chance of a reconciliation, not that he cared anyway, all things considered: he wanted for nothing. Thus freed from – almost – all work and all chit-chat, he could daydream and observe. Over the past weeks the staff at Magistrale had grown appreciably in ugliness. Paul had never before paid attention to it, but now it hit him. They were probably not aware of it either; they contemplated themselves in mirrors that aged even faster than they did. Beautified by love, Pervenche took delight in counting the balding pates, the bulging paunches, the double chins and the leaden eyes around him – symptoms of an affliction he knew he would escape.

On Wednesday afternoon Pervenche had returned from the toilets and was leafing through a file, his head full of music, when Frigo called on him. He had something important to tell him, he whispered: Pervenche's presence was requested on Friday at four in Jourdan's office. Frigo was quaking less at the name of the big boss than at the day and time: Friday afternoon was the ideal moment for averting scenes by sacked employees with nothing to lose who might create havoc in the office. Pervenche greeted the news with detachment. The following evening he was going out with Marie-Ciel, his exhibition had been a success. As for anything else . . .

# — 17 —

Late, but with rose in hand, Paul entered the Montparnasse café they had made their headquarters. She was quick to dispel the hint of sorrow in her eyes. Paul watched fondly for her switching between moods he could only suspect, shades of mauve. They had known each other for ten days, had talked little of themselves yet were unsurprised by their collusion: same tastes, same games. They guessed and out-guessed each other. She was becoming a little less the girl on the cassette and much more Marie-Ciel. But for him she remained the fiancée or girlfriend of a silhouette sprawled across a flawed photograph. As he chatted with her, as she held the rose to her lips, Pervenche's crime insinuated itself into his world like a print emerging from a negative; insinuating itself into a palpable reality. Paul was holding the hand of a woman whose lover he had murdered. Until then the dead man had hardly stepped out of the photo, so preserving a certain abstraction and improbability. That was over. The mysterious tie which linked him to Marie-Ciel would some day have to transform itself into a terrible secret which would unite them forever. Some day he would tell her everything. Would she realize before then?

He looked at her through his mug of beer. The dimpled glass and the amber liquid distorted everything around him. He would have liked to go through life with a glass of beer in front of his eyes. There was no need. Marie-Ciel served just as well. Seen through her, the world sparkled: an extravaganza. Sparing no expense, he ordered two more drinks. She insisted on paying for her own, she knew the form. They left for the concert aglow with an intoxication made headier by their complicity.

Paul had not set foot in a church since Armand's death. The American church, although it also served as a place of worship, was less than mystical. On the right were four windows, their arches straining to appear Gothic, their painted panes longing to pass for stained glass. Their green and their violet – pardon me, Pervenche upbraided himself, their celadon and their violaceous – matched perfectly the prevailing mood and clashed atrociously with the yellow radiators below, which in winter enabled the pious to inject some sincerity into their prayers. Much wainscoting, a huge mirror for the benefit – judging by the barre fitted to it – of young girls eager to admire the image of a ballerina. Paul managed to sit with his back to the interloper: for the evening he had agreed a truce with his reflection. At the far end, the stage and the curtains of a theatre. Acting in a church, or praying in a theatre – the Americans had failed to resolve the dilemma.

A redhead, Marie-Ciel's friend and by no means unbecoming for a flautist, was having an altercation with a period harpsichord, witnessed by Gluck, Mozart and Bach. The alcohol still coursing in Pervenche's bloodstream brought shameless thoughts to mind. The fingers of the instrumentalist displayed a dexterity guaranteed to make Frigo dump even his girlfriend. After glancing to make sure that Marie-Ciel was not watching, Paul approached the artiste and began to remove her clothing, which was superfluous in this context of music, mirrors and voyeurs. He encountered difficulties in accomplishing his task: the performer could not be disturbed. Too bad. He finished the job with scissors, very slowly, in time with the Bach sonata. He stopped to savour the joy of the instruments. They were frolicking like two children, without jealousy, each taking their turn, their fair share. They chased and caught each other, rolled entwined down a grassy bank, got up laughing, stood and inhaled the breeze, watched a flock of flying birds. They raced away again, the flute playful but a little better behaved, the harpsichord mischievous and lively, always ready for a tiff, but good-naturedly taking no offence at the flute's appeals to behave. Each appreciated the other's qualities, without an eye to faults. In any case, there are no such things as faults at that age. At the bottom end of a field – a stream with stones cleaving the ripples, trout, water-spiders, dragonflies, beaches for lilliputians, tiny waterfalls and a blonde head resting on his shoulder. Marie-Ciel gave Paul a nudge.

'Do you like it?'

'Yes, yes,' stammered the culprit sheepishly, caught scissors in hand.

After each piece the musicians disappeared through a small door, concealed behind the harpsichord. Fulsome applause accompanied their departure, and equally their return, which must have been reassuring. They had acquired a taste for it and – Paul had his suspicions – would interrupt a piece to go off-stage, be applauded, kiss behind the door, come back on and be applauded again. Marie-Ciel clapped louder than those around her in an attempt to attract the flautist's eye. Paul had been disappointed not to detect in her face the sorrow which a particularly moving passage of Mozart should have painted there. He had watched her on the sly; throughout she had worn a sociable, forced smile that she had chosen for the concert. The setting did not lend itself to the efflorescence of the soul. Musicians should be uncompromising; they should build watch-towers from which marksmen would blow out the brains of anyone who had not fallen into the mandatory day-dream.

The congratulatory ceremony abounded with superlatives. Paul relished the light thrill as he shook the redhead's hand. A reception pepped up concert-goers who were, they had to confess, fatigued from clapping so much. Paul and Marie-Ciel slipped away and set up residence by candle-light in some corner of a restaurant. Paul forced himself to step back in order to savour more fully this first real evening out in his life. The dressing-down in store for the next day was the last thing on his mind. What would be would be. There were more important things now, like Marie-Ciel's knee against his and the smile she was giving him – a Florentine smile, no less.

They had an intimate dinner. The candle-flame flickered in their wine, its shadow played across the cheek and neck of the young woman. Around them it was business as usual, with waiters dressed for a flute and harpsichord concert following perfect trajectories. Pervenche lingered over their bustling to-ings and fro-ings. With years of practice and a crystal-clear highway code, the free-flowing traffic was the pride and joy of the maître d'hôtel, a retrained gendarme. There was no grinding of gears, they accelerated smoothly out of the bends, a muted toot of the horn requested, from the kitchens, 'One special, one rabbit for number eleven.' Having eaten, Paul and Marie-Ciel got up to leave. On his way out Paul stopped beside a table occupied by an elderly couple. He said, 'Excuse me,' took the gentleman's glass of white wine, drank a mouthful, gurgling like a connoisseur, pronounced, 'Yes, it's good,' finished the glass, put it back, courteously took his leave and rejoined Marie-Ciel. Between two fits of the giggles she described to him first the shock and then the horror on the old fogies' faces. Pervenche admitted that as a precaution he had picked on someone scrawny.

Before leaving her he dreamed up an excuse to make her listen to *The Blue Raincoat* on the Walkman, which went with him everywhere. The air was sweet, the place was right. He strained to listen in order to reclaim his property before the next extract, the counter-tenor; he wanted to instil his poisoned secret one drop at a time. Marie-Ciel's expression stiffened, she handed back the Walkman. Her eyes were full of tears; the lights from a café imbued them with a furtive glimmer.

'I know it. I love it.'

Pervenche almost replied that he knew. They had reached their destination. He leaned towards her, placing his hand beneath her ear, on the curves and the shadows; he kissed her. Her mouth tasted of mint and cherries. She ran from sight without turning round.

Pervenche did not feel like singing or shouting. If he had been at home, he would perhaps have danced, solemnly, silently, because this was a love to be lived in solemnity. He realized it was becoming too important to nurture only levity.

In order not to lose her but to preserve the imprint of her kiss on his lips, he returned home on foot, treating himself to the boulevards: Courcelles, Batignolles, Clichy, Rochechouart. At Pigalle he was solicited by some prostitutes. He could no longer remember the Rue Saint-Denis or Claire's warmth and perfume which he squandered there. He asked the going rate of the ugliest just to cheer her up. The night bestowed its illusory consolations on those whose prayers no longer knew who to offer themselves to. The half-wrenched-off door of a phone box swung in the wind. The manholes showed him, at distant intervals, their glinting round covers pierced by a hole in the iron, like an eye riveted on Paul. He quickened his pace, crushing underfoot – sometimes at the cost of a sidestep that startled a few late-night walkers – the gaze of these vigilant Cyclops.

Pervenche painfully flushed the toilet. The interlude was nearing its end. Three forty-five: he could still enjoy the peace of his hiding-place for a while, listen to his songs, think of Marie-Ciel. He had relived the previous evening in detail. Not a single false note from beginning to end. From the rose to the kiss, from the flautist to the old man deprived of his wine, the emotion and the awareness of winning a decisive battle had plunged her suitor into a state of beatitude from which even the prospect of the little chat with Jourdan had not distracted him.

No one at the office had even mentioned it. Frigo had advised Paul to enlist union backing, but he had refused. He pulled the chain again, it was cleaner that way; the sound of the flush was refreshing.

The secretary asked him to wait a few minutes. Monsieur Jourdan was busy. Paul did not dare take the Walkman out of his pocket: no point in being provocative. He waited. Eventually he was summoned. The vast, austere office was not to Pervenche's liking; he would have preferred something more imaginative. Jourdan seemed on form. Along with poring over the files of overawed trainees, the Friday afternoon appointments constituted what he termed his last contact with the shop-floor. For the occasion he sported a mouse-grey suit – and a neurasthenic mouse at that. He was peering over the top of spectacles perched on the tip of his nose. His hairdresser had carved out around his ears a perfect crescent, as clean as a whistle: it looked like a deserted beach in the middle of which was embedded a nicely polished sea-shell.

He began by informing him that Monsieur Jaubert, the head of personnel, could not attend but had delegated to him all his authority. Without asking Pervenche to be seated, he placed his elbows on his desk, erected at chin level a sort of nave with his fingers, frowned and fell silent, to lend great weight to his words. Paul was admiring. He had already seen that intense forethought, or pretence thereof, imparted to the inanities which followed a semblance of judiciousness. By the time one reacted, the speaker had waffled on to a new topic.

Jourdan had opened hostilities: Pervenche's backlog of work, his general attitude over recent weeks, it couldn't go on. He spoke well, articulating clearly, displaying his lower incisors in the manner of all those who like to talk and hear themselves doing so. A small green fleck – a piece of parsley? – lodged between the very white teeth undermined his credibility. Paul forgave him and told himself to pay attention. He articulated well and expressed himself felicitously. And so Jourdan talked, deploring the backsliding of a loss adjuster of whom he had come to expect better. What he wanted was fighters. The telephone allowed him to add gestures to his words. He grabbed the handset, stood in a boxer's stance, right fist poised to strike, guarding with the left, dancing from one foot to the other: Yes? What? No! I said no! He sat. What was I saying? That's right, I want fighters.

Paul was thinking that matters weren't looking too bad after all, when there was a worrying silence.

'That was the first point. There's worse to come, alas. Much worse. About twenty files have been found hidden in a cupboard in an unused machine-room. Most of them are yours, the rest Le Nabec's. Well?'

Pervenche had foreseen that one day the cache would be

discovered and had sketched out a defence. Even so, he improvised, gutlessly putting the blame on personal problems. He'd taken some hard knocks and, yes, there'd been times when he'd thrown in the towel and got rid of files he couldn't sort out. But if something urgent or serious cropped up, he could always retrieve them straight away. He did not mention Chantal's role and, while he was at it, he asserted that Le Nabec was blameless, that he, Pervenche, had hidden the files in Le Nabec's absence.

Jourdan had resumed his meditative pose. Pervenche awaited the verdict, but with curiosity rather than trepidation. The sack, a warning: he couldn't care less. On Monday he had a date with Marie-Ciel; he was longing to taste her lips once again. More mint or more cherry? The divisional manager was now speaking. Paul heard him invoke the higher interests of Magistrale. He missed the rest, he had just noticed the ring Jourdan wore on his little finger. This distressed him: he had been told that a ring on the little finger indicates sexual problems. Yet Jourdan had everything going for him. He was filled with sympathy, he would have liked to talk it over with him, help him get over his difficulties. Another silence, for Pervenche another alarm, but short-lived. Jourdan was preparing to sneeze and did so, with class: handkerchief, head half-turned, no anxious glance into the handkerchief, a mumbled apology, perfect. However, he did not take up his monologue. He waited a few seconds. Nothing rash, he knew himself, indeed that was one of the keys to his success; he knew that he had two sneezes still to execute. He closed his eyes, abandoning Pervenche to his fate, focused on the build-up to a climax no worse than many others and, thanks to this meritorious concentration, took his pleasure twice over: as calculated. 'Yes, as I was saying, I don't want any black sheep in my division.' Paul recalled that Roupette had referred to him as a wolf in the fold. He had moved on, it was a good sign.

'. . . one week.'

'Sorry?' What with wolves in folds, Pervenche had missed the punch-line.

'Suspended for one week. Your candour has saved you, this time. But, Pervenche, don't tempt fate again.'

'Thank you, sir.'

Pervenche crossed the secretary's office without seeing Le Nabec, who had also been summoned and was biting his nails. He went home rather disappointed. The sanction lacked weight. He would have preferred either acquittal or dismissal – a touch of showmanship. Don't be a jerk: he admitted to himself that he'd got off lightly. What was more, he'd be able to take up bodyguard duty for another week. He donned his Walkman and, humming, bit into mint and cherries.

No Ella in sight from the top of the footbridge. Nothing unusual in that; he had never spotted her from so far off. Nonetheless, his stomach was in knots as he hastened to the square. He hadn't seen her at the school entrance all week. His premonitions from the previous Saturday came back to him. Her gang was already racing about. But no Ella. Her brother wasn't there either; Paul regained hope and strolled around the square. It contained children and old people: old people ambling slowly, unhurriedly towards death, children rushing towards it heedlessly. A man was walking along the far pavement with a small boy, stopping every ten yards, squatting in front of his son, talking to him, clasping the boy's head in his hands; unhappiness was written all over his face. On a nearby bench two lovers were consoling one another for all the sufferings of the world. The girl was running a feverish hand through the hair of her man, who was much more restrained. Paul sauntered past to make sure that she wasn't very pretty and that her passion was fired by a feeling of inferiority. Sportingly, he recognized that on Thursday evening he had been the one overacting. On your best behaviour, Pervenche, watch out on Monday!

He deigned to take a seat on his bench. Ella's bench, despite the presence of an old man with a waxen complexion. The minutes accumulated pointlessly. He rose to interrupt the little girls' game.

'Ella? She's not well.'

Voices chimed in from all sides, vying to get in the first,

and longest word. She had been in bed since Monday, no one knew what was wrong with her nor when she would be better. Paul would have liked it to rain; he found it hard to bear the mocking lightness of the air, the uneasy bitterness that swept over him with the news. He could feel Ella's intense gaze on him. He was sure she had guessed the photo's secret. Last Saturday she had interrupted him just as he was going to tell her about Marie-Ciel. She had guessed that too. She knew that Claire had never been more than a shadow; she knew that she would become Marie-Ciel's shadow. So she was stepping aside, there was no room for them both in Pervenche's heart. Paul felt like shouting she was wrong, he needed her. But who to? To the old man who gave him a welcoming grimace as he shifted along to make room? Paul sat. He'd visit her on Sunday if she wasn't back. The idea calmed him. He sneaked a look over the shoulder of the man next to him, who seemed electrified by his reading, craning his neck: 'Why not eternity?' Why not, indeed? Paul cleared his throat to disguise an unsuppressible snigger. The old man was right, you had to believe in it to the very end and not let mere contradictions stand in your way. Philosophy, even in small doses, can improve your life. The episode bucked Paul up. Ella would soon be better. He headed for the *çay salonu*; he had some details to sort out for the trip this summer. Above all, would it be okay if he took a girlfriend?

Instead of making the most of Sunday and relishing each minute to appreciate more fully the slow, irresistible approach of Monday and its treasures, Paul frittered away his day, like one of those songs whose verses go unheard because one is obsessed by the refrain. He wandered, called on the Turks, played cards, lost but in good heart, listened to his music, returned to the *çay salonu*, then followed a demonstration which was blocking his way. It occurred to him that some people did actually celebrate May Day. He celebrated it too. There was an aura of good humour over the long column: stewards clutching microphones, wearing forced smiles in deadpan faces, launched into easily remembered songs; the rank and file swigged bottles of beer, red-nosed and unbothered by the froth clinging to their chins. Police feigning nonchalance – desist, their commanding officers had drummed into them, from anything resembling irony or provocation; drivers adopting a sympathetic air to avoid damage to their property while muttering 'bloody demonstrators'; passers-by with condescending yet wary faces; leaflets bearing the prose of little-known writers, read and discarded on the spot; the cacophony of loudspeakers; the jealousy of spectators' children on seeing other children perched on marchers' shoulders, waving colourful flags and wearing swish caps. The enormous flagship was crying victory. There soon remained no more than its wake strewn with empty bottles, tracts, pieces of bread, placards, shouts of hatred and fraternity chanted, sung and borne away by the evening. Paul was rapidly bored.

He finished his Sunday in front of the television and was even more bored. But this was a boredom to be savoured for its hint, already, of sweet anticipation and for its leisurely passing which was now nudged forwards with growing insistence by impatience and its attendant snares.

— 18 —

The bodyguard hummed to himself. A short suspension never hurt anyone, especially in May. He spurned the creepers hanging from his tree and left instead via the stairs, swapping the Gautiers' mat with their neighbours' and in the street making an obscene gesture to anyone who felt it was for them. Another celadon-pink day: this was his new compulsory colour, his private vintage. In the métro he familiarized himself, over a shoulder, with the events shaking the world. The paper concealed the meagreness of its news behind the disproportion of its headlines. Still no mention of the murder in the Rue Monte-à-regret in the news-in-brief section. What on earth could have become of the guy?

Paul killed time until his spell of duty opposite Marie-Ciel's. He sat outside the café. The steam from his coffee spiralled in the sunlight; the cassette led him by the hand, dissolving walls, streets and sky; he was overcome by a gold- and azure-studded lethargy. Marie-Ciel appeared, dressed in gold and azure, without a second glance for the walls, streets or sky; she lived elsewhere, Paul alone knew where. He stood; she was already crossing the first junction, the lights turning green for her. What should he do? Catch her up and breathlessly explain that he had been suspended for a week for hiding files? That he was a loss adjuster by profession, that he composed stylish letters – I acknowledge receipt of yours of, I shall be contacting you as soon as – sent out handsome cheques, answered the telephone politely – Magistrale. Can I help you? He had come to know and then love her thanks to music, thanks to death. And here he was preparing to demonstrate that a suspension isn't the end of the world? A touch of dignity, fuck it, a touch of class!

This talking-to whipped up his pride. He followed Marie-Ciel at a distance, slipping into the shoes of some middle manager who would pass her, turn around, admire her walk, her dignity, her class, desire her passionately, concede that she was too good for him, and envy the lucky man of her choice. He walked a long way, aimlessly, decided the manhole covers looked more friendly, then suddenly remembered he had a film to see. He had been scouring the cinema programmes for ages before finally being rewarded. *Hôtel du Nord* was showing in the Latin Quarter. Despite his prejudice against a part of town where his straightness was uncomfortably apparent, he settled in his seat with the firm intention of panning the poseur in the gallery who had cast aspersions on his talent.

From the opening dialogue and images he stifled his aggression and abandoned himself to the film's old-fashioned charm, to this union of tragic and comic which Armand had repeatedly told him governed the world and its masterpieces. He laughed a great deal, wiped away a few tears, recognized his neighbourhood but not, to his great joy, his photograph. No footbridge at night, no fog, no mystery, but conventional sentiments, a tight plot, everyday heroes – Gautiers, nobodies, never-have-beens. Carné's work in no way detracted from the originality of his own. Simply, the two of them, like many others, had taken to this part of the city. He had stolen nothing from Carné and Carné nothing from him. They were quits.

The mauve outshone the blue when her eyes smiled; she permitted him to ascertain it at close quarters. Their Montparnasse hideaway had flung open its doors to the spring. She had forgotten to ask if on Thursday the old man's wine had been really that good; she'd had the idea on her mind all weekend, funny things ideas, aren't they? Paul talked about Turkey, his trip there in the summer – it was all poetry.

He held back the coup de grâce – an invitation to the Orient – for another evening. Near her apartment, in collusion with the shivering night, Paul made her listen to the counter-tenor. He was a little afraid: was he going too fast? She was liable to suspect something. Had he prepared her sufficiently? He examined her face: her features seemed to have hardened. She removed the Walkman:

'It's strange. What is it?'

'Don't you know?' Paul almost shouted. He felt a vast emptiness inside. 'Don't you know?' The imploring tone of his voice made her think she had upset him.

'I like it though. It's nice but – what should I say? – it's strange. I can't define what I feel.'

'It's Vivaldi, sung by a counter-tenor. A counter-tenor is a bit like the castrato of bygone times, neither male nor female, and . . .' Paul was numbing himself with words; he felt at a total loss. Everything had been so simple until now; each stage in the conquest of Marie-Ciel had seemed a foregone conclusion. Now suddenly nothing was left standing, except himself, lost in a sandstorm. He played her *The Blue Raincoat* solely as a branch to cling to: oh that one, yes she knew it well, she was crazy about it. Marie-Ciel went over the top to prove her goodwill. She was positive she would soon adore the counter-tenor's voice, once she'd got used to it.

At the door to her apartment building it was she who kissed him, lingeringly. The mint had lost its freshness.

On the other evenings of the week Paul avoided all reference to music or his Walkman, into which he now inserted only harmless cassettes. He was shaken by the blow but not floored. Lying to himself – but what's a white lie between friends? – he concluded she'd recorded the piece in a rush one day, without paying attention. And then she had recognized *The Blue Raincoat*, straight off. So why go on with this fruitless dissection, or vivisection? Their conversation clothed itself once more in graceful garb, her hand and mouth melted beneath his. Pervenche was forgetting.

But when he opened the door of his bedsit, his small

clique was waiting: Rimbaud and Petrushka, the cassette and the photo. Opening the window to the night, lying on the floor, he listened over and over, questioning all the songs in turn. Over and over the soft voice murmured: 'As it perchance reveals me.' Who was lying? The girl on the cassette? Marie-Ciel? Or both? He turned up the volume. The sky, torn between blue and mauve, made his head spin; the whole world hung on the thread of an answer. Paul begged for it before the start of each song. The silhouette of a chimney on the roof opposite bristled with two metal stalks, the alert antennae of some monstrous insect, messengers of death. Paul clenched his fists: he would not backslide, trusting to signs and omens that made no sense, he would not sink back into the rock-bottom existence that had led only to dead ends.

He even contrived to disown his reflection: what image would a bakery window show of an artist in love, shaken but not floored? Nothing real? He finally sweet-talked himself into agreeing that there was a doubt, no denying it. So make the best of it, and see later. Not that it diminished Marie-Ciel's charms or the pleasure he derived from being with her.

Yet each morning his good resolutions flagged. On the footbridge a violaceous hue was already making a comeback despite Pervenche's choruses of 'celadon, celadon'. More than anything, the wasteland of the Rue de Marseille was starting to smother his horizon. Paul had glimpsed Ella's brother, alone. That Saturday he gathered his courage and accosted the unsmiling little so-and-so:

'Is Ella still poorly?'
'Yes.'
'What's the matter? Is it serious?'
'Yes.'
'She's not going to hospital, is she?'
'No.'

Paul could have hit him. But he couldn't get a thing out of him. He strolled around the bandstand, spent ten francs on the wheel of fortune, fancying that Ella was holding his hand. He really missed her. What if he went to visit her?

Why not, after all? Hello, I'm a friend of Ella's, how is she getting on? And her smile when she saw us – the sweets and me! Or flowers? Yes, flowers: she loves them and she never sees any. But only the best, no rubbish. Pervenche was overwhelmed with joy. What a fantastic idea. He would see Ella tomorrow! Imagine her face.

He organized himself accordingly, everything in its own time. He waited patiently until the little bastard had finished playing, tailed him home, rang the concierge's bell to ask where two children, Ella and Julien, lived. Now stage two, Austerlitz for the train-times and the ticket. Spare no expense. Ella's face tomorrow! As for this cassette business, it's all a misunderstanding, Marie-Ciel doesn't remember, or else the boyfriend recorded it without her knowing. Ella would talk to him about the tunnel, definitely. Any sweets too? No, just flowers.

The countryside was awakening unhurriedly. Through the window of a train showing scant concern for the surrounding calm, Pervenche watched the last patches of mist skim by. The Beauce took on the air of a sports field. A sort of concrete bridge beside the tracks spanned only fields, telling for mile after mile the tale of an unfulfilled dream. So much the better, Pervenche consoled himself, those are the most beautiful dreams. The thought suddenly struck him: he hadn't taken the train since his last visit to Armand's. He realized, too, how much Armand had remained a part of his life. In fact, Armand had hardly left him. He followed his every deed and move, intervening on occasion through a gallery director, a surprise photo in a magazine, or, like this morning, popping up with no warning from the monotonous unfurling of a plain studded with copses and large farms. Paul's programme suited him, he was along for the ride. Paul shared his secrets with him: the photo, Marie-Ciel, the exhibition, the dip in the flooded meadows which had resulted in only average photos, in a feverish cold, for nothing. He said goodbye before Orléans and donned his Walkman, closing his eyes to concentrate fully on the music, and almost missed La-Ferté-Saint-Aubin. He tumbled off the train and went to pick up the bicycle available from the station for a laughable sum, given the bouquet of flowers he would be bringing back.

It was striking nine when he set off along a small road which could have led straight to Meaulnes' château. He was gripped by a sudden emotion: it was the first time in seven years, since his arrival in Paris, that he had encountered the spring. He had soon realized that in the city there is no spring, no more than there are dawns or stars, which was fine by him. Then the high grass of the ditches had sharply whipped his legs. He was disappearing under a verdant canopy pierced here and there by the sun, which illuminated the way just as the Holy Ghost, in paintings seen in churches, illuminates God-fearing souls. That morning, way back, the high grass had also whipped their faces through the open car windows. He was driving as close as possible to the verge in order to feel the gentle switching. Her hair streamed in the wind, she had put one arm around his neck, she was laughing, then there had been only silence, shards of glass glinting beside her head, some drops of blood and, far off, birds flying away.

Paul wanted to dismount, sit on a bank and not budge. He hesitated. A little further on at the bottom of a meadow someone had lit a fire of grass or ferns. The graceful rising smoke stood out against the black bulk of the forest. Smoke from such fires, aromatic and joyful, was a particular pleasure of Paul's. He pedalled harder, suddenly bent on embracing this spring day as if it were the first, as if it were the last. He had been deprived of them for too long. Thanks to Ella he had broken the spell, he had transgressed the forbidden frontiers. He experienced elation fanned by vain gusts of sorrow and hope.

He concentrated on watching and listening to everything. He had already been avoiding the trap of the Walkman for some time. Nature was in full cry. Now and then he passed a small, isolated building with walls of brick and a roof of flat tiles. Adventure-starved sheep in a field watched longingly for the wolf. Lilac and wisteria made a welcome change from the unrelieved assault by the colza on the plains he had just crossed. The railway bike was going well; Pervenche put in a short sprint to beat Armand on the line. Two squashed hedgehogs marking the spot confirmed Paul's victory. The winner awarded himself a rest beside a pond. It was the perfect place, with a riot of flowers around it. A small island in the centre of the pond harboured a statue of the Virgin. The white vapour trail of a plane trembled on the surface of the water; the shadow of a crow who hadn't fully understood traced a dubious perpendicular. Paul climbed over a wall, skirted the pond and advanced into the meadow. The grass came up to his knees. He was rediscovering forgotten smells and images. The wind caused a silver rustling of the leaves on the trees. On each daisy, small green beetles with blue legs were rehearsing a declaration of love. Ducks hurried across the pond, nodding their heads like cyclists struggling up a mountain. Paul let himself be overwhelmed by myriad sensations heightened by unexpectedly vivid memories. He recalled the bitter taste of grass chewed with bovine application many years back, the sponginess underfoot of the moss in the undergrowth. He took a dirt-track leading to the forest. The laugh of a jay made him jump. A snail was causing consternation among a posse of beige mushrooms. Nature's good humour was proving contagious. He found himself singing, and leaping for buds that stuck to his hands. If only Ella had been with him. Happily, that was only a matter of time.

A butterfly arrived in welcome: it had come to the wrong place. Paul waited for it to alight before pouncing. Two bungled attempts forced him to take drastic steps. Undoing the pullover tied around his waist, he gripped it by the sleeves and, thus armed, remorselessly waged war on the beast. The battle raged. Pervenche chased his adversary like a madman until, finally exhausted, it made the mistake of recuperating on a thistle. Thinking itself safe, it had already forgotten the hunter and was devoting itself to the flower and the breeze. Paul envied its receptiveness to the present moment, contemplated this minute particle of tranquil existence that he was about to annihilate. It was a swallowtail. Its large yellow wings striped with black closed and opened with delight, while its double tail splashed with blue conferred prestige among its fellow butterflies. Paul wondered if swallowtails liked Elvis, spared a touching thought for Anne-Sophie and brought his pullover violently down. He took great care in picking it up, ready to act if the butterfly made any attempt to escape. It did, but without illusion. Ensnared in an inextricable tangle of broken blades, it was flapping spasmodically. *Love me tender, love me sweet, never let me go.* Paul felt stupid, leaned over the emerald cage, prised the bars apart and released the victim on to his open hands. Its scales deposited on his fingers a kind of golden pollen. The swallowtail righted itself then fell back on its side. It had one tail ripped off and a torn wing. What could it hope for now? A cripple's existence, life at any price? A glorious end? A muffled buzzing surrounded the two enemies, like the sound of high-tension cables. Two flowering acacias were being visited by scores of honeybees and bumblebees. The company was busy interpreting the *Te Deum* requested by the butterfly, which had tried to escape. It fluttered around for a couple of yards, lost height and managed to cling to an obliging stem. Hanging on, it made the best of its laughable freedom. The acacias smelled good; Paul vowed to buy some honey. He flung a stick into the humming branches simply for the pleasure of allowing a few soloists to express themselves: the monotonous discipline of the orchestra got on his nerves. And indeed the buzzing was punctuated by the outraged recriminations of those apidae prevented from working; then order was restored and the trees resumed their threnody.

Coming up to eleven: the mischief-maker set to work too. He unfolded the large bag he had brought and began to lay waste the meadow. After some debate he went for the daisies, despite the protests of the small beetles, and the buttercups. Out of the question to take back cornflowers or even pervenches that would have tried to compete with Ella's eyes. No, yellow and white to bring out the blue. Red too: a few poppies, which wouldn't travel well. But surely he'd manage to preserve three or four? He would teach her how to transform them into dancers with brown hair and red dresses. And she would be the dancer. To avoid any risk of failure in his forthcoming demonstration, Paul sat by his bag and went to town on a poppy. He turned back the petals, successfully joined them and admired his dancer. What a surprise for his young patient.

Flowers, birds, insects, blue skies, celadon everywhere: the spring welcomed the prodigal son with open arms. His bag was respectably full. Pervenche with buttercups and daisies: he regretted having no one to share his wit. The sun shone a little less brightly: intellectual pleasures thrive on applause. The sun also shone less brightly because a nasty twinge in the back reminded the insurer that picking flowers requires fitness. Paul resolved to resume his jogging, and more, forthwith. The bag was now brimming with flowers; Paul could hardly get his arms around it. He tied it up as best he could and walked back towards the road. The pond, which had only just emerged from a refreshing night, was preparing for a siesta. Beside the old wall separating it from the road, Paul noticed a drowned fledgeling, wings spread, beak and head dipped into the water as if it were exploring the bottom. The spring had not given it many grounds for satisfaction. Paul would have preferred to take away a different image from his escapade.

The countryside had lost some of its innocence and Paul his stamina. The size of the bag didn't make things any easier. He had balanced it on the frame and handlebars and could just see the road over the top. What a sight, thought a gentleman delighted by the diversion. That's true, it's Sunday, Paul realized, not unhappy that some picnickers should distract him from the memory of the drowned bird. He had spotted them by the roadside ahead. A model family: mum was giving the folding table a last wipe, the kids were playing, dad was getting bored. He had plonked himself by the roadside, bare-chested and in shorts. The pallid paunch on display was blessed with a lighting softened and subdued by the foliage, as if in a cloister. Some weirdo, he concluded as Paul cycled by, what an idea to pick flowers like that. The cyclist – nose in the flowers, head in the clouds, heart with Ella – did not know who to award bottom marks to: the bird or the picnicker?

The train dawdled, solely to torture Pervenche in his concern for the flowers, which he kept shifting about. A granny opposite could not contain her admiration:

'What a beautiful bouquet.'

'It's for my fiancée, she's ill . . .' Paul was fond of these nice lies that aren't really lies. His fellow passenger melted into a smile. There are still some decent people after all. The two travellers were patently delighted, pleased with themselves, pleased with each other, optimistic about the future of the human race.

It was almost six o'clock when Paul rang at Ella's door. Six: with a bit of luck her father would offer him an aperitif. That would be the moment to sound him out on the trip. He had removed the string holding the flowers in, they kept spilling. The distrustful face of the lady who opened the door brightened at the sight of the flowers:

'Ella? No, sorry, try opposite.'

She kept her door ajar in the hope, perhaps, that Paul would present her with part of his bonanza. But he had already rung at the right door, his bag jammed between his feet, his outlook cheered by the morning's impressions and the pleasure of seeing Ella again.

'Hello, I've brought some flowers for Ella. Are your parents in?'

'Wait a minute.'

It was the brother who had answered the door. Paul waited. He peeked inquisitively into his playmate's world. Not bad, nothing out of the ordinary: which increased even more her merit for being what she was. He thought he overheard a confabulation in the kitchen, then a voice spoke out:

'That'll do, I'll go.'

Paul suddenly felt less at ease. Should he proffer his hand first? Should he talk about their meetings in the square? His plans for a trip? The father arrived, quite young, tall, a little tubby – but less than my picnicker, Paul joked – pleasant features:

'Hello . . .'

Paul gave attention to his smile and eye-contact, prepared a firm handshake. His host had halted six feet away, looking first at Paul, then at his bag. He finally came right to the door, which he opened wide, and immediately began to yell:

'Who the hell do you think you are? What the hell is this? Are you completely crazy, or what? You need your head examining.'

Paul listened but could hear nothing but shouts and incomprehensible noises. He was devastated, unable to move or speak. The man was ranting; Paul's silence breathed greater fury into him. He had known for a long time; if he hadn't stepped in earlier, it was out of kindness or weakness, but this was the last straw.

'If you go near my daughter once more, I'll call the police, you'll pay for it. I've got connections. Anyway, she won't be going out any more, or only with me. It's easy to show off to a six-year-old, you bastard. What's this tall story about a journey through a tunnel? I had to explain what the tunnel really is. I don't know what's stopping me from smashing your face in. Clear off! And remember what I told you, next time it's the police.'

He kicked the bag, as if afraid it might obstruct the door, and slammed it shut. Pervenche still did not move. He thought he heard a small voice call, had the feeling it was him it was calling. He gathered up the scattered flowers one by one, piled them into the bag, abandoned on the doormat a few poppy petals, a few dancers' skirts. He hadn't noticed the mat outside the door before. Ella wiped her feet on it when she came back from the square. The white ankle-socks skated to and fro while she gleefully pressed the bell. She would cram in one last sweet and chirpily enter her nest.

Back in the street, Paul came to. He still could not comprehend what had happened. Maybe he should have given Ella's father a hiding? Or tried to calm him and explain? Perhaps all was not lost. Somehow he would see her on the way to school, he would make amends, they would work things out. Paul felt ready to make any concessions to avoid admitting he would never see Ella again. He reached the canal and made for the footbridge at the Rue Monte-à-regret. He sat by the water, the bag on his knees. He was hugging it to him and rocking slowly. He thought of the doll Ella had won on the wheel of fortune, of the dreamy look in her eyes when she comforted it. It was she who had called him just now ... What if she came and joined him here on the canal side? He would see her coming, unbalanced by the weight of her bag. H-hello Paul: she would have the breathless voice from the finish of her victorious races. I-I've brought my scrap-book and my water-pistol, and my brother's torch. No, instead she would sneak up and place her hands over his eyes, crying, 'Guess who?' And this time he would not disappoint her, he wouldn't give the same, silly answer 'It's a little girl called Ella.' No, he'd keep guessing for some time, saying every first name under the sun, and then give up to hear her laugh. She would sit beside him, watching him make the poppy into a lady. He would lean towards her to collect his reward of a noisy kiss. The island at the end of the tunnel, the beaches and the sweet-seller would dance in her eyes. He would say, 'Come on, let's go,' show her his room, pack his things, throw the cassette and his camera into the grey waters as they passed. They would cross the footbridge and never return. From the now-entangled bouquet there still rose the song of the birds, of the bees, of the whole countryside. The mist was probably settling over the Beauce once again. He took large handfuls of flowers and let them slip into the water. He had the silly feeling he was laying flowers on a grave; but he didn't know who this one belonged to. The unknown shadow of the Rue Monte-à-regret? Claire? Armand? His neighbourhood, dying from Ella's absence? Without her there would remain only stones and water – nothing. The flowers were drifting sedately away on the dark water, forming a flamboyant wreath. Passers-by halted near Pervenche, watching him, then moving on to more sensible activities.

'Mummy, look. The pretty flowers!'

A little girl tugged at her mother's hand to get closer to the spectacle. With the last bouquet in his hand, Paul hesitated; then he threw it too. It was more than the girl deserved.

He returned home. He was wearing the Walkman again. The counter-tenor was mocking the theatricality of Paul's gesture. Opening his eyes wide to hold back the tears, Paul gorged himself on memories in order to forget Ella. He thought about anything but her, denied himself the doubled-edged joy of opening the door to her and spending the rest of the evening beside her. He saw once more the drowned bird, the discarded flowers, the martyrdom of the butterfly. He murmured, 'Ella, Ella.' Stars were already quivering behind the rooftops, but Paul turned his back on them.

# — 19 —

'Paul!'

The familiar voice had reverberated in the street. Several heads, including Paul's, swivelled towards Le Nabec sitting outside the bar. Paul had to steel himself to drink the coffee and chaser already awaiting him: François could not contemplate a reconciliation without a drink. He pleaded guilty on all charges; he would never be able to thank Pervenche enough for what he called his 'sacrifice'. Jourdan had explained Paul's version of events. He wasn't stupid but, in the end, this solution was convenient for him. The matter would be a lesson to all concerned. He had advised Le Nabec that he too should keep his head down.

'Come on, make me happy, one more, we've got time.'

Paul made him happy. Taken aback by the warmth of the rekindled friendship and the morning drink, he was sliding into a listlessness that he planned to nurse between his two stacks of claims. He was pleased to be friends again with François.

At the office he was greeted as if nothing had happened. He felt a momentary weariness as he took his seat: the others couldn't guess that, in fact, everything had happened, everything was finished. He dismissed the image of Ella asleep on his knees, looked forward to seeing Marie-Ciel that evening and opened the first file, which absorbed him fully. Magistrale was right to rely on him. His conversations with Le Nabec – brief at first, because they both felt shy, like two kids in front of a Christmas tree – quickly regained the old joviality and complicity. Made circumspect by an alert that showed the hitherto underestimated precariousness of a post-probationary loss adjuster's situation, Calot dropped his pens on the floor more frequently. But Blandine still poked her tongue out at her claims; the two secretaries were locked in their never-ending confidential tête-à-tête: no, nothing had changed.

Paul faced the days with resigned confidence. Each morning he went to the footbridge for an update, but the colours lacked definition: albuminous crossed with violaceous, or violaceous tinged with peonin. He left it at that. He halted there out of habit, out of a sense of propriety. Then he loitered near the corner of the Rue de Marseille, ready to provoke, if he should meet him, that bastard he ought to have thumped; ready, if he met Ella, to melt. But she had not returned to school. Patience. His itinerary offered its usual opportunities for preciosity: the roast chickens and the dog turds tried hard to distract him; he exercised himself by fabricating the life-story of a girl walking in front of him. He would have preferred to tell her his own, edited here and there.

After work he would hurry to Montparnasse. An already tanned Marie-Ciel would order her cocktail and he his pastis; then he would escort her home. From this fresh routine they derived a continually renewed pleasure. He took her hand and in her street they embraced by some railings. He felt she was waiting for him to take the initiative; he did not care to. His desire to keep some doubts alive was waning. He did not dare ask the questions he constantly brooded over, but he knew that ultimately he would and that it would be over. So he kissed Marie-Ciel even more passionately, as if to prevent her from speaking, before dashing away. He ran his tongue over his lips to taste once again the cherry and the mint, inclined his head to his shoulder to smell once again the perfume, adjusted his Walkman to hear yet again *The Blue Raincoat* and Vivaldi. He would go straight home, sometimes stopping for a sandwich, and stretch out under his window, with his photo nearby. The music soon painted across the sky a huge embankment, a footbridge, cobblestones, street lamps and trees. And there was nothing but that, the cassette, the photo and Pervenche in the middle.

On Thursday he concurred with the footbridge: peonin. There was dynamism in the air, people greeted one another, ribbed one another. After a routine glance towards the school, Paul backtracked and headed for the métro. He occasionally used it when the weather was too good, as a precaution: he mistrusted the languor trailing behind a song escaping from a window, the day-dreams prompted by a girl's walk, the desire for happiness fanned by a fresh breeze. But the underground tunnels failed to provide the hoped-for tranquillity: an accordionist was going full-tilt. His nostalgic music – Tour de France and Sunday fishing – splintered its bones against the walls of its jail, wore itself out appealing to the commuters and was swallowed in the racket of a train. Le Nabec had once explained that there were two accordions – the lively, carefree Sunday-morning one, and the melancholy one of sailors' laments as they set to sea. The first had lost its identity and was pleading for the right to stop searching for it.

Paul was not that far-gone: he had made up his mind. That evening he would talk to Marie-Ciel; he would talk to her about this bottle thrown into the sea by a sailor in the Rue Monte-à-regret, the message it contained and the terrible journeys it foretold.

He waited until she had finished her second cocktail. She was radiant, lightly made-up. For the first time since he'd known her, Paul wanted her. It seemed a bad omen. Until then he had attached too much importance to Marie-Ciel to desire her so soon. That would come later, or never – it didn't matter. Her lips, her hands, her neck were arousal enough. There was all the rest that made their relationship unique: the cassette, the songs, and death. She was radiant. The spark of vulgarity which had struck him the first time and brought him to heel had now taken on some substance: she chewed gum and it didn't suit her. Paul thought of Ella and her g-gum: Marie-Ciel was left in the shade.

'Don't you ever make cassette recordings?'
'No. Why?'

'Because you could have lent me some. I'd like to get to know what you enjoy. Haven't you ever made any, not even a long time ago?'

Marie-Ciel shrugged:

'I don't even have a cassette deck. I listen to records or the radio.'

Paul was not disappointed. He already knew the answer. Yet he persisted, as if to punish himself for his past illusions.

'Have you ever encountered death?'

'Death! I'm not with you.'

'Well, have any members of your family or any friends died?'

Instinctively, she crossed herself. That hadn't yet happened to her and she was in no hurry. But what a funny question. Why was Paul asking?

'No reason. I just asked. Because it can influence one's tastes in music.'

'Do you think so? As far as I . . .'

Paul was no longer listening to her. He was looking at her, looking at a stranger, a pretty stranger who had deceived him. The mauve eyes, turning celadon, the peonin fingernails: the colours had misled him. 'Oh this reveals my delight, As it perchance reveals me.' He almost climbed on the table and started spouting her verse. Just wait till he caught the artist in love outside a pharmacy. He'd make him look a fool!

At her door he gently unhitched the arms she had put around his neck, with the excuse that Le Nabec had invited him for dinner. Just as he had earlier used the excuse of a weekend with some friends near Meaux to decline her suggestion of a meal out on Saturday evening. He avoided her lips, put his mouth to the join of the neck and the cheek, the place he liked.

'See you tomorrow,' he said.

He looked back at her slim silhouette, answered her wave, heard her footsteps echoing still in the darkness of the courtyard. It was over, he wouldn't see her again. This stark truth filled him with strange excitement: a confused feeling of being cut off yet free, sad yet elated. He saw it as the expression of a mystic temperament. He could not help smiling as he gloated at a bakery window: the mystic artist only recently in love didn't cut such a bad figure. Paul congratulated himself on seeing the good side of things, on having the intelligence to distance himself. Though intelligence was the last thing he'd shown in taking this gamble with Marie-Ciel. How could he have believed for a moment that with a surname and two letters assumed to be the initials of a first name he could in five minutes – because that's all it had taken -- lay hands on a superb woman who would love him, thank him for killing her man and live life with him as an amazing adventure?

Paul was not hungry. He went home, deaf and blind. He recalled returning from Armand's funeral, the rain and the spray thrown up by the cars on the motorway. This evening, the cars raised no more than the odd puff of dust. End of the road, or a fresh start? We'll see. He did not listen to any music but fell asleep in his armchair, facing a sky blotted out by the city.

The next day the office buzzed with unaccustomed warmth. It was as if the word had gone round for everyone to join in the party. The slightest hint of a joke brought the house down. Calot found takers to count the number of revolutions completed by his projectiles, a new girl chatted with Le Nabec, Frigo complimented Blandine on a dress fit for an English rose, really. Little Bruno phoned Pervenche to demand a visit. He was fine, starting to get around, still having fun with his darts. Paul promised to call in the next fortnight. He bumped into Chantal in the corridor; his trusted filer gave him an enigmatic smile. François recounted a few memorable booze-ups, and what everyone was hoping for – except perhaps Frigo – happened. At sixteen forty-five he carefully cleared his desk and displayed his nautical portrait. And at seventeen hundred hours precisely the fog-horn boomed to general jubilation.

Pervenche joined in, but the siren call had caused him pain. So too had François's beaming face. His spree in the country the previous Sunday had reawakened things he had chosen to forget; the tatters of another life had cracked like flags in the wind. At that time he was able to disown it, he held the trump cards – Ella and Marie-Ciel, a cassette and a photo. And now, while Le Nabec celebrated his childhood and his future, Paul was discovering that he had mislaid his own childhood, that he had lost Ella and Marie-Ciel, that his future was not exactly brilliant.

As he took his leave of his colleagues, shaking distracted hands, Paul's gaze took in the sheep-pen in which he had burned himself out over the past months. He had never been able to isolate the flame that consumed him. Yet he was going to have to contain it, moderate it, adjust it to this chair, this desk, these files to which he had given his all. He would erase the past, win back the confidence of his superiors and look forward – for good, this time – to a transfer away from Paris. Why not try to start over again with Claire? He had changed in a short space of time, he saw things differently. Marie-Ciel was no doubt looking out for him, cocktail in hand. When she left, would she have that sadness in her eyes he had seen at the very beginning, the sadness that had led him astray?

He saw Saturday through with less trouble than anticipated. He didn't even need to resort to the traditional expedients: wandering around, cinema, Pompidou Centre... He got up late, pronounced – to intrigue the footbridge – that the day would be yellow, drank his coffee sitting on the window-ledge and tossed two sugar cubes near Madame Gautier, who had to haul on the lead to stop her diddums from gobbling these sweeties that must have been poisoned by the good-for-nothing on the fourth floor. The Martin girl was late. He saw her run out of the building and knock into Madame Gautier, who feared for her dog. He listened to a lot of music, especially the records he had just bought, and was moved yet again by the story of Eurydice, his sister. But why look back? Why not keep going forwards, filled with love and scepticism?

In the afternoon he tried his luck. He went to the square, determined to throw a punch if need be. He sat on his bench, their bench. A game of football was in full swing.

Paul's heart skipped a beat: there was the brother. He suddenly stopped playing. He had seen Pervenche. Their eyes met. Paul no longer felt obliged to be the first to divert his gaze to flatter the youngster; he held out in the hope that the contempt he felt actually showed. The kid cracked and, no doubt upset, missed two crucial passes, which earned him the jeers of his team-mates. Paul would have split his sides if Ella's absence had not disheartened him. The thunder of the father's insults had died away; his optimism led Paul to imagine that he would not match his words with deeds. But no, Ella wasn't there. Still ill, probably. Two little boys on the next bench were blowing into a plastic ring dipped in soapy water. Bubbles rose tentatively and floated unhurriedly away. They glinted fleetingly and abruptly gained height; the square and the houses were mirrored in miniature until suddenly they burst. Armand had taken a superb photograph of a child trying to catch a soap-bubble: it was floating between his hands, which were eager to enclose its magic, while his eyes said they didn't dare. Paul curbed the ludicrous idea of helping the boys: although it dismayed him, he knew not to believe in bubbles.

Leaving behind the bubbles and the ball, he climbed one of the footbridges for the hell of it. The end of May was not providing the neighbourhood with the uplift it was entitled to. It was not the fault of the spring. The sickness was incurable, this was no place for rejoicing. The canal, the embankments and the bridges felt hemmed in. Roll on winter. And in fact, those who had shown an interest in this part of town had latched on to its lugubrious side, from the gibbets to the *Hôtel du Nord*. Even so, he reproached the film for its closing line, which he thought played to the gallery. 'Dawn is breaking, it's going to be fine': the words had stuck in his craw. They probably didn't detract from the film, but by kindling a glimmer of hope, they betrayed the truth of the area. Ella's illness didn't help things; she alone could have changed them. Paul missed her more and more. And he was reluctant to call on Claire. A small yacht with its mast down was entering the lock; the Rue Monte-à-regret was hiding behind the leaves on the trees. Everyone was singing and smiling, especially on the hoardings, where perfect couples were head-over-heels in love. Paul envied them.

In the *gay salons* the countdown had started. Already the presents were piling up here and there – the stuff of the dreams of those who had stayed at home and who would bemoan their fate, while their benefactors would gloss over eleven months of humiliation and dejection. Genghis insisted that Paul should accompany him to a restaurant in the Rue d'Enghien. One of his friends was playing the *saz*. One glass of raki, and Turkey invaded the small room, just as Brittany had flooded the office the previous day. Paul did not stay long. Pointless torturing himself. The sky was turning violaceous, a rather grubby violaceous soiled by the hatred and misery that welled up from the city. Heavy clouds announced a storm, Paul thought he'd glimpsed the lightning. It was like a stage set by a director not quite on top of things. It all seemed artificial and overdone.

Paul woke earlier than usual. Encouraged by the silence of the street and the ease with which he had sailed through Saturday, he opened his curtains. The clouds had disappeared, the storm had confined itself to an admonishment. He went out for a coffee at a pavement café near the Rue du Faubourg-du-Temple. From there he could view the deserted square. Invisible birds seemed in disagreement over their day's programme. Squabbles meant peonin to Pervenche, although he couldn't really see who he could discuss it with. A beetle had dropped on to the next table. Curious, he picked it up and put it in a white saucer which brought out the metallic green of the shell. A rose-chafer in the middle of town, would you believe it! It must have gone through hell to reach him. Bearing what tidings? He prodded it to no avail, it did not move, it had come to die near the Rue Monte-à-regret. The message lost some of its appeal. Paul paid and abandoned the corpse in the middle of the change: a green coat instead of a blue one. That was it, the message had got through to its destination, the beetle had come to tell him of corpses.

Pervenche devoted the rest of the morning to his photo and his cassette, they had become inseparable. He told his secrets to the girl on the cassette. 'Will you then confess your plight, The day you know my ennui?' His plight he repeated over and over again, and she replied from one song to the next. But soon that was not enough. He wanted to talk, to squeeze a hand, to feel a breath on his neck. Marie-Ciel had vanished just when he thought he had triumphed, just when he was preparing to reveal everything. Ella, who knew, who had unmasked him, had been snatched away. Armand remained silent. So Paul did not talk; he wrote. He cut out some long strips of paper, wrote down his adventure in black felt-tip pen, then chopped the narrative into countless rectangles. He opened the window and launched on the wind, one after the other, a string of words, of cries. Night, fog, club, photo, cassette, corpse, name of the killer, first name: it all fluttered away like a cloud of butterflies gone to tell a story that might not be his. A startled swallow swooped at one of the butterflies, wheeled and departed screeching. Two of the pieces of paper landed on the window ledge. Paul snatched them up – 'blue raincoat', 'Ella' – and put them in his pocket. The eddying wings met various fates: some were already lying on the pavement or a car bonnet, others were still whirling over the roofs, at the end of the street and along the walls. Would someone take the trouble to gather them all up? Should Paul post his photo in the window in full view to put Maigret on the scent? And so he amused himself, leaning out of his window. No one seemed to notice the strange butterflies, no one looked up to the fourth floor.

In the afternoon he set off for the square, climbing one of the footbridges to stand watch, acting as if Ella were waiting for him. She was not. The wheel of fortune was closed. He opened the small gate behind the statue of la Grisette, who was still oblivious to the leering actor, and was engulfed in the unavoidable atmosphere of boredom and lethargy which emanates from any square on a Sunday. A fat black woman had fallen asleep on his bench, her arms folded on a shopping bag. Paul walked around the square, something he had never done; he had never felt the need to go beyond the bandstand because Ella never went beyond it. He met an old man shod in pink plastic sandals, he looked a shady character. In the absence of a mirror, Paul had a moment's anxiety about how he looked himself. Shady or not? Two Arabs on a bench, their eyes sparkling with pleasure, were conversing in low voices; next to them a mother was knitting. Children played with tennis-rackets or raced on four-wheel bikes. A gaggle of little girls had taken over the bandstand, the queen's throne was empty, it always would be. Pigeons being fed glided in wide, greedy sweeps; a family was picnicking. Toddlers occupied themselves in the sandpit while their mothers made acquaintance. A debonair gendarme, carrying his képi as a sign of peace, strolled up and down giving the most attractive mothers the eye, counting on the lure of the uniform. A couple followed a new pram; the wife had put her arm on her husband's shoulder, conscious of being in the mainstream, of being one of those who set the standards, of being in control of her world.

Since the empty benches did not inspire him, Pervenche again found a table outside a bar. Business was slow, service fast: the patron didn't want to miss the next episode of his TV serial. Elbows propped on table, chin cupped in hands, Paul watched time pass by without moving or turning his head, like one of those dogs – nose on paws, motionless – who follow with a roll of the eyes the comings and goings of their master. He affected a blasé interest in the exciting things on offer in town on a Sunday afternoon: a car pulling away, sallow passers-by, a snatch of music. It felt close, the storm had still to say its final word. The green liquid, rose-chafer green – so much celadon for an albuminous day – was gently lapping the inside of the glass that Paul did not dare drink. Without thinking, he had ordered a mint cordial; now he was dreading the taste on his lips. Mint and cherry: he remembered the walk back to his bedsit trying with his tongue to preserve the taste of Marie-

Ciel's kiss. He left his table to check that the small white thing on the far side of the street wasn't one of his butterflies. Slightly disappointed, he returned to his seat. What had become of the butterflies? What had become of his story, the true one? What had become of the corpse? Had he died for nothing? The prospect troubled Pervenche. He had never lost sleep over the stranger's fate, never regretted his act; but he did deplore its pointlessness. He didn't hold himself to blame for killing someone, but he did for making a hash of a photograph. That was more serious.

'One day I will stride naked and unbowed into the sea and I will drink it. I will, I swear.'

Startled, Paul observed the two men coming out of the bar: two tramps, obviously the worse for wear, one propping up the other and telling his secrets. The roar of a car prevented him from hearing what came next; he almost followed them. Beauty was not without cunning, it was hiding everywhere, especially in unexpected places. The photographer promised to learn his lesson and tried to make a connection with his current preoccupations, with his one photo that was a failure and the other almost a success. He was unable to, which seemed only natural since he was insensitive to coincidences.

He went to fetch his photo and his Walkman, returned to the square where his bench had been vacated by the overweight sleeper. There was almost no one about. The mums had gone home to cook dinner, the dads for an aperitif in front of the telly, the kids because they had to. Paul studied his photograph yet again, as if it could shed light on fresh mysteries. The music did its best to help. The golden rain, the patch of light: the riddle stopped there. Armand's voice in his friend's cellar: 'A corpse.' Paul began to cry, not knowing why. His tears came from afar, taking their time. He didn't hold them back and through them the photo took on phantasmagorical forms. He ripped it up. He wondered how many times he had torn it, how many times he had reprinted it. He clenched the pieces in his fist. Gusts of wind announced the storm, a piece of paper swirled in a cloud of dust and wrapped itself around a leg of the bench. Paul wiped his eyes, picked up the scrap of newspaper: racing results; the killers of an old lady had been turned in. He let it whirl away. He crossed the street, threw into the canal the remnants of his photo. He was throwing everything into the canal – the chaff and the wheat. They were carried slowly by the current; the blackness of the tunnel swallowed one by one the small patches of light.

Where the remains of his photo had just disappeared, a band of light dislocated by the troubled water scarred the tunnel entrance. Paul had never noticed it before. Probably a light bulb inside the vault that hadn't been switched off. He realized it wasn't a bulb, it was a ray of sunshine, a ray from the sun he had promised to Ella, at the far end of the tunnel, with the island, their boat with the multicoloured sails, the orange peel and the packets of sweets. Heavy raindrops started to fall. Paul hurried to his room.

He forced himself to cook something, palming himself off with a tin emptied into a saucepan. He ate out of the pan, standing at the window. The storm was already abating, night was falling early. He put on the cassette: Vivaldi, *The Blue Raincoat*. The counter-tenor's voice suddenly sounded unworldly, dangerous even; the singer of *The Blue Raincoat* was urging him harder than ever to find his soul-mate. What soul-mate? Paul silenced the tape and tried to sleep. He surprised himself adopting a curled-up position unusual for him, like someone seeking warmth. Old age, no doubt, or the storm. His humour fell flat. Yes, things could be patched up with Claire. With Ella too, why not? He thought of the sunbeam shining through the tunnel. He would have loved to show it to her. He thought he heard footsteps in the corridor; he held his breath. There was a knock at his door. He froze. There was another knock, more insistent. After a pause the footsteps could be heard again, then faded. Paul dashed to the window. Claire? Marie-Ciel? François? He was about to open it when he saw that a light fog was hanging over the street. He forgot his visitor. His heart was racing, this was totally unexpected. It called for a beer. Slumped in his armchair, he drank from the can. He had put on the cassette. The girl spoke to him again, he was moved by her voice; Elvis made him feel like dancing. He closed his eyes, rocking himself as he sang *Love me tender, love me sweet*. It was all beginning over again. He held her tight, her lips did not taste of mint. It was all beginning over again, and he had no cares: his photo would turn out well, he wouldn't make the same mistake as last time.

He prepared his equipment calmly and efficiently. He changed his shirt, took out his combat jacket. It was eleven o'clock, perfect. Out on the landing, Paul turned round. The bedside lamp bathed the walls in a soft glow, the cassette continued to summon apparitions, the window hovered between black and gold. Petrushka shed a few tears at this, a draught gave life to the shade of the unlit ceiling light. Rimbaud was thinking of Ethiopia: the time for follies was past. With his foot Paul straightened the old carpet, then he slowly closed the door on posters, ribbons, chair and curtains, on this small boat adrift on the ocean. His room was waiting for him, dull and reassuring.

He did not forgo the pleasure of alarming the Gautiers. He had been too gentle on them for a few weeks now. He pressed the bell: there was a loud ringing as joyful as Easter chimes. The warmth of the air outside surprised him. The storm had brought wet and fog but the temperature had not dropped. It had also brought silence – the silence of peace regained – saluted briefly by a distant blackbird. A blackbird at this hour? Paul wasn't too sure. Shaken fitfully by a nonchalant breeze, the branches cast raindrops on his face. They streamed down his neck, disappearing over his shoulders and chest. Each time a slight shiver went through him. He opened his mouth as he walked, to catch some water from the heavens.

He set up his tripod with the confidence of an old hand, adjusted the camera and examined the scene. It was strange: there was an almost delicate fog, and then a vapour rising from the ground like wisps of smoke to meet the fog at the height of the street lamps. It was like being in a cavern with an opalescent roof and quivering stalagmites. Everywhere there was the impalpable presence of the golden rain that had stayed away the night of the second photo.

Paul took another look through the lens. Framing spot on, settings perfect: it was all looking good. Leaving nothing to chance, as scrupulous as a professional or a recognized artist, he lay in the centre of the pool of light. He felt against his cheek the damp warmth of the tarmac; he inhaled the smell of earth and of the spring, which was pushing its way through to him. He felt good. *Never let me go*, ample-thighed women, God they'd laughed that day, and what an idea, the ample-thighed women slithering silently by, he never had known where they were slithering to. He could recall it clearly now, it was when the teacher had made the class laugh that she had taken Paul's hand, without any warning, *Love me tender, love me sweet*, how he would have liked to dance to that song with her, her blond hair against his lips, close his eyes, hold her tighter . . .

Paul stood up, a bitter taste in his mouth. For form's sake he re-checked his camera. He wound on and set the self-timer. That would give him fifteen seconds, ten to be on the safe side, to be sure of not moving, and five to spare. He thought that maybe he would resolve the problems posed by his reflection, that his image would at long last match his expectations. If he didn't resolve them now, it was a lost cause.

He pressed the shutter release and hurried to lie down. Fifteen seconds – an eternity. The heady smell of earth persisted; the fog outlined the footbridge, the angles of the canal side, the haloes of the street lamps. Reassured, Paul fumbled in his jacket pocket. He cradled the butt of his revolver in his palm: it was warm and soft like her hand on the school bench, warm and firm like Armand's. Paul closed his grip on this hand in his. He saw Armand open his arms, he heard him say 'Come on, let's go home,' and roar with laughter. At the far end of the street he could sense the poplars rustling by the riverside. His left hand clutched Ella's small blue handkerchief. Paul was going home. The echo of the report overtook Armand's laugh in the night, rolled long among the trees.

Abacus now offers an exciting range of quality titles by both established and new authors. All of the books in this series are available from:
Sphere Books,
Cash Sales Department,
P.O. Box 11,
Falmouth,
Cornwall TR10 9EN.

Alternatively you may fax your order to the above address. Fax No. 0326 76423.

Payments can be made as follows: Cheque, postal order (payable to Macdonald & Co (Publishers) Ltd) or by credit cards, Visa/Access. Do not send cash or currency. UK customers: please send a cheque or postal order (no currency) and allow 80p for postage and packing for the first book plus 20p for each additional book up to a maximum charge of £2.00.

B.F.P.O. customers please allow 80p for the first book plus 20p for each additional book.

Overseas customers including Ireland, please allow £1.50 for postage and packing for the first book, £1.00 for the second book, and 30p for each additional book.

NAME (Block Letters) ..........................................................

ADDRESS ..........................................................................

..........................................................................................

☐ I enclose my remittance for  _____

☐ I wish to pay by Access/Visa Card

Number

Card Expiry Date